# DISCLOSURES

*The Harpur and Iles Series by Bill James*

*\* available from Severn House*

# DISCLOSURES

Bill James

**Severn House Large Print**
London & New York

This first large print edition published 2015
in Great Britain and the USA by
SEVERN HOUSE PUBLISHERS LTD of
19 Cedar Road, Sutton, Surrey, England, SM2 5DA.
First world regular print edition published 2014 by
Severn House Publishers Ltd., London and New York.

British Library Cataloguing in Publication Data

James, Bill, 1929- author.
    Disclosures. – (The Harpur and Iles series)
    1. Harpur, Colin (Fictitious character)–Fiction. 2. Iles,
    Desmond (Fictitious character)–Fiction. 3. Criminals–
    Fiction. 4. Attempted assassination–Fiction. 5. Police–
    Great Britain–Fiction. 6. Detective and mystery stories.
    7. Large type books.
    I. Title II. Series
    823.9'14-dc23

ISBN-13: 9780727872463

Severn House Publishers support the Forest Stewardship Council™
[FSC™], the leading international forest certification organisation. All
our titles that are printed on FSC certified paper carry the FSC logo.

Typeset by Palimpsest Book Production Ltd.,
Falkirk, Stirlingshire, Scotland.
Printed and bound in Great Britain by
T J International, Padstow, Cornwall.

# Author's Note

Some material from my short story in Italian 'Arriva Natale eccetera, eccetera', published by Sellerio Editore, Palermo (2013) in their collection *Regalo di Natale*, has been adapted for inclusion in a chapter of *Disclosures*.

# PART ONE

Reminiscences

# One

Now and then, during a quiet spell at home in his authentic, multi-chimneyed, paddock-graced manor house, 'Low Pastures,' or, say, when business went sluggish at the club he owned in Shield Terrace, Ralph Ember liked to think back to certain, undeniably very rough, handgun episodes in his past. Liked? No, not quite that. In fact, not that at all. He didn't enjoy recalling those harsh times. The memories could cause near-paralysing pain, and possibly some shame. He had to compel himself to re-run them in his head.

So, why do it? Why pipe torment aboard? He knew the answer. Of course he did. He wanted to check something, recheck something – something crucial to him, something sensitive, something non-stop fucking troublesome. He had to prove that nothing in his behaviour during those lawless, violent capers long ago could justify the disgusting nickname some still vilely blessed him with: 'Panicking Ralph,' or even worse, 'Panicking Ralphy.' In Ember's opinion, this foul, dangly 'y,' stuck on to give an entirely unwanted jingle, made him sound feeble and pathetically childish, a gibbering kid.

Very few – other than that insolent, eternally savage, bombastic sod, Assistant Chief Constable Desmond Iles – would call Ember Panicking Ralph or Ralphy to his face. But he felt certain

3

the slur circulated as more or less routine abuse among his enemies; and probably among some of his seeming friends, too: anything for a smirk, disloyalty included. Although this hurt and angered Ralph he obviously could not prevent it. But he searched for solace. By going over and over the ancient details he tried to convince himself he'd never in fact actually faltered, had never chickened, despite terrible, salvo dangers in some of the gang jobs then. 'Panicking Ralph,' 'Panicking Ralphy' – these were surely utterly undeserved smears, weren't they? Weren't they? The word 'Mondial' kept recurring among his memories – kept badgering and taunting him.

Ember had a high business status now (income, six hundred thousand plus a year, and rising, the bulk untaxed, naturally) so that those contemptuous nicknames seemed especially offensive to him. And he enjoyed an admirable civic status, too, frequently publishing very heartfelt and constructive letters in the local Press on environmental and pollution matters. The signature he used for these was 'Ralph W. Ember' – such an immense distance in tone, import, quiet dignity from 'Panicking Ralph' or 'Panicking Ralphy.' Befouled rivers he particularly focused on. He felt more or less sure his wife, Margaret, had run across at least hints of those cruel names, but she had the decency and kindness not to mention them to him.

Ralph's social club, The Monty, also brought him a kind of distinction. It used to be a select, comfortable haven for local professional and commercial people, and, although the clientele

4

had changed since Ralph bought it, he was careful to preserve the rich mahogany panelling, spacious, marble-themed lavatory-cloakrooms, and excellent brass bar room fittings, which he would often polish himself. Ambience. He longed to create the perfect ambience: vital; indispensable for any communal meeting place. This objective had the irresistible strength of a grail for Ember.

Not long ago he'd decided to fix a heavy metal sheet aloft between a couple of pillars. He thought it would baffle any attempt by envious, recession-poxed rival trade colleagues to rip him apart with sudden automatic fire from just inside the club doorway, before hoofing it to their getaway car, the murderous bastards. Without that elevated defensive barrier he'd be a simple target, seated at his little accounting desk behind the bar.

Of course, he could have found himself a less exposed position in the club, somewhere not so easily targeted. This, though, would have been a virtual admission that the label 'Panicking Ralph,' or even 'Ralphy' was spot on. Ralph at his miniature desk, very obviously presiding over things at the club, had become part of Monty tradition. To wilt by seeking out some obscure, sheltered corner would indicate a sickening collapse of courage and of dignity. It would, in his opinion, be like the master of a ship abandoning his sinking vessel in a storm before making certain all the crew and passengers had safely taken to the lifeboats. This didn't mean he should casually leave himself vulnerable. It was only intelligent and realistic to establish basic precautions. And so, the metal umbrella.

But to offset the rather chilling impression it might give of The Monty's character, he had arranged for this rectangular, three-centimetre-thick, anti-dum-dum screen to be covered with enlarged prints from the poet and illustrator William Blake's famous work, *The Marriage of Heaven and Hell,* in a sort of montage. These sketches had a real, swirling power to them, inevitable if you merged two opposites like heaven and hell; there'd be aggro; it would be no tranquil marriage, and this was before the time of Relate counselling. If anyone quizzed him about the purpose of his decorated metal slab he'd say it was to do with controlling the air-conditioning currents. 'Please don't ask me how, though! I obediently do what the experts recommend.' Or he might reply that he'd introduced this shield to match the club's address in Shield Terrace. He would have been interested to know why the terrace had that name. Perhaps in another century there had been a battle hereabouts, with shields used against longbows and/or halberds. He felt that this possibility gave the club extra significance. History could thrill Ralph, make him feel part of what he called 'a grand panoply'.

He had very major ambitions for The Monty, but occasionally he'd wonder whether it was grossly and stupidly optimistic to think he could bring about the enormous changes he wanted. This deep doubt made him more determined to buttress his identity in other ways. One of these was to abolish if he could his dread that those smelly monikers, 'Panicking Ralph' and/or 'Panicking Ralphy' might be terribly accurate and justified.

He sometimes sensed a gap inside him where his hopes for The Monty had previously thrived.

He used to believe that one day he'd raise the social and intellectual standing of his club to match The Athenaeum's or at least The Garrick's in London. Ralph intended to chuck most of the current Monty membership and put a definite end to many types of rowdy shindig he tolerated there at present. Although some of these festive functions might be absolutely OK and acceptable – wedding receptions, christening parties, post-funeral get-togethers, gatherings to honour Her Majesty the Queen's official birthday, or the anniversary of Trafalgar – others were not. He had meant to exclude what he thought of as definitely 'non-Athenaeum, non-Garrick' type celebrations marking, for instance, prison releases; turf war victories; paroles; acquittals; bail awards against all the odds; effectively silenced and/or retracting witnesses.

He could still think along those lines, but not with quite the same bounce these days. Ember didn't understand how it had come about. For the present he'd lost some of the absolute, bullish faith in his scheme to lift The Monty to a different class. He knew that most people had always regarded as utterly and preposterously loony this dream of Shield Terrace transformation. Until recently he'd discounted their view: treated it as malicious, negative and defeatist. There was a phrase in the commercial realm 'to turn a company around'. That is, to take a failing firm and revive it, bring it back into profit. This was the sort of conversion he sought for The Monty.

7

On a special trip back up to London not long ago he'd gone to look at some of these clubs, from the outside, naturally. He'd needed to see the facades and doorways and, indeed, doors, and members entering and leaving, some with walking sticks, some taking taxis, vans delivering newspapers or new chalk for the snooker cues; or possibly the more traditional billiards cues in this type of club. He'd needed plain, physical expressions of what he was aiming for. Templates. Concreteness. He'd felt, here it really was! Actuality. Achievable actuality for The Monty. These London buildings were simply that – buildings. The Monty could equal this: it, too, was a building. The members going and coming were, obviously, people, and so were the Monty's members, people.

But in retrospect this seemed to him sometimes now a sad, pitiable visit, like that famous picture of salivating urchins at night with their noses against a restaurant window, watching the customers inside fill themselves with expensive food and wine under bright, cheery lights. At moments he feared The Monty was The Monty and would stay so. Ember realized he'd better try to get some of his prestige from elsewhere now. He should struggle to annul anything that brought him disrepute, such as, yes, the grossly slanderous tags 'Panicking Ralph' and/or 'Panicking Ralphy.'

He was Ember, or less formally, Ralph, or in those press letter columns, Ralph W. He didn't mind any one of these. He liked to think of himself as easy-going, unfussy, without side, yet possessing fully earned self-esteem. When someone asked him what the W stood for in 'Ralph W. Ember,' he would reply either, 'Wait and see,' or 'Who knows?' Humorous quips Ralph loved. Weren't they part of his wry, amused, laid-back approach to life? Weren't they? The satirical magazine, *Private Eye,* ran a supposed letters-from-readers feature where the signature of the writers comically echoed the topic of the correspondence. In a witty mood, Ralph had sent in one about gross vanity as from 'E.G. O'Tripp'; another dealing with behaviour of the work force on a construction site from 'Bill d'Urs-Kleevidge'; and a third bemoaning broken government promises, from 'J.A.M.T. O' Morrow'. None was printed. Probably too subtle for those infantile buggers, Ralph decided.

# Two

Now and then, during a quiet spell at home on a day off, or when matters at the office were not too pressing, Esther Davidson liked to think back to certain handgun episodes in the past. Liked? No, not quite that. In fact, not at all like that. Not as planned as that. She didn't exactly *think* back. Her mind would seem to return of its own accord, frogmarching her memory to one or other of these incidents, as if responding to a prompt she was hardly aware of. It troubled her. She wanted to be in control of what her brainbox did. The word 'Mondial' kept badgering, taunting her.

Well, didn't everybody have this sort of weird experience occasionally? A borrowed French phrase covered it: déjà vu, meaning 'I've seen this before.' Usually it was spoken as, 'I had a strange, unexplainable feeling of déjà vu', so possibly the best translation with trimmings might be 'I've seen all this before, haven't I? Haven't I?' People would observe or hear something now that in totally unpredictable style triggered a memory of a similar happening previously. Or seemed to. This needn't be anything massive or striking or unusual, but it would appear to match and reproduce conditions of an earlier date, utterly forgotten until now. It *was* forgotten, yes, but not lost. Instead, it had lain stored somewhere in the subconscious, very ready to pop out on cue, the process more or less subliminal. Esther didn't feel comfy with subliminal stuff. For her, extremely slight, even trivial, occurrences would set this mysterious type of sequence off: say the sound of a revving, low-powered car; or sight of a starling formation buzzing the street below; or a rush of jagged, dark cloud blanking the sun; or the crying of a child. She'd find herself transfixed for a moment, trying to locate where, when, originally she'd registered something similar without knowing she'd registered it at all: a comparable car engine din; glimpses of an identical bird patrol; the abrupt onset of shadow when the sun got lost; the yelling of a baby.

Today, a starling squadron criss-crossing not a street but the Davidson rear garden three or four times bamboozled Esther into revisiting some violent, bloody, mini-war minutes in her history. She lay stretched out, fully dressed – jeans, woollen socks, desert boots, polo-necked dark sweater – on a lounger in the conservatory. It was sunny but December sunny, pale-sunny, and she had a Calor gas stove alight. She'd been a detective superintendent in the Metropolitan force then, not long before she was promoted and moved here, away from London, to take charge of Operations. She'd learned a lot about such duties with the Met.

Possibly it was the gunfire that day, in the jumbled, rambling district between Peckham and East Dulwich, south of the Thames, that disturbed the starlings and got them formation flying; some of the bullets from Esther's people, some not. Like most police hits of this sort it originated

11

from what was called 'advice': a bland, seemingly harmless term, but meaning a confidential tip-off, or confidential tip-offs, from an informant or informants. 'Advice' was graded as to quality.

There were – and still were – four categories. The lowest rated as R-minus, rumour so frail and unverified that it hardly added up even to rumour. But best not ignore it. Suddenly, there could be a jump up the league to a more compelling status. Stay watchful. At the level above came plain R – rumour, but with a possibility of turning fairly soon into something more than that. If it happened, this would then become category three: R-plus, which allowed for some rumour still present, but with more than three checked certainties. In police work three checked certainties stood fairly close to Gospel truth.

And then, at the top of the whisper scale, stood classification AREA, referring not to a patch of ground, but Advice Requiring Emergency Action. It had been a flash flood of AREA-quality signals from their voices inside a couple of the London gangs that led to the SWAT move with Esther in command. And to the starling street theatre that day.

# Three

Ralph Ember was at his accounting desk behind the bar at The Monty, business slack just after opening at noon. He felt it necessary to spend time at the desk to check over the previous night's takings and do some stock ordering by phone or email. But, of course, he meant his spells seated there to be about more than club management: those deeper things. To be installed here, unruffled, in an open, potentially hazardous position surely made those sickening nicknames, Panicking Ralph, or Ralphy, totally misguided, and vicious slanders. Ralph was coolly maintaining a core Monty feature; a feature he, personally, had initiated and would now honour. This captain wouldn't ditch his responsibilities but was on the bridge, so to speak. And those speaking it would say 'Ralph' or 'Ember' not 'Panicking Ralph,' or 'Ralphy'.

He had command, and, more important, it could be seen by anyone about that he had command. Admittedly, there weren't many to see him at present, but enough: the word would circulate – Ralph was where he should be; where his social standing, his character, his robust temperament said he should be, regardless. All right, so there was the thick, inter-pillar metal extra up there offering a degree of protection. Ralph regarded that, though, as simply a bit of basic strategy. Panic it certainly did not signify. Panic took away thought and rationality, but that fortification was the *fruit* of thought and reasoning. When a jet fighter pilot strapped on his or her parachute this didn't indicate cowardly terror. It was necessary preparedness; it could save his life and enable him to fly and fight again. When a surgeon pulled on his face mask before operating it was to avoid contagion, giving or receiving, so that he or she and the patient might go on unimpaired in their careers. The shield at Shield Terrace was comparable with that type of professional counteraction against risk.

If those cruel labels, 'Panicking Ralph/Ralphy', were even very slightly appropriate he would never have sat at the desk, whether or not the life-preserving fixture were up there. His body would have refused to let him remain in that target situation, stalwart, calm, defiant. An uncontrollable trembling and sweating might have disastrously weakened him. In any case, that custom-made flying buttress was not there only to ward off attacks, was it? Didn't it have a decorative, mind-widening factor, an instructional factor? How many of The Monty's members would have heard of William Blake, let alone his *Marriage Of Heaven And Hell* without those gutsy, collage pictures near the ceiling? This brought a touch of culture to The Monty.

He liked to think of the club as something of an educational beacon. Ralph had begun a mature-student degree at the local university – suspended now because of business pressures – phenomenally expanding Charlie sales particularly – and felt a duty to pass on to The Monty crowd some of the points he'd picked up in his Foundation Year there, such as the remarkable poet and illustrator, William Blake. OK, obviously, The Athenaeum and The Garrick didn't need to do that because most of their people would already know about Blake's importance, and his campaign to stop children getting pushed up chimneys by sweeps. The Monty was different and had quite a number of ignorant, unalterable slobs on its books, mostly male, but not all. If some of these louts had been around at the time of Blake and were working as sweeps they would most likely have pushed kids up chimneys themselves. Blake was a Romantic. This didn't mean he wrote slop, but Romantic poets wanted folk to let it all hang out, long before this slogan was 'invented' in the twentieth century.

*Great Expectations* by Charles Dickens was another work studied in the Foundation Year, and Ralph had heard that film posters for a movie version of this with John Mills and Alec Guinness, could be obtained from a special relics shop in Hull. He thought that after a while he'd have *The Marriage Of Heaven And Hell* scraped off, using hot water suds, and a fish slice, and replaced by this alternative reference to literature. Probably Monty members would understand about great expectations better than marriages of heaven and hell, although some of their marriages turned out fairly hellish, resulting in home-based abuse. Ralph hated to see women with black eyes in the club bar.

Many Monty regulars had great expectations, although it wouldn't be in exactly similar ways as in the Dickens book. They had great expectations of a fine price for valuable items they managed to get possession of and brought to their

15

middleman, their fence. Usually, the price from fences was not very fine, but the great expectations in the book took hundreds of pages to come good and, in fact, were shown up to be not at all what Pip in the story imagined.

It might seem disrespectful to get a fish slice going on a soaked William Blake, but this work, *The Marriage Of Heaven And Hell,* had such a splendid regard from university scholars that nothing could damage its brilliant essence. The Monty would be extending its role as a subtle, committed teacher. Ralph had now and then lost the full urge to bring The Monty up to scratch, but he could never lose that impulse altogether.

In fact, the need for the Blake or Dickens bulwark in The Monty had helped persuade him to moderate the overall improvement plan for his club. He had been fairly sure that The Athenaeum and The Garrick, nor any of the other top London clubs, did not have to rely on an added aerial rampart to ensure management didn't get slaughtered on the premises. This realization need not prevent him, though, from bringing at least a morsel of refinement to The Monty. Prisoners at the time *Great Expectations* covered were kept on hulks or shipped off to Australia, and some Monty members should be glad it wasn't still the same. If any of the film posters showed hulks he'd cut them out.

He glanced fondly up at the Blake now, and then brought his gaze down to bar level so as to greet with a nod and smile and pleasant, 'Afternoon both,' a couple of regulars ready for a lunchtime drink or two. Yes, he did feel it pleased and reassured them to see him on his usual perch, relaxed, ready for anything. But, of course, *sangfroiding* it at The Monty couldn't eliminate altogether for Ralph the stink of those 'Panicking' insinuations. He still needed to travel back for that. But to be at his desk, bold, undeterred, resourceful while he assembled his unblemished memories, made travelling back so much more tolerable than it might have been. These two said as they always said, 'Afternoon, Ralph,' but might be thinking, as perhaps they always did, 'Afternoon, Panicking.'

On that far-past evening, where he compelled his mind to go, the firm had given him a choice of handguns for any future exercises. He'd known something about weapons, but very little. He didn't rush to pick out one or the other though – Browning, Walther or Beretta automatics. He wanted to seem experienced and particular, so he delayed a bit, as if working out in his head which would be most suitable for the jobs they might be going on soon, taking into consideration calibre, chamber capacity, recoil. He'd talked to people in the outfit about guns as if pistols were what he'd been brought up with, instead of Farley's rusks. He'd needed to establish himself with these folk.

Ralph was the new boy. He'd more or less drifted into the firm. At the time, he'd been living in a flat with Margaret and the two kids near King's Cross station. Some of his friends then were serious users. He'd done a bit himself, naturally, but only grass. Charlie was too dear and H scared him, thank God. One winter week the supplier failed to show. People grew despondent and restless. Ralph said he'd go and see what he

17

could discover. It hadn't been difficult. He found a lad corner-street trading and told him of a new, enthusiastic, established long-term market, backed by fairly reliable money from various ploys, not all of it dubious and precarious. This acquaintance mentioned there'd been a drugs squad onslaught and four pushers were taken in and remained in. Ralph reckoned the previous supplier must have been one.

Ralph's pals were pleased and grateful for the new arrangement. If there'd been a Nobel Prize for salvaging drugs commerce he reckoned they'd have definitely nominated him. This replacement pusher worked for the Pasque Uno – Single Flower – firm, and Ralph's part in the minor crisis got him some notice by the chiefs there, favourable, positive notice. He could tell they admired his initiative – his willingness and ability to remedy a bad situation. He was a locally unknown face so could courier and trade unspotted by the troublesome, anti-business cops. As he'd understood it, the main troublesome, anti-business cop was Superintendent Esther Davidson, a bit of a monster. Ralph had told the Pasque Uno board that OK, he'd noted the possible difficulties and would go 'very judiciously'.

'Yes, go very judiciously,' someone replied. Ralph had arrived. But he still had his way to make as to, for instance, weaponry. Therefore, the confident talk and seeming fussiness about choice of pistol. Although he knew next to bugger all about guns then, he had to pretend he knew bugger everything.

# Four

Esther, on her conservatory lounger, turned up the gas heater. December was December even if the sun came out. Her recollections could continue to sprout, though, never mind the season.

Back in those Met days rumour grades R-, R, and R+ had been saying for weeks that a battle might be imminent between the Opal Render and Pasque Uno firms. Oh, really? Without dates, times, names, this alert didn't go much beyond the obvious, the customary, the useless, like a forecaster announcing there'd be weather tomorrow. Two outfits dealing drugs in districts alongside each other were sure to try for some – all? – of the adjoining ground and customer base. Hitler's quest for *Lebensraum* – living space – by taking over neighbouring countries was the same kind of colonizing.

Esther also thought of that Colombian 'godmother', Griselda Blanco, and the welter of killings she'd done, or ordered, of rival drugs gang members, until she got drive-by machine-gunned herself, very suitably, when leaving a butcher's shop, though she might have had no time to enjoy the in-joke. Griselda knew a company must expand or dwindle. It couldn't just flatline. This was a fundamental commercial, private enterprise law. Hence, Tesco – all those new stores. Flatline had two meanings, as Esther understood it: (a) to stay static; (b) to die, when the heart meter flatlined for a hospital patient, an image and continuous pinging sound much loved by movie-makers. In business, the first would cause the second.

R-, R, and R+ had agreed with one another that this fight would be 'all-out', 'final', 'decisive', 'bloody', 'critical', 'definitive': impressionistic, woolly terms that didn't help much with forward planning. Ultimately, it had required the AREA service to come up with reliable detail. This guidance had given absolutely correct date, time, location for the fight, and thirteen names, seven from Pasque Uno, six from Opal Render. These companies went in for fancy, mystifying titles – Pasque Uno, the single or unique flower; Opal Render, a glistening, glinting surface. Esther thought it was probably her handling of this lethal, territorial, street super-spat that put her name in lights for a while and helped with the steps up from detective superintendent to her rank now, Assistant Chief Constable. She'd set herself up as Gold – supremo – in a unit command vehicle that day, and had been able to see most of the action direct, or on screens taking filmed coverage from police cameras already in place to survey the probable battle area. There'd been five deaths, two hospitalizations and subsequent jailings, five arrests at the scene, also with subsequent jailings. That added up to twelve, not the AREA figure of thirteen.

She had an idea – less than an idea, a hindsight inkling – she had an inkling that the subconsciously noted starlings had appeared at one of the hottest and noisiest moments in the action. Squawking well, they'd soared and dived, effortlessly keeping their brilliantly tight squadron formation. Below them, Paul Elroy Stanton, leader of Opal Render, took four very cumulative rounds in the face, admirably close-grouped, and fell to the pavement, probably not recognizable any more, even by his mother and/or debt collectors.

Although it was a while ago, Esther recalled that he had on a magnificently cut, custom-made, dark, double-breasted, three-piece suit. His shoes were Raymond Roundel black lace-ups, the undersides showing hardly any wear and glossy with newness. About two centimetres of white shirt cuff fastened by silver links protruded from under the suit jacket's arms. People in these firms tended to be very meticulous about their clothes, shoes, haircuts and appearance in general. They could afford it. They accepted one of capitalism's wisest and most fundamental rules: plough profits back in; nourish the companies. They unstintingly invested in their firms. And since the firms were themselves they spent like crazy on tailoring, et cetera. He'd held an automatic in each hand, at least until he hit the ground.

Esther, mulling things now, could still have named all twelve either killed or convicted, and also someone called Ralph Wyvern Ember, listed as in the Pasque Uno contingent by AREA, but apparently not present for the confrontation. There had seemed to be six against six from the firms, plus, of course, Esther and her people, reinforced by marksmen and markswomen from the Met's specialist firearms consistory at Lippitts Hill in Epsom Forest. Because of the source's usual excellence on detail, they had done a rapid but very thorough post-op examination of the battle streets and lanes, in case R.W. Ember lay injured somewhere or dying or dead: nothing, though, and all blood and other leavings on the ground, walls, cars and front garden lawn patches, traceable to the twelve. Esther could find nobody of that name in the police national crime computer. Wyvern – the legendary armless dragon: what were his parents thinking when they called him that?

She'd ordered a detective to go back to the AREA source and find what was known about R.W. Ember. Not very much. He'd established a recent connection with Pasque Uno, but where he'd come from and where gone nobody knew. There might have been a wife or partner and children, more than one. Possibly a flat some-where near King's Cross station. Apparently, the source oozed apologies for his error. But Esther recognized that thirteen might have been sched-uled to take part and something prevented it; perhaps something too near the date for the source to know of; possibly, even, something on the very day of the set-to.

Esther sent a soft-soap, sophistry message to him saying the information had probably been basically right originally but put marginally out of date by an unanticipated change. This was like telling someone who thought it was Wednesday, although, in fact, it was Thursday, that he'd made no mistake because today would have been

Wednesday if it were yesterday. She assured him his AREA ranking remained unchanged and that, in fact, he'd be getting a one-off bonus. Her remarkably talented fink had helped neutralize twelve members of two gangs, and must be cherished and, in this instance, excused a gaffe. Clearly, thirteen would have been better, but twelve rated excellent and had led very soon to the extinction of both firms. A detective was as good as his or her informants made him or her, and this operation had placed Esther high, and due to go higher, thanks in part – major part – to a fine, only slightly overstocked, AREA whisper.

She had genuinely wanted her source to feel OK, and not to have worries about his reputation. To achieve and keep top billing an AREA informant must get things continually right and, preferably, completely right. Although major informants would not have 'By appointment to the Metropolitan police' nicely displayed on their stationery – or gravestones – a good history was crucial. Mistakes by a previously AREA-level informant could mean a tumble to category R+, or even lower, with a consequent fall in snitch salary; and the demotion very hard to reverse.

Esther remembered from school that Shakespeare had a character called Rumour at the start of one of the plays. Rumour got a pretty good kicking because it stuffed 'the ears of men with false reports.' Police didn't like getting stuffed, and they bore grudges. But the small error in this case could be tolerated, overlooked, and had set up no resentment in Esther.

# Five

Yes, back then, Ralph had needed to pretend he knew a real whack about guns. He tried to see himself as the Pasque Uno people would see him. For them, he'd be someone from nowhere who'd done a minor job quite well – fixing up some regular buying from PU by several of Ralph's friends. It was a start, but only a start. He had to plump up his image, get some solidity into what these others saw when they looked at him. And they *would* look at him. Maybe 'scrutinize him' was a better way of describing it. So, he'd try to seem gun-wise, gun-experienced, gun-choosy.

Of those three pistols available for the immediate situation – Browning, Walther, Beretta – he eventually picked the Walther. He'd acted very much from a gut feeling: that is, he could imagine some Opal Render bastard with a couple of Walther bullets in his guts and, just before he hit the ground, dead, probably deciding to ditch all hope of absorbing any of Pasque Uno's territory. Ralph liked the look of the P38 model, and it felt good in his hand, as if the metal of the butt had been fashioned specifically for his grip and now radiated a genial welcome to his palm, almost a kind of unstoppably fated fusion, like successful sex.

The P38 was biggish – more than twenty

centimetres long, Ralph guessed – which would make it difficult to conceal. The barrel must be about twelve centimetres. But it wouldn't matter that the gun was fairly obvious; and, in any case, the Beretta and the Browning seemed about the same size, but, somehow, didn't establish a rapport with him like the Walther. The kind of operation getting cooked up now would have firearms very much in view, nothing furtive or discreet. When you fought a war your weaponry was likely to be on show and as effective as you could make it. Think of propaganda scare pictures of that enormous piece of artillery in the Great War, 'Big Bertha'. And there was something else from around that era. Even as a teenager, Ralph had liked to read history and he'd been impressed by words from an Admiral of the Fleet, Lord Fisher: 'The essence of war is violence, and moderation in war is an imbecility.' At the time, that had seemed to Ralph very acute, an uplifting call for total win-win-win commitment.

Ralph currently, though – Ralph mature, Ralph reminiscing in the Monty bar – would regard matters differently. These days, he hardly ever carried a gun. For him, guns were the past, and not a past he felt any link to now. *Any* link? That so? None at all? Well, only intermittent. Very intermittent. No nostalgia. It would have been what the French called *nostalgie de la boue* – a longing to get back to degradation: to lawlessness and mayhem. That wasn't for Ralph, thanks very much. Juvenile. Uncivilized. He was Ralph W. Ember who wrote heartfelt, constructive letters to the local Press about environmental issues, and knew quite a number of French phrases.

And he considered it would be utterly off-colour to have a loaded, shoulder-holstered pistol nestling chummily under his jacket either at home in Low Pastures or at The Monty. Anomalous. He'd come across this word lately, meaning grossly out of harmony. So, yes, anomalous. In Ralph's opinion, a property like Low Pastures, with its notable history and Latin inscription on the main, tree-swathed gates into the grounds, deserved something finer than . . . indeed, something finer than an owner who went about with a secret shooter on his chest like some heavy. It was a matter of taste and tone.

He regarded both as deeply important, even vital. He had no aversion to guns in general. Obviously, a hunting rifle or shotgun would be absolutely OK and acceptable at Low Pastures, a country manor house or *gentilhommière* – more French! No, it was concealed, street-fight hand-guns he regarded as anomalous in a distinguished residence three hundred years old and more.

Similarly, he'd consider it inappropriate to go armed to The Monty, unless it became necessary, of course: that is, forced on him by extreme events and dangerous people. After all, this was a true and popular social centre, although admittedly not quite as he would have liked it, owing to present high yob, slob, slapper and villain membership levels. By introducing *The Marriage of Heaven and Hell* as a literary-visual, bullet-proof chunk up there, he hoped to thwart an enemy's guns; but this didn't mean that he himself had to come armed every day to what was acknowledged as a kind of comfortable, community haven. It would be crude. It would be unforgivably naff. True, The Monty had its smelly aspects, but Ralph didn't intend adding to them now by behaving like a gangster.

The plaque with a Latin quote on it must have been fixed to the gate by a previous occupant, who included, over the centuries, the local Spanish consul at one time, and, later, a county Lord Lieutenant. Classical languages would be right up their alley. The inscription said: '*Mens cuiusque is est quisque.*' To his abiding regret, Ralph had never learned Latin, but he found a translation on the Internet. 'A man's mind is what he is.' Ralph loved the blunt, straightforwardness of 'is what he is.' The repetition and simplicity really grabbed him. No weaselling. No 'possiblys' or 'perhapses' or 'on the other hands'.

He, personally, *wanted* to be judged on his mind, though many unfulfilled, copiously over-juiced women thought he resembled the young Charlton Heston, and craved intimate physical not mental contact, some calling him, 'The Last Hard Man' or 'Ben Hunk,' or 'El Stud', after several of the star's film roles. Some seemed fascinated by a scar down one of Ralph's cheek bones and would finger it unhurriedly. All this could be an embarrassing pest. He put up with it and, anyway, as he grew older his mind – the Ralph mind that *was* Ralph, the very essence of Ralph, according to the Latin – his mind made him unhappy, even queasy, about certain species of firearms.

27

He remembered and loathed one sentence from a novel called *The Grapes Of Wrath*. He'd read it during the American literature side of the university Foundation Year – 'a gun is an extension of themselves.' The tale showed families forced off their land and trying to settle in California, despite resistance from the locals. Someone said the immigrants could turn difficult if it came to a fight because they'd been brought up to regard guns as 'an extension of themselves.' Guns took on their owners' characters? Guns were natural to them – like a limb? Ralph W. Ember could never feel like that.

He cleaned the blue plaque every couple of weeks to keep it legible, and checked that the screws didn't corrode and let it drop into the dirt. Although hardly any visitors entering the Low Pastures spread via these gates would get the meaning of the Latin, they'd realize from it that they must be approaching a distinguished home, strongly respectful of education and learning. For its owner to be tooled up – even if imperceptibly – would bring an unwholesome, brutish, cordite factor into things, Ralph thought. 'Tooled up' – hell, such an ugly bit of phrasing. No taste, no tone. The search for these qualities never left Ralph alone. He didn't understand how others could fail to value them, too.

But this was now. Way back, when he'd only just landed a place with the elite Pasque Uno substances firm, at the beginning of a career – rather than today, at its pinnacle, or, at least, immediately pre-pinnacle – yes, in those earlier, different times, handguns had clearly figured as a routine necessity. It would have been impossible to trade efficiently and reasonably safely without the proper, fully loaded aids. An usherette in an old-style, traditional cinema, serving ice creams and so on in the interval, couldn't operate without a torch and that tray contraption hung around her neck. Likewise primed firearms in the pushing game.

The magazine of the P38 Walther he'd picked held eight rounds and he'd have a dozen replacements in his pockets. He could use a single or double hold, copying stances he'd seen in movies. The actual process of selecting the Walther had given his morale a nice boost. An extra boost. It was already high. Choosing, assessing, comparing, rejecting, put him in control. He was doing something to shape this coming war, shape his response to it, and, he hoped, decide its outcome. This had to be exhilarating. This had to strengthen self-hood. Several times lately he'd found himself humming that famous nineteenth-century song about the prospect of taking on Russia in a dispute: 'We don't want to fight, but by jingo if we do!' They'd enlisted him for the job. They trusted him to contribute. The shoulder holster struck him as bulky, but that didn't matter, either; on the day, his Walther wouldn't be in it for long, would it? 'The day' was due in just under a week.

There was a task ahead. He had been selected to take part. And, in turn, he had selected the elegant Walther to help him. The comfortable step-by-step logic of this sequence delighted and reassured the young Ralph. He'd seen that here was the kind of life he'd been born for – to guard and improve the interests of those who'd taken him into their team. He would deliver fearlessness, flair, fealty. He owed these. Ralph had fondled the Walther for a moment and given it a quick, jovial smile. Allies. Then he fixed the harness on and holstered the pistol.

But less than a week later he'd come to feel he didn't owe Pasque Uno anything at all.

# Six

Esther left the conservatory for a few minutes and went into the house. She unlocked the study wall safe – combination 'Hosea', her favourite Old Testament book, with its enraged toughness on 'transgressors', promising them a fall – and brought out a couple of cassettes. Of course, the prophets were on to a sure thing by promising a fall. Everyone would fall eventually or sooner. Life presumed death. Esther was fond of profound thoughts now and then. At her rank she felt entitled to them.

She took the playback machine from a shelf. In the kitchen she drank a glass of lemon squash and then returned to her lounger with the audio gear, old hat by present standards. She fitted the earpiece and began listening – re-re-listening – to the first of the cassettes. They contained the full briefing and debriefing material she'd used for the rumble on that day when Opal Render met Pasque Uno by appointment for street warfare. Esther and her armed troop had lurked hidden nearby at two locations, then suddenly intervened from both sides and cleaned up. She reckoned Hosea would have loved it: a right, tripartite smite, eliminating villains in their prime.

Esther had code-titled the operation 'Chastisement', a theme in quite a few O.T. books and sex guides. Incidentally, regardless of the

31

thump, thud and yell nuisance sometimes hesitantly mentioned to Esther by neighbours, she and her husband, Gerald, enjoyed a decent amount of intimate, erotic rough stuff, biting and, yes, chastisement. The houses were detached so the din for their next-door families shouldn't be all that bad, surely. Afterwards, either she or Gerald or both might have visible scars, and/or plasters, but, to date, definitely not splints. They had never explicitly discussed injury limits – that would have seemed corny and legalistic – but a kind of tender, instinctive agreement existed that they would not deliberately attempt bone breaks, nor gouging.

For one thing, Gerald needed his hands, arms and eyes OK in case job offers came. He was a professional bassoonist and was away on orchestral duties at present. Esther had done a full, systematic inspection of her body lately, with mirror use where necessary, and found herself almost totally unmarked except for two commingling, purple-edged bruises on her left inner thigh, fading very nicely. She wondered whether if she changed into short shorts to expose this area, the sun – made more powerful through the glass sides of the conservatory – would act medicinally and speed up the return to normal. But she had to wonder, also, whether glass-boosted winter sunshine would bring the affected skin location a fertilizing heat that restored the bruising to its full, foul picturesqueness. Could be the second. She instinctively pulled at her jeans, as though she had changed into the shorts and needed to cover the discoloured patch. The move reminded her of Marilyn Monroe in *Some Like It Hot*, tugging her skirt down to a primmer length when she discovers she's alone on a yacht at night with Tony Curtis.

Nowadays, Gerald had to take whatever jobs he could get. Esther would hate to hinder his search for work. His morale always slid if he could find none. He hoarded a bumper stock of self-pity, which he referred to as artistic temperament. Whatever it was called, Esther would have liked to lock it up in the Hosea safe and change the combination in case he had discovered what it was. How about a switch to 'Weepy?' Esther did not want Gerald at home too much. He would lie on the living room carpet and intone and/or scream the names of those who had refused to employ him recently, giving each a different mix of filthy curses – the same words, but in their own, personalized, made-to-measure order. He had a musician's sense of rhythm and memory for sonic patterns, and would repeat without notes or autocue the identical sequence of profanities for each of these targets, although there might be days between one grief-and-hate session and the next. She considered his paranoia to be top-notch, king-size, gilt-edged. She used to call the noise he made sometimes during a crisis his 'scream of consciousness': i.e., he had become conscious of what she had been conscious of for ages, that the best orchestras no longer wanted him. Busking next?

These Chastisement recordings were her private souvenir made covertly. She did that now and then on a case – a successful case. They provided

33

a memoir, a safeguard, a chin-up tonic if she felt low: masturbatory, maybe; she played with herself, but her past self. They offered a change from the formula, Jack and Jill brutalities with Gerald. She believed in looking all-round for satisfaction opportunities. *Carpe* fucking *diem.* Seize the day.

Back then in London, her much shorter, formal, typed version of the ambush had been lodged in Scotland Yard's computer data library, as was required. Esther had shaped and edited that to her advantage; a survival spin skill she'd taught herself over the years, and essential for promotion. Smart presentation was so crucial, nice packaging such a dinky art. To disclose the full, verbatim reproduction of those Chastisement meetings, though, could have started trouble. Esther had discovered that a main quality of good leadership was the ability to spot possible setbacks for her career and snuff them out early. If she ever needed a motto for her escutcheon, she felt it should be tersely, cogently, 'Me, I pre-empt.'

The tapes showed, didn't they, that she'd had very strong, timely evidence of exactly where and when the scrap would occur; and who'd take part; and with what weaponry? But she'd done nothing to forestall it, despite the stark, acute-carnage danger. This had menaced not just gang personnel and police, but utterly non-involved citizens, unluckily in one or other of the streets at a bad moment, to shop, or get coiffured, or buy stamps; a bad moment being a crossfire moment. In such a very limited area, that kind of disaster had been obviously possible. Some of the gunplay might be from gang crud with only sparse weapon training, and sparser accuracy: very uncool shoot-bang-fire merchants. They knew how to squeeze a trigger and that was it. Their bursts could go more or less anywhere and cut down more or less anyone. Collateral damage? Their speciality.

Why had she run the hit like that, then? Answer – *obvious* answer, she'd say – because Esther wanted the beautiful, holy simplicity of confronting both firms while they were clearly and undeniably on the job, *in flagrante delicto.* That is, openly, plainly, blatantly committing firearms crime, maybe maiming, maybe killing. Result, say: seven arrests and seven successful convictions. Stuff the bickering and pious defence QCs! Stuff identification difficulties! Bravo, Esther! Give the girl a coconut! She'd mock herself like that now and then.

This catch-'em-red-handed-at-it tactic was known as 'over the pavement' policing, and originally applied chiefly to bank hold-ups. Following a tip-off, bandits would be surprised and nabbed actually scurrying out to the getaway vehicle with their sacks of sterling. In the Pasque Uno/Opal Render case it would have needed to be 'over the pavements', plural. The action had snaked and billowed and erupted into several streets, red trails tracking the punctured. Yes, the phrase meant collaring villains while they were there, deep into the villainy, or starting their flit. This cut police dependence on witnesses, a real plus, a rare, splendid boon, because witnesses might

35

be terrorized or bribed or both into silence and/or selective blindness, by relatives or mates of the accused. And the glaring actuality and conspicuousness of the offence compelled juries to convict, even juries likewise nobbled by bribes and/or threats to themselves, their loved ones, property and long-haired dachshund.

OK, neat and tidy. But in the Pasque Uno and Opal Render clash there were also five deaths (three PU, two OR), an amputation (OR), a de-nosing (PU), and a permanent wheelchairing (PU). Some judges, some juries, some Press commentators, and a sanctimonious troupe of politicians didn't care for it when officers let a clearly hazardous situation build uninterrupted to such a bloody toll. The police might be accused of favouring this ploy because, from their angle, the more hazardous it was, the sweeter. All those arrested could be charged with something big and meaty. Gunfire on the streets was big and meaty, and therefore gorgeously apt for the heaviest, double-digit slammer sentences.

During several of the trials, there had, in fact, been what Esther considered nauseating, unworldly quibbles and whines about police set-ups and entrapment. Defence wigs did their usual trite, sententious, expensive bit about good ends never justifying questionable means, though they knew, of course, that sometimes they did. Anyway, as it turned out, they produced nothing strong enough to make judges stop proceedings, or to win not guilty verdicts. It helped that no officer was hurt, nor any innocent pedestrians, except very temporarily in their nervous systems.

Their bowels might have suffered some loosening, but also temporary.

Esther had calculated she'd probably get away with it. As she saw things, that's what high rank was about – guessing how near the knuckle you could go, and then going there and winning. She'd read a clever book describing the kind of leadership brain needed to estimate risk and intelligently calculate possibilities. True, Hitler, the Führer – super-supremo – had held high rank – none higher – but guessed rather poorly – calculated badly – when he decided to invade Russia, despite history and blizzards. OK, such occasional slip-ups would happen, yes, but the general principle of bold, properly informed chance-taking by top commanders stood. Best example? D-Day, when the Allies invaded France.

Although courts might get sniffy about situations that seemed deliberately allowed to reach outrage and slaughter, in the sly hope of making prosecutions easier, some courts might get even more sniffy about suburban shoot-outs. This, after all, was violence and chaos brought to ordinary people's doorsteps. The havoc reeked of civic and social breakdown; house-to-house mayhem; an Englishman's castle turned into a rat-run. It was ominous. It had bigger implications than itself, but was itself barbaric. It should be corrected by chastisement, and Chastisement.

# Seven

Esther's Cassette One covered an early, standby meeting when the AREA (Advice Requiring Emergency Action) information was promising but not yet complete. The emergency action would have to be only a prospect, a promise, at this stage.

She'd had a street map of the Dorothea Gardens, Mondial Street, Baste Lane, Meadow Street, and Trave Square area projected on to the conference room screen. 'Good morning. I've called you together today because we have very credible intelligence that an armed, territorial, face-to-face gun-engagement between Opal Render and Pasque Uno is imminent in the district shown. May I offer an explanation of the names in case it's necessary? "Opal Render" means "glinting surface" but is also an anagram of "Nepal Order", apparently a kind of Gurkha military formation that Piers Stanton, Opal's founder, thought suggested discipline and purpose. "Pasque Uno", a single flower, therefore unity.'

The kind of voice that came over to her on the replays always astonished Esther. It was younger, of course, and had picked up some traces of cockney during her Met postings, now more or less gone following her move to another force. But it was the casualness of her tone – bland, chatty, almost throwaway – that seemed so strange in retrospect. Detective Superintendent Esther Davidson, of those days, was announcing what would possibly rate as the most violent and lethal showdown ever seen in south-east London, although there'd be plenty of competition for this blaze-away tag. Inevitably, she'd realized at the time that this was how things might develop: she'd only have to note the weaponry listed, and consider the amounts of cash involved. Yet she spoke as if about some minor lawlessness problem, regularly dealt with and resolved, like bike theft or pissing in shop doorways by drunks.

The formal, ponderous 'gun-engagement' phrase sounded like officialese, an attempt to downplay the dodgy realities. And Esther felt the words, 'I've called you together today,' had a sort of churchy, pastoral flavour – 'where two or three are gathered together' – as if she were telling a group of the faithful which streets to letterbox-leaflet touting the next Roof Fund jumble sale.

'We think the activity will start at the corner where Mondial Street joins Trave Square. Most of you will know this has been a disputed strip of territory for at least months, even a year, characterized by isolated, fairly trivial barneys between dealers from the two firms. It now looks as though both sides have decided such recurrent, flea-bite aggro is anti-commerce and has to end; and that the way to end it is by moving in with numbers and challenging the opposition to dislodge them. We are not sure so far which firm will act first. They might even agree a time for confrontation, like people fixing a duel. It would be a properly staged honour fight. We do know they are equally alert to the possibilities and are ready to resist any major grab by the other. So, yes, probably a macho pride issue as much as a business and money matter.

'This is two champions – Piers Elroy Stanton, heading Opal Render's contingent, and PU's Dale Hoskins (Gladhand, as he's known) – these two with their minions, aiming to wipe the other out, and *his* minions. The encounter would be required by both sides to prove courage, flair, decisive chiefdom, charisma, and, as an extra, to consolidate fully a hold for one of the firms on these few hundred magnificently fertile square metres. That bit of ground linking Mondial and Trave has become symbolic for both firms, and symbols are always a massive pain, able to motivate all kinds of mad extremism, frenzy and barmy heroics. This location includes, of course, The Bouquet club and The Mall and Red Letter pubs, all significant trading centres. We'll take a look now. Next please.'

The voice on the tape paused. She had called for the screened street map to be replaced by a colour photograph of the Mondial-Trave corner. It was a picture she could still more or less visualize even so long after, idling here in the conservatory, half hearing the repetitive five-note racket made by pigeons in the winter-shrivelled trees. God, didn't they bore one another senseless? She heard, too, from somewhere over the back fence a car engine start up, and the crying of a child – faint through the conservatory glass wall, but audible. The tape, when it resumed, helped her memory, of course. She had given a detailed commentary on the buildings and road where the information said it would all most likely start, and where now, later, comfortably on the conservatory padded lounger, she knew it certainly did start.

Architecturally, Mondial-Trave had been quite an impressive spot. Four high, grey-stone Victorian warehouses stood tastefully converted to flats, with the ground floors shops, a hairdresser's, post office and a new car showroom. As a token, they'd left a projecting derrick near the top of one of the ex-warehouse facades. It would have been on a pivot and used to haul up goods for storing, and for lowering purchased loads to waiting carts. It didn't function like that any more, of course. The derrick and its pulley were there to give a reminder of local history. Esther had liked this preserved link with another century.

She didn't sentimentalize that period, knew some people, most people, had a hard, deprived existence then, and had very bad times at the dentist's. But she admired the soaring tallness and solidity of these structures. She found their businesslike, towering proportions a sign of confidence, resolve, progress. And the fact that they could last so well and take on recently a new, modern role and nature had heartened Esther, brought her a good helping of general optimism. Plans could work out OK. Some plans, anyway. Her plans.

'We assume – and it's only an assumption – no information on this – we assume Pasque Uno will come in from the south via Baste Lane and

Bertram Street, and Opal Render from the west via Charlton Road and Billigod Terrace. These estimates are based on the belief that each will start from their own established city sections, their home bases. My present thinking is that we'll have two police units waiting out of sight, each of fifteen officers, seven armed in each, one first-aid trained in each. One party will be positioned behind foliage in Dorothea Gardens, the other in the basement of one of the apartment blocks.'

Her voice speeded, lost some of its casualness. She didn't like talking about guns. 'Our armament will be the Heckler and Koch MP-Five carbines and Glock Eighteen automatic pistols. Information so far ties Gladhand Hoskins and two others in his group to Beretta Ninety-Three-R automatic pistols, usable for single shot or three round volleys; and at least two Swiss MP-Nine machine pistols in the Opal Render team, though we can't say yet who'll have them. There'll also be other pistols with both units, Brownings, Walthers, and Smith and Wessons. We count on being able to offer at least twice as much firepower as the two firms together.

'We should have surprise. PU and OR will turn up very single-minded and focused, expecting to confront each other. The third party will confuse them. They'll have to switch to wondering who's the enemy. We should be able to let them know the answer to that while they're trying to adjust.'

That had been a good prediction.

# Eight

More Monty staff arrived, ready for when the heavy business of the day began. Ralph remained seated at his little desk behind the bar, reminiscing under *The Marriage of Heaven and Hell*. He took a mouthful now and then from a bottle of sparkling spring water. It was too early for his favourite serious drink, black-labelled Kressmann's Armagnac.

He had a strange mixture of reactions as he thought back to earlier interesting moments in his career. Well, more than just interesting. 'Important' might be a better word, or even 'crucial'. He'd certainly regard that body-bag kerfuffle around Mondial Street and Trave Square during his south-east London days as important *and* crucial to his personal history. No wonder that word 'Mondial' kept popping out from the back of his mind somewhere to disturb him. He felt more or less sure it was from this episode that the rotten, cruel, grossly unjustified nicknames, 'Panicking Ralph,' or 'Panicking Ralphy', had their disgusting, slanderous start. He must try to establish this, and wipe it out for good.

In some ways, he envied his younger self, the up-and-coming, very confident, but still novice, Ralph. And, as to names, for a while then he'd considered asking Margaret and other people to call him Raef, rather than Ralph. That alternative spelling and pronunciation of Ralph seemed to carry more class and pep. He'd had the idea it was adopted in many distinguished families, especially by a son commissioned in, say, the Horseguards, or a similar glam regiment: Captain Raef Longville-Chase, that kind of thing. He'd liked the sound of 'Raef W. Ember'. The sharper, cleaner impact of the vowels in 'Raef' seemed to suggest someone gloriously devil-may-care. And the 'f' when it was 'f', not 'ph', had a more dashing, sexier edge. He had been so positive, forceful, optimistic then – 'comfortable in his own skin', as that weird modern phrase would put it. Who else's skin could you be in, whether you were called Ralph *or* Raef?

During that Foundation Year on his mature student degree course he'd had to do a bit of everything, and, as well as phrases from *The Grapes Of Wrath*, Ember recalled and responded heartily to lines in a chewy poem that went something like this: 'It was bliss in that day to be alive, but to be young was very heaven.' Or possibly not 'day' but 'dawn'. That was stronger, stressing the marvellous newness and unfolding promise of the experience.

And maybe 'bliss' came earlier, to emphasize it: 'Bliss was it in that dawn to be alive,' et cetera. Poets did that kind of thing. They were very used to dealing with words. Well, obviously: you couldn't have a poem without words. They'd put them in a certain order, possibly an *unusual* order, to get extra impact. Probably, writing a poem could take weeks. The poet here wanted what might be termed a double whammy from 'bliss'.

So, 'Bliss was it in that *dawn* to be alive.' But to be young then produced not just bliss but bliss-plus; a big plus. Absolutely!

Ralph shared the heartfelt, nostalgic emotion. It matched his memory of a continuous rapture he'd enjoyed during the first year or two of his entry into vigorous, very private, private-sector, commercial life, dealing capably in the substances, cash only, same place and time next week, 'and have the money ready in your hand so we're not hanging about and obvious doing the deal.' Yes, private private-sector. This had been his splendid 'dawn'. He came to realize then that he'd been born with a vocation for such work, similar to a priest's in the church, or the poet's. It had made Ralph feel chosen, privileged, separated off from the general crowd. He'd sensed he had a special destiny, and he had been entirely ready to go out and meet it.

Obviously, the eight-round Walther P38 automatic hadn't represented the essence or core of that wholly satisfying commercial life he was starting, but it *was* a significant fringe factor, more than an accessory. And so, Ralph had decided he should get nicely familiar with it. The prospect delighted him: first, careful hesitation in picking the right gun and then swift decisiveness. He'd immediately planned a practice shoot in a stretch of woodland he'd walked near Orpington to improve aim and to gauge and cater for recoil. Accuracy beyond six or seven metres with a handgun was worryingly unreliable, unless you'd been marksman trained. But, he'd thought – correctly thought, as things turned out – he'd

45

thought the action around Mondial-Trave would be within that kind of distance, truly face to face, face to blast-away face and, therefore, half a day spent getting to know the Walther had to be worthwhile; getting to know not merely its comradely feel and shape, but its practical, wipe-the-Opal-Render-bastards-out-before-they-can-wipe-you-out potential.

Although he still disliked the description of a gun as an extension of some people's actual physiques, a well-managed pistol could be a valuable aid, a vital standby. Bliss was it in that dawn to *stay* alive, and a Walther nine mm might help. This eager wish for intelligent mastery of the gun was part of his happy approach to the grand business chance he'd been offered. He would strive to excel. This would be like an apprentice ballet dancer practising, striving, yearning for perfection and ready to work at it unrelentingly. Bliss was it in that dawn to be alive, but to be young and part of a dynamic, established, commodities trading company, supremely ready to hit shit out of any dangerous, invasive competitor, was very heaven; especially if sweetly backed by an automatic and a good stock of ammo. Obviously, the poet couldn't go in for that kind of thinking.

And, as William Blake had noticed when doing Ralph's overhead, sheltering, Monty collage illustrations, there was heaven but also hell, and the two sometimes lay very close together, as in what he termed a 'marriage'. Yes, it had been fine – very heavenly – to become part of the Pasque Uno organization; but what about the appalling, vindictive – very hellish – results of that PU

46

operation, and the contemptuous name-tab/-tabs, stuck on him afterwards: the dual-version 'Panicking' smears?

And they *were* smears, weren't they? They had no basis in truth, surely. Occasionally, in rather harsh self-scrutiny moments, he did wonder whether only someone deranged by panic could have had the William Blake anti-hitman, save-my-skin bastion installed. Would the *young* Ralph have caved in so flagrantly to fear like that? Would he have cowered under it, as some would say Ralph was cowering now? Yes, some *would* say it, some *would* sneer and insultingly deride this special defence device. It was as if they thought he should have it painted yellow, to proclaim his funk.

Not long ago a rum-sloshed, giggling Monty member wagging a pistol like a sword had fired a couple of shots from a .38 Smith and Wesson at *The Marriage of Heaven and Hell* from the bar, holing one of the Blake figures very badly in the beard and creating a real hazard for club customers through whining ricochets off the impenetrable metal. Those bullets came back with ten times the power of a returned service in Grand Slam tennis. An almost full bottle of Worcestershire sauce used in Bloody Marys caught one of these diverted rounds, causing glass splinters to fly as well as brown liquid to splatter on another member's T-shirt and arm and on the play-surface of a pool table, which would require delicate cleaning.

The sod responsible was instantly banned for ever from The Monty, on health and safety grounds, although he apologized almost at once and offered to get the T-shirt laundered and find and pick up the sharp, Worcestershire shards. He wanted to pay a thousand compensation into club funds – meaning Ralph's – for the distress and peril involved, and vulgarly brought a roll of fifties and twenties from his pocket, but Ember refused. For one thing, how could he tell where that loot originated?

Altogether, it was one of those incidents that Ember considered could never take place at The Athenaeum or even The Garrick in London; the kind of incident he was determined to eradicate. The Athenaeum might have members who routinely packed a piece – say top officers from one of the secret security services – but they were unlikely to get pissed and then start pot-shotting at something designed to bring security itself, supposing The Athenaeum had such an item of decorated strategic equipment; unlikely, he thought.

Yes, didn't that S. and W. idiot typify other idiots who seemed set on offending Ralph? They could be squashed, though. He began to recover from his doubts and self-blame. OK, maybe the younger Ralph would not have had the bullet-blocking strip put in place. But the young Ralph had been . . . had been . . . young. That meant gravely lacking experience. That meant casual-ness, carelessness, foolish blaséness. It meant the passing wish to be audacious, cocky Raef, aiming to win a peerage for services to snorting. It meant having collected few serious enemies, if any so far. It meant no proprietorship of a famed,

48

esteemed club, such as The Monty, and the target this might be to such enemies. It meant someone only at the bottom of the career ladder and unable to see from there the absolute need for that benignly robust, hoisted barricade.

The name Ralph, as Ralph, not Raef, had its own considerable qualities. He'd been told it came from the Norsemen many centuries ago and one half meant 'counsel', as in worthwhile advice, and the other half 'wolf' – so, maybe, 'wise wolf, leader of the pack.' That was quite an impressive reputation, and one he believed suited him so much more than 'Panicking Ralph' or 'Ralphy'. He believed most reasonable people would agree.

# Nine

Just before the Mondial-Trave set-to Dale Hoskins had taken Ember and a couple of the others from Pasque Uno out to reconnoitre the slice of ground where the fighting would most likely centre itself. They knew the area well already, of course, because both firms did a lot of dealing there. It was the natural site for any confrontation. The Bouquet Club and two pubs provided true hives of rich business. Also, street commerce went on very vibrantly there, and in Dorothea Gardens, a delightful park with mountain ash and eucalyptus trees, a clear water stream, a bowling green and children's swings and climbing frames. Ralph thought it immensely heartening to see such a beautiful environment on the one hand and the trade on the other brought happily together like that.

But now they had to look at Mondial-Trave and the Gardens as a probable urban battleground, not a prime, consistent marketing venue. Ralph felt the roles were utterly different, just as in the Great War a field at, say, Ypres, could have been regarded originally as simply a field, part of the agricultural scene; but later only as a key piece of no man's land to be battled for by mighty armies.

A monument of Richard Robert Laucenston, a Victorian alderman wearing robes, stood in front of the converted warehouses, perhaps the owner when they ran their former trade. Ralph had seen

50

the sculpture before and admired it: another link with that bustling, workaday, enterprising past. Feet wide apart, crouched slightly forward, as if about to bullock his way ahead for further business quests and triumphs, the alderman usually gave Ralph a terrific thrill of fellow-feeling, a kind of across-the-decades empathy. This was entirely selfless admiration because Ralph believed that unless there was real progress in legalizing the substances he was never himself going to get a city monument. It would be tricky for Ralph or anyone else in Pasque Uno, or for any other devotee of the trade, to be given that kind of recognition if attitudes remained as they were at present.

Now, though, Ember experienced more than a brotherhood bond with the alderman. He noted the stone impenetrability of the monument, saw it as a good piece of cover, something you could pop out from behind and fire your burst, then nip back fast and get the hard bulk of the plinth and Laucenston's legs and lace-ups between you and retaliation. The retaliation could be severe if rumours about Opal Render's weaponry were correct.

Alderman Laucenston, 1847–1899, had obviously been a solid citizen in the sense of public spirited and honest, but now that solidity had taken on a new meaning – a more concrete meaning, you could say – and might get helpfully between Ralph and an Opal Render bullet or – more probable – bullets. Ralph thought the alderman would understand totally the need for his statue to be adapted to this particular use for a day. Wasn't substantial commercial progress the purpose of PU's and Ralph's coming fight? That must have been the main theme in Laucenston's own fine career. In fact he would return – reciprocate – the deep approval *Ember* usually offered to *him*. He'd prize Ralph as someone who knew how to live with the changes of time, such as the presence of machine pistols, blood on the pavement, perhaps, as well as cascading fragments from a monument and its plinth caused by volleys.

Which pavement, pavements? They'd try to get an idea of that during their visit now. Hoskins drove. He had on one of those rural county, ginger tweed suits he fancied, waistcoat included, with pocket-watch gold chain across it. They were in a stolen Vauxhall. Hoskins' big new Mercedes could have been recognized, and Hoskins' big new Mercedes with four men in it intently eyeballing the street-scene might indicate something beyond a pleasure jaunt. Ralph thought the precaution was not much more than a twitch, though, forced by the long habit of business secrecy in that private private-sector. Didn't everyone in both firms know there'd be an absolute, winner-takes-all tussle here soon? Ralph had amused himself with the fancy that the head-on clash was so inevitable there might be a foreboding of it in one of the Old Testament prophets. 'For Pasque Uno had a little army and Opal Render did, too. And, yea, they did fall upon each other at the place called Mondial-Trave in the land of Peckham-East Dulwich, OK, not quite a holy place, but up there among the tops for grass and coke. And Pasque Uno said this terrain shouldest be theirs, but Opal Render said, "Stuff

52

that, mate, it's ours," so get your catapults primed and go to Daniel for training if you like.'

Secrecy hardly mattered, and, naturally, some reconnaissance was bound to take place by each side. It would have been a dark laugh if PU met an Opal Render vehicle doing the same sort of survey. *'Well, what ho there, gents! Are you looking for an idyllic picnic ground, like us?'* But it didn't happen. Opal Render had possibly already conducted their on-the-spot tour, or would come tomorrow, or the day after.

Ralph was in the back with Greg Mace. Quentin Stayley had the front passenger seat. This had been Ralph's first experience of major work for the firm and he'd felt excited, proud, determined to learn. Although he'd been in stolen cars before, it had never been for such a momentous purpose as this. His mind had been wide open and events and conversations imprinted themselves vividly there, imprinted themselves deeply there, imprinted themselves more or less immovably there; he could still do something he believed fairly close to a detailed recall.

Hoskins had said it was pointless to pretend they knew how the opening moves would go. Nobody could prescribe in advance the detailed moves of a battle. He saw variable elements depending on all sorts. They had to plan fluid, play adjustable, get at them how they *could* get at them – *'ad* fucking *hoc,* like.' It had always seemed bizarre to Ralph when someone like Gladhand in a ginger, Royal Ascot Enclosure suit, and with the watch chain meaningfully across his waistcoat, broke up a word or phrase to stick 'fucking' between. But perhaps Gladhand had *wanted* to unsettle Ralph and others by the sudden mauling of the language style expected from someone in that sort of suit and with a fob watch.

Then Hoskins had gone on with an analysis along the lines of, 'It's possible we'll destroy them right away and totally, which is, obviously, how we'd like it, nice and tidy. OR RIP. But maybe the luck don't look after us quite so complete at once and what we got to do is impose ourselves, take over the shaping of things, drive any still-resisting remnants down into—'

He'd glanced right and briefly took a hand off the wheel and pointed with his thumb. 'Here it is now, we're just passing – drive them down into the *Red Letter*'s car park which, of course, is high-walled so we got them cornered and a final wipe-out can take place there. Again, nice and tidy, though not quite so simple as if it had happened earlier. Except at evenings the car park don't usually get many vehicles. There shouldn't be much for them to hide behind. Quentin, Greg, this is your position, the car park.'

'Message received and understood,' Greg said. He sounded relaxed, playful, ready to accept whatever Hoskins ordered. Greg was mid-twenties, very pale skinned, a good bit overweight, wearing a long navy jacket and khaki chinos, old suede desert boots, crimson, open-necked shirt, small, silver cross on a silver neck-chain resting on his chest.

Hoskins said: 'You're waiting there and you don't stop them coming in, not at all, it's what we want, but once they're in you've got them, no exit. This should be the final ploy. You'll be on foot, Quentin, Greg. We don't put one of our own vehicles in the car park owing to possible gunfire damage making it undrivable, in which shitty case you two could still be there with your armament and them bodies when the 999 emergency call police arrive. It would be *you* who was trapped then. No trouble for them proving murder. But we'll have a donated Lexus ready to pick up the two of you and disappearing as soon as you've done a neat and full wipe-out in the car park – chauffeur for this exit, Hector Lygo-Vass.

'Hector's not with us today, but he'll get down here later and have his own squint, with good concentration on the *Red Letter* locality, to note what might turn out to be any special problems for a getaway motor, like some road-crossing patrol who thinks she got a right to step out and stop the traffic. Hector would prefer not to hit someone like that at speed. Hector's a brill Wheels, thoughtful, twenty-twenty eyes, unflashy. Acceleration is his brother. His right sole got perfect intimacy with that pedal, like fused.

'OK, landlord and owner of the *Red Letter*, His Royal-*fucking*-Highness, Clifford Grange, won't be pleased at first with this outcome on his premises, the car park being, clearly, part of them premises He would rather not have artillery and subsequent deads and wounded littering that car park. He got notices up on walls there saying the pub can't be responsible for no damage caused, but that's only to do with bumps by vehicles, or vandalism. That sort of warning don't really mean corpses in the car park, though. All right, all right, understandable. It's unkempt and don't do the reputation of a pub good, even a pub like *Red Letter.* But sod Cliffy. We can't hardly go to him in advance and ask would he mind if we use that patch of ground to carry out a rather essential slaughter programme? There got to be a certain degree of confidentiality re these tactical plans.'

Ralph remembered that Greg Mace gave a big, deep chuckle. It had seemed wrong for someone so pale. He said: 'We could tell him, "Cliffy, you might have thought this was a car park, but, really it's an abattoir, though only on a temporary basis, so don't get all fretful."'

Hoskins said: 'He got to be instructed how to think long-term, not just instant reaction to what will be a hot eventuality, I admit. Clifford should take into account that them few minutes of undoubted stress will lead to an enduring period of settled peace, not just in the car park but for the pub itself and the general Mondial-Trave area. Once these crisis minutes are over he can get his pub back to its settled position as a grand facility for sale of the substances, along with the beer and crisps. And that settled position will be even more settled and safe from aggro because there'll be no other firm to jostle PU and cause division and upsets.

'The short, fracas period of gunfire and disturbance should be regarded as a cleansing operation. Now, it's plain I don't mean what was called "ethnic cleansing" in the past such as around the Croatia and old Yugoslavia region. This is not to do with race, it's about peaceful, untroubled trading, something, surely, to be desired by all, but unfortunately not available to all yet – and I stress, yet – because one firm got a kind of survival duty to squash the other. Goodbye OR, and God bless. Basically, the minutes of acute conflict and anxiety – nobody can deny they'll come – but them minutes are ultimately a gain for Cliff Grange and the *Red Letter,* as well as the totality of the general environs. This will be the land of milk and honey and money.'

Gladhand had been gentle and persuasive, very suitable for the brave, perfect logic of his argument, Ralph thought. Ember had always been a great fan of logic. He loved watching, and even taking part in, the methodical, stage-by-stage progress towards proving a conclusion. Most probably humans were the only creatures in the animal creation who could do logic. Other animals acted very logically, yes – such as a fox killing a chicken, because the fox and its family had to eat, and the fox was stronger than the chicken. There wouldn't be that stage-by-stage, but-on-the-other-hand move towards deciding to kill the chicken or not, though, because it came completely natural to the fox to kill chickens. No logic was needed and there was no other hand to supply a but. The fox just got its teeth into the chicken's neck because that's what foxes did and why they had that sharp muzzle so they could be theirselves and bite necks.

Dale would have been mid-thirties then, young to head a company. Possibly he chose the fogeyish, squire-type suits and the antique-style watch and chain to mimic more maturity. He had circled the big roundabout at the Dorothea Gardens end, then taken them back for another gaze at the *Red Letter,* the car park and the approaches.

Quentin Stayley swivelled in the passenger seat to talk to Hoskins: 'I suppose what we got to hope, Dale, is that it's not *us* who get pushed back into the terminal car park.'

Hoskins said: 'Right, Quent. That is definitely a danger.'

'Dale, we have exactness and precision about what occurs at the later stage, but an absence of that exactness and precision as to the opening minutes of the conflict,' Stayley said. 'The sequence is not clear. *Il y a des lacunes*, as the French would say. There are considerable gaps. I return to my recent remark: how do we get to the situation where we are pushing the OR lot back towards the *Red Letter* car park and are not pushed towards the *Red Letter* car park ourselves?

'A spot-on observation, Quent,' Hoskins agreed. 'It's why I said we got to plan fluid, play adjustable.'

'It's vague and chancy, Dale,' Mace said.

'It *is*, Greg,' Hoskins replied. 'I could see that, but your comments make me even more aware of them uncertain elements. Thank you. I'll give further thought.'

This was so like Dale. He hardly ever got ratty and injurious because someone put a question mark on what he'd just said. Up to a point, up to quite a point, Hoskins could cope with others' views on a situation. It was one reason he had the nickname 'Gladhand'. He'd treat with civilized warmth and a decent smile almost anybody, even those in disagreement with him, and even those below him in the firm, which meant everyone in the firm.

All this was a long while ago, of course, and Ralph realized he might not have all the conversations absolutely as they were. But he certainly had their drift right. And, over the years, he'd continually gone back in memory to those days and nights, so things had remained pretty accurately, nearly verbatim, in his head. Some of the phrasing was so important that Ralph couldn't have forgotten it, anyway, even if he'd wanted to. And the phrases acted as sort of bullet points to bring the rest of it back: 'acceleration is his brother' (Gladhand); 'thought this was a car park, but, really, it's an abattoir' (Greg Mace); 'fracas period of gunfire' (Gladhand); 'terminal car park' (Quent); that bit of French from Quent that sounded like something to do with lagoons; 'vague and chancy' (Greg).

There was quite a whack from Quent Stayley on that Vauxhall saunter. He was about forty-five, thin framed, thin faced, maybe not too content with getting bossed about by someone ten years younger in a farcical suit. Quentin himself had on dark-blue jogging gear and red and white training shoes. He didn't seem to have lost any of his fair-to-mousy hair and wore it in a ponytail fixed with a thick, red elastic band, probably discarded in the street by a postman. Ralph knew Quent had education beyond comprehensive school. He could get very articulate and bring in those bits of French without any special fuss. This seemed to show not just that he knew some French but that he thought the people he was with, such as Gladhand, Ralph and Greg, could also do French and would be familiar with the lagoons and how they came into the reckoning. He obviously had a certain kind of background. That day, he had moved about too much in his seat, as though pent up.

Ralph had felt a bit the same. Rehearsals and reconnaissance always bored him, though he recognized they might be vital. Ralph kept reasonably still and observant, memorizing systematically streets, buildings, the sculpture, that he already knew, but which he'd know with a lot more detail after today. Quentin also gazed about, but apparently had to move his whole body to cover the various perspectives, as if needing to see around lagoons. This restlessness in Quent didn't appear to trouble Gladhand. He could be very patient and tolerant.

But, of course, to speak of someone glad-handing had a half suggestion that the display of friendliness was *only* display, a meaningless gesture, even phoney: for instance, politicians glad-handed among supporters so as to keep their vote. And *only* to keep their vote. They forgot everyone they'd glad-handed as soon as they'd glad-handed them.

Dale Hoskins could switch to very rough. Now and then it had been as if a knuckleduster figured on the gladhand. He was founder and leader of a firm and Ember realized this job needed more than the milk of human kindness, and less. Many nicknames radiated a pleasant, unhurtful nature, such as 'Tiny' for someone 200lbs and 6' 4" but several had a taint, or more and worse than a taint, such as 'Panicking Ralph,' 'Ralphy'. Nobody called Hoskins 'Gladhand' to his face. Its tone was too uncertain. Best not to upset Hoskins, Ralph thought. Dale might garrotte you with that watch chain using both gladhands.

60

# Ten

Esther on her lounger listened to a younger, lower-ranked, London-based Esther on tape: not someone she felt totally fond of. The gas fire fought a losing battle against the conservatory cold. Cloud blanked off the feeble December sun for a few minutes. She felt her voice came over as brisk, a bit clangy and know-all, maybe designed to shiver into fragments the glass ceiling that kept women from top police jobs then.

'I want to talk today about Pasque Uno and Opal Render personnel,' the recording said: this was more from the pre-operation briefing. 'We have names – some names – of those likely to be involved in any confrontation. The list is probably not exhaustive and might contain occasional errors, but I think it's broadly accurate. You will be notified of any necessary amendments.' *Lads, lasses, you can rely on me. I'll decide what you can be told and when you can be told it.* That was how she sounded, Esther thought. *Listen up, underlings.* She hoped she'd learned something about humility since then, or not so much humility itself but the semblance of humility. Top cops couldn't be genuinely humble, for God's sake. After all, the job was about going one better than the crooks – at least one better. Humility wouldn't do.

'Two sources, wholly independent of each

other, naturally, have produced the names, and there's a good measure of agreement between them. The sources are: (one), our original informant who also defined the likely location. That is, the Mondial Street-Trave Square junction and corner; (two), our own observation. We have maintained a continuous, clandestine watch at Mondial-Trave since it was tentatively identified, as itemized at (one).

'I'll take Pasque Uno first. Our informant gives the following line-up: (a) Dale (Gladhand) Hoskins, age thirty to forty. This, of course, we would expect. He is head of PU and accustomed to leadership, compelled by leadership: the *noblesse oblige* of the gear game.'

There'd been a projector to screen pictures of some of the people she mentioned, photographic quality variable. A few were official police mugshots. Others looked as if they'd been snatched, the target apparently unaware of the camera – angles sometimes awkward, a face and/ or physique, part-obscured by other, irrelevant people or foliage or vehicles. That seemed true of the Gladhand pictures: two in the street, one with a dog, some sort of terrier, on a leash, and walking in what could be a park, possibly Dorothea Gardens. Rhododendrons blanked much of his jaw and upper body, though the dog came out well. One of the street snaps got him only in half profile, with a Royal Mail van and a billboard touting final days of a sofa sale behind. This sofa sale was always in its final days.

Esther said: 'The heavy, three-piece lord-of-the-manor suit on Gladhand is more or less a constant. Social ambitions. I mentioned the *noblesse.* Middle height, square built. He can present a mild, genial personality, but has ample, standby stocks of grade-A savagery. Without it in that trade, he couldn't have got to where he is so early. As a matter of cred and self-respect, he must accept the same risks as his people, anyway. He can't abstain. He'll be there, no question. Preferred armament, Springfield semi-automatic. No convictions. Married. Infant twin sons, teenage daughter. Lives in large Cheyne Walk, Chelsea, property (four to five million pounds) containing a meditation suite, gym and indoor pool, stylishly minimal lounge furnishing – the "Black and White" room. Butler, Pedro, possible illegal immigrant. Continuously waistband armed.

'(b) Hector Lygo-Vass, age twenty-eight. Specialist driver. Some rally experience. Family significant in Cumberland, at least until the war – a sizeable estate and mansion. Sir Brandon Coss Lygo-Vass big in two Wellington campaigns as young cavalry officer, including Lines of Torres Vedras victory, Portugal. Family in bad tangle with the Revenue over tax 1950s. Enforced sale to settle and meet legal costs. Possible injustice – or probable: Inland Revenue official sacked for some sleight of hand but no redress for the Lygo-Vasses. Resultant hatred-stroke-contempt in Hector for legality and due procedure. Also Springfield. Maybe PU got a two-for-the-price-of-one deal. No convictions. Separated. No children.

'(c) Gregory Francis Mace, mid-twenties. Accountancy background. Accompanies Hoskins as negotiator on trips to bulk suppliers. Instant mental calculations. Uzi machine pistol. Served one year of two-year sentence for embezzlement. The picture is standard mugshot. Skin showing cell pallor? Gay partnered by general practitioner.

'(d) Clive (Aftermath) Palgrave, thirty-four. Street pusher and general heavy. Possession and dealing convictions. Mugshots ahoy. Married, one child (d), one stepchild (s), both at school. Has survived several rough episodes, hence the nickname: always alive at aftermath, so far. Unrelated to *Palgrave's Golden Treasury* poetry anthology, though doesn't personally deny the link.

'(e) Ralph Wyvern Ember, mid-to-late twenties, young Charlton Heston lookalike. Unclear background. No convictions. Big ambitions. Married, Margaret, but wanders: women keen for experiences with El Cid, Ben Hur and Moses, in any order. Two daughters, Venetia and Fay. Probable nine millimetre eight-round Walther automatic. PU could be his first contact with major commerce. Untested in street warfare? Lives near King's Cross station.

'(f) Quentin Stayley, age forty-five. Oxford literature degree. Boxed and golfed for university. Briefly public school teacher. Expensive divorce beyond teacher's salary. Entry to the trade via a pupil's sympathetic parents. Present partner, Lucille Eldon. No children from any relationship. Mac Ten machine pistol. Possible hostility, envy, towards Gladhand – boss though younger, and fertile, Stayley sterile?

'Mimi Apertine, age fifty-one, street and rave pusher and occasional Gladhand bodyguard. Divorced two husbands and reverted to maiden name. Served eight years in Israeli army, rising to sergeant-major equivalent. Uzi machine pistol and grenades. Sister of Lester Apertine (stage name, Nascent), pop musician and singer. Scarred right cheek and ear lobe missing, as pictured, following shooting range accident. Two grown-up children in Israel. Fancies Ralph W. Ember, but age precludes.'

Now that Esther was older she found herself resenting the offhanded terseness of that comment by her less mature self, like fifty-one was death. 'Age precludes' – so final, so absolute as if everyone would take it for granted. Time, a sod. On the tape a pause followed. Then: 'I revert to (two), our observation unit and camera at Mondial-Trave. On the screen now you see film of a stolen Vauxhall, presumably chosen for anonymity. Almost certainly the four men in this car are conducting what they intend as a secret reconnaissance visit to the probable fight site, some listed names missing. A vehicle belonging to any PU member might be recognized and its purpose obvious. The security obsession seems superfluous, though, as the battleground is apparently agreed on.

'The photograph shows the four occupants fairly clearly: Gladhand at the wheel in a ginger three-piece suit, Hector's high-grade driving flair not required. This is just a jaunt. Stayley alongside Hoskins, Ember and Mace in the rear. Stayley seems to do most of the talking. That would be in character. Has possible ambition to lead Pasque Uno. Stayley's babble attritional? The four appear to be much focused on the *Red Lion* pub, and possibly its car park. This is ground they must all know well already from ordinary trading routines but, of course, they need to look at it differently today. Concealment nooks, cover spots, fields of vision, to be noted and not forgotten. The Victorian alderman's statue and its big, square, granite plinth are significant only as a potential useful sniping position: a quick volley, a quick withdrawal behind the stonework, count to ten slowly, maybe reload, then emerge and blast off again. Perfect action examples for *The Urban Warrior's Manual*. There might be a few chippings knocked off the alderman in any shooting activity, but he'll survive. He's from a robust Victorian tradition of service and self-fulfilment, a lesson to us all.'

# Eleven

Thinking too much about the past could make Ralph Ember jumpy and restless. In an attempt to steady himself he glanced up to where the vandalizing bullet rip in *The Marriage of Heaven and Hell* beard was hardly visible. Some beautifully skilled patching had been carried out by an interior decor firm Ralph trusted, not just for its flair but its empathy. These were people who understood Ralph's deep fondness for certain art work and steel.

Enjoyment of the restored illustration only halfway calmed him, though. Ralph found it impossible to sit still any longer and he stood up from his chair under the William Blake and had a little walk around the bar area of the club, into the kitchen then back to the pool table corner. The Worcestershire sauce staining on one table's baize had taken the form of a large, brown exclamation mark with dot. No trace of that remained now after successful cleaning, but he did a token examination, really only to justify his ramble to any of the staff or early customers who might be watching him. The repairs here and overhead were excellent. He should have been relaxed and at ease, but still wasn't.

The past harassed him. Yet, during that drive years ago in the stolen Vauxhall with Gladhand, Quentin Stayley and Greg Mace, he had felt at first entirely relaxed and at ease – excited, yes, favourably excited, full of optimism and a kind of derring-do. This cheerful confidence seemed foolish to him now, youthful, green. It made him edgy, in retrospect. Perhaps this was what happened when you grew older.

In the rear of the Vauxhall, alongside Greg, he'd relished early on not just the thrilling sense of comradeship and that glorious shared purpose – the sweet and timely blasting of Opal Render – but also an awareness of his own special role; unique role, in fact. He would change his attitude a fair amount soon, but for the moment he felt very content. He had been chosen for this excursion today because he would be looking at the layout with comparatively new eyes. The others had seen Mondial-Trave innumerable times, since so much business was done there. Ralph himself had been here more than once since he joined PU, but not very often – not to the point of staleness. He might see things others would miss owing to overfamiliarity.

Dale Hoskins obviously realized Ralph possessed a precious sharpness of view. It heartened Ralph to think he must radiate valuable qualities he was not previously conscious of. He thought 'deft and original' would be the correct terms for his examination that day of Mondial-Trave.

Yes, yes, Quent had been allocated the front seat next to Gladhand while Ralph was stuck in the back with Mace, but this hardly proved that Gladhand regarded Stayley as superior, as his deputy. The seat surely brought no co-pilot status.

All right, Quent had a literature degree from Oxford. That didn't mean he could create an innocent-seeming, unruffled manner doing the Vauxhall formalities, so as not to draw public curiosity. Ralph regarded the word 'create', as vital here. Quent lacked the kind of creative impetus which, clearly, Gladhand detected in Ralph, and which must put Ralph far ahead in Gladhand's grading of staff. The front-seat position had no significance. Ralph could do his survey duties quite effectively from the rear windows and could also put on a casual kind of air so that nobody watching the Vauxhall would think it a reconnaissance vehicle.

In any case, Quent used his situation to nag Gladhand – to turn, and from right alongside harass him with miserable suggestions that PU might get slaughtered at Mondial-Trave-*Red Letter*. Although this behaviour didn't seem to trouble Gladhand, it was idiotic, potentially harmful pessimism by Quent – even alarmism. It showed jitteriness, poor spirit, disbelief in Gladhand's grasp of tactics for a built-up-area clash. Quent had more or less said that what Gladhand envisaged for OR could possibly get neatly, disastrously reversed on the day, so it was PU that went under, not OR. The obnoxious, tidy tit-for-tatness of this argument was bound to upset and enrage Gladhand, although on the face of it he treated Quent with politeness – a politeness Quent did not deserve, even though forty-five at least, the prat. Gladhand would get back at him eventually and in his own manner. Ralph had looked forward to watching that, known as comeuppance.

Stayley reeked of uppance. It had a rubbery whiff because of the elastic band holding his pigtail. Ralph had thought, what a comedown for that rubber band. Yes, it had probably been a postman's and would have held a clutch of what might be very important, even valuable, letters. But now its only role was to get a grip on that rubbishy sheaf on the back of Stayley's neck.

The Vauxhall was due to be dumped at least a day before the actual combat rendezvous. Gladhand and Mimi had worked out a quite detailed programme for everybody and everything to be part of the Mondial-Trave fight. She could help with such planning having had a lot of logistics experience in the army. Naturally, other stolen vehicles would be used on the actual day – probably vans, able to carry half a dozen or more people. There wasn't going to be any link between the Vauxhall and a gunfight at Mondial-Trave-*Red Letter.*

'Worry not, Ralph,' Gladhand had said.

'I don't, Dale. I'm confident. I know everything's been done to keep us undetected.'

'Right. Mimi's great on spotting potential difficulties and countering them in advance'

'Who'll get the vans?' Ralph said.

'The operational vans?' Hoskins said.

'Yes, the actual. The stolen ones.'

'We got specialists in that kind of thing, so necessary nowadays. Car and van locking – they've really improved it. But it's routine to our people. They keeps ahead of manufacturers' new anti-theft tricks. I want to stress, Ralph, it's our own in-house team who do the taking. I can tell you're very conscious of security matters. Wise, Ralph. But we'd never outsource car and/or collection to freelancers. We couldn't be totally certain of their ability, could we? Plus, I'd fear leaks. They wouldn't be bound by loyalty to the firm. Our vehicle/car acquisition lads do other, ordinary tasks within PU normally. It's not economic to have staffers whose only job is taking away. But, when the occasion comes, as now, they're ready, on standby, and will switch very smoothly to picking up suitable reliable motors for us. They knows exactly what to get, as according to the particular demands of an operation. Them demands will vary, but that will all be taken into account perfect by our people. Each vehicle we claim requires two of our people, naturally. They reach the location in one of our cars, then one hops out, does the magic on a door and the alarm, more magic on the ignition, checks the fuel then drives it back here.

'The timing got to be totally right. If a car or van's took too early, with a waiting around period, there's obviously increased danger of reg recognition. The owner of the vehicle will have reported it missing at once and police all over will be alerted. "My precious motor gone, officer!" Sometimes we'll change registration plates, but that's not the perfect answer because, of course, the reg probably won't tie up with all the details of the car or van. So, no hanging about. We get the vehicles one day, operate the next and ditch them also the next.

'They might have belonged to, say, a bakery in Ruislip or a stockbroker in Swindon, or a media exec's in Dorking or a builder's yard in Watford. We favours a considerable spread, so the steals won't be linked. If four vans was took from the same area police would start thinking there must be a jolly job on somewhere, and they'd get alert. The Vauxhall came from Islington. Next, them four vans are needed, two for the action, two to switch to after. Plus, the Lexus for Hector subsequent.

'As I said, routine. Haven't we done similar operations in the past when other firms try in their filthy way to come nosing in? You bet! They got to be dealt with. And when I say "dealt with" I don't mean do a deal with them. They got to be persuaded this is not the right spot for them. We persuade them by terminating a few lives. This gets the message over beautiful. They worry about their women and kids. Most people can be helped to see what's all right and what isn't. Believe me, I hate doing domestic but you never know when it could be necessary.

'We got to look after ourselves, haven't we, Ralph? I heard of a book way back, *The Territorial Imperative*, about animals fighting to guard their ground with everythink they fucking got. Nothing else makes them fight so fierce. Well, think of that famous speech by Churchill in the war – "we'll fight them on the beaches" and all that. This is the territorial imperative, which was why they invented what the TV called "Dad's Army" – proper, unjoky name, "The Home Guard". Guarding homes – territorial. Same for us. The imperative, signifying it just got to be, no alternative. We're born with it, Ralph, that urge to look after our patch. A mother don't have to teach us that, like potty training. We got it there already, from what's known as our genes with a 'g'. It's a noble, brill urge and we'd be nowhere without it, nowhere at all, sleeping in cardboard boxes under rail bridges.'

In the Vauxhall, on the re-run past the Mondial-Trave corner and the pub, Gladhand said: 'Hector will take our lead van, transferring at a proper point in the action to the Lexus. Mimi says she'll do the second van. I'll have to think about that. She might be used to driving a tank over there in Gaza armed with a seventy-five millimetre anti-brick-wall gun. This will require a different technique and the weaponry lighter!'

'Mimi?' Quentin snarled. 'She probably just wants to impress Ralph. It's pathetic. "Look at me, do look at me, Ralph! I'm as good as Hector, a hotshot Wheels!"'

Greg and Gladhand didn't say anything at first. Maybe they felt things had become a bit sensitive. They had. Ralph wondered what that meant, the 'It's pathetic.' Was Quent saying it was pathetic for a woman in her fifties to want someone in his twenties like Ember, which Ralph would more or less agree with, though he'd never be rude or hurtful to Mimi? Or did Stayley want to suggest it was pathetic for any woman of any age to see something in him, Ralph W. Ember? This second interpretation seemed more likely to Ralph, because that sod Stayley was driven by malice, contempt and envy. When Stayley said, 'It's pathetic,' that was the moment Ralph's total happiness about being in the Vauxhall began to shrink. He could recall it very well, and all the chat surrounding this cruel comment – cruel whatever it meant.

Ralph would bet no woman ever told Stayley he *doppelgänged* the young Charlton Heston, especially as El Cid. Ralph reckoned most women would be too busy sicking up at the sight of that disgusting ponytail to say much to Quent at all, or only 'Good-fucking-bye, mate.' He had the Oxford degree they'd all been told about, and often, so he'd know who El Cid was; but he wouldn't have a cat in El's chance of being mistaken for Charlton as him.

Mace said: 'Mimi's a warrior.'

'She knows about the territorial imperative,' Gladhand said. 'She's lived it, out there in the mid-East.'

# Twelve

Esther, on tape, her tone still clipped and matter-of-fact, announced from deep in her Metropolitan Police past: 'The screen shows a fresh car, ladies and gents, a black Mazda, also nicked, this one by Opal Render, though. It's a day later, the objective identical – a reminder of the street layout around Mondial-Trave, but viewed as a future battleground now, not a brilliant, famed, druggy, trading venue. You'll see there are only two men in the car, but our source provides four more OR names and faces certain to be involved. This will be a full-scale set-to.

'The driver, under the big-peaked blue cap, is Luke Gaston Byfort, age thirty-four, general duties operative, with OR from its beginning, no convictions, divorced, present partner Naomi Trent, divorced, son, aged eight, by previous, baby son by Luke. Beretta automatic. Teetotal after alcoholism treatment. Has become local prize-winning ice skater since dry: limbs now better coordinated and fit for purpose.

'Piers Elroy Stanton in the passenger seat, chief and distinguished founder of OR, aged thirty, married to Veronica (Marshall) pregnant. Byfort his assistant-stroke-aide from the creation of OR. Two arrests for supplying, one for menaces, but no charges or convictions. Several properties including three-floor home in Hampstead

75

(uncheap), holiday villa, Esposende, North Portugal; similar, Abersoch, Wales, this sometimes rented out to yachters (uncheap). Owns two race horses, Dombey And Some and Colonel Jackeen, stabled Newmarket, several wins at minor events. Heckler and Koch nine mm automatic.

'It could be significant that OR's survey is done by only two people. In fact, it's effectively, by one – Stanton: Byfort not much more than a flunkey. It looks as though OR's tactics will be very tightly controlled by Stanton. He doesn't want others in Opal Render on his reconnaissance and guessing how the fight will go. He'll *tell* them how it will go. Contrast the Vauxhall with its team of four aboard, plus Hector due to make his own visit later, which we've also filmed.

'We deduce that PU's action on the day will be flexible. Gladhand expects his group to adapt, improvise, according to how things develop. And how things will develop can't be predicted or pre-controlled. True, the Vauxhall four seemed compulsively interested in *Red Letter's* car park. Possibly there's an overall scheme to push OR, or the remnants of OR, into it as a handy, cloistered slaughterhouse. But I don't think Gladhand will lay down categorical orders on the way that's to be done. He's a democrat. He's an empiricist.

'Meanwhile, Stanton's method assumes he sees more clearly than anyone else, and knows better than anyone else how to cope. *Heil, mein Führer*! That's certainly one kind of leadership: confident, autocratic, vain. But putting so much on to a single figure raises a big question, doesn't it: what if Stanton gets hit, or taken, early? Suddenly,

OR would lose its captain, and – because he's a one-and-only chief – there'd be nobody else with enough knowledge and grip to replace him. No Hardy to direct things like after Nelson's death. So, parallel collapse of Opal Render. Stanton *was* Opal Render. Farewell, OR.

'This prospect will guide our tactics. The priority must be to remove Stanton.' She hooted, making fun of herself. 'Wow! A revelation! Some would argue that in this kind of conflict one objective is *always* to destroy the kingpin. It is, but more so here then ever. Stanton will impose a plan, his exclusive plan, and there'll be no alternative if he is negatived and it comes adrift. We make sure he is and it does.'

A male voice, just audible, spoke on the tape. She remembered him. Martin Wilcox, a detective sergeant, gun-trained. Of course she remembered him: after promotions he'd gone on to big things with cold case reviews nationally. He'd been sitting midway back in the briefing, eyes unfriendly behind Himmler rimless glasses – cold, colder than any cold case. 'So, you're saying, are you, ma'm, that we intently, single-mindedly, target Stanton from the start and try to snuff him out?' he said.

In her sunny, chilly conservatory now it sounded close to a snarl, an accusation, as it had live, at the time. He meant, did he, that *she* might theorize and talk tactics to them, but *he* might have to do it – set out to kill someone as a pre-selected 'priority?' Mr Nitty-Gritty was quizzing Madam Backroom Thinktank and Command Vehicle. *Sergeant* Nitty-Gritty.

'This is warfare between two firms,' she'd replied. 'We are a third party, present to protect the interests and lives of the public.' This didn't seem like an answer to what he'd asked, and she'd realized at the time that it didn't. A vital part of management and political practice was the skill at reshaping a tricky query into something easier to deal with. She'd wanted to guide things on to more favourable ground: some safe, trite waffle, something non-hecklable.

But he hadn't looked the type who fancied being guided. 'Protect the public by knocking over Stanton?' he'd asked.

'We must adjust to whatever is happening on the day between those two firms. We shouldn't get into the kind of narrow, constricting, set attitude that will probably characterize OR, as I've said.'

'Yes, but when you call for Stanton to be "removed" – this might be regarded by some as a deliberately imprecise term, surely, and—'

'As I've said, our source names four other OR people who'll be at the confrontation: three men, one woman,' she replied. 'They will appear captioned in sequence on the screen. I don't think I need to give detailed backgrounds. They will all be armed, two with machine pistols, two have done time. In other words they are what one would expect in this standard scramble to extend a firm's sales patch. We can leave it at that, I feel.'

End of meeting. It sounded as though she was shaken by the questions and had abandoned the session in a panicked rush. She'd brought the four's biogs and should have read them out; had intended reading them out. They could be as significant as Stanton's and Byfort's. Instead, she'd gone for rapid withdrawal, hasty closure. It was a while ago and she couldn't altogether recall her state of mind then. But she recognized, of course, that the questions went some way towards the truth: recognized it now and had recognized it then. Awkward? An invitation to a killing? Perhaps. She considered she'd had things at least halfway right: the police *would* be the third party, not a main contender in the battle, Esther's task to put an end to that violence by suppressing both sides. But Wilcox was correct, wasn't he, to suggest she required the first stage in their operation to be the wipe-out of Stanton, on his own account, and because the disintegration of decapitated Opal Render would follow?

Then Esther's platoon could turn everything against Pasque Uno. The classic, acute danger from being caught in the middle would disappear. The defeat of both firms should mean safety for law-abiding people on the streets and peace in at least that corner of the city. Yes. Perhaps it was the crude directness of Wilcox's language that had rattled her badly – the 'snuffing out', the 'knocking over'. Probably, they hadn't sounded suitable for an official wish-list. No. She wanted Stanton 'removed', 'neutralized', 'negatived', or in that CIA code, offered 'extreme prejudice'. Superfluous to state how. Too much information. Wiser not to overdo the detail, or to gloat about a scheduled execution.

Esther stopped the tape, ran it back to where

the Wilcox questions had begun and listened again. Then she switched off once more. Although she couldn't remember exactly how she'd felt at the time, she knew his interruption had troubled her badly. Forcing a premature end to the session like that must have made her appear weak and wrong-footed. She *had* been weak and wrong-footed. She could recall the look of shock on some of the faces there.

A couple of hours after the briefing she'd gone alone in civilian clothes to the Mondial-Trave junction. She parked in a side street and did a sort of slow inspection on foot. It was her way of trying to counter the Wilcox hint that she lived and talked in a woolly, evasive, theorizing, HQ realm, whereas the people she'd been addressing had to prepare themselves for some very real rough stuff here, either giving it or taking it or both, body armour on, helmet chinstraps tight. She wanted to prove that this, also, was her realm: the streets, the buildings, shops, businesses, pavements, kerbs and gutters. Prove? Who to? Well, to herself. Nobody else knew she'd made the little, self-comforting, but – she'd admit – basically meaningless, possibly ludicrous, trip. And not many would understand her thinking if they *did* know about the visit.

It was true that she wouldn't be with her people and among the bullets when the fighting began. Superintendents planned and briefed but as a rule didn't get physically into gun play. She would be what was called 'Gold' – the highest level of authority during an incident – but she'd be in the Command Vehicle, keeping in touch by

80

electronics and radio. There was a joke about the appalling London riots in 2011. A constable, in this story, grew so scared by the violence and burning that he turned and ran to another district, finishing up tearful and broken in a shop doorway. After a while he heard a stern voice say: 'Get back to your duties, lad.'

Too ashamed to look up he replied: 'I can't, can't, sergeant, it's too terrible.'

The voice said: 'It's not your sergeant speaking, lad, it's your superintendent.'

'My God,' he said, 'I didn't realize I'd run that far.'

Esther's command vehicle wouldn't be all that distant from the action, but nor would it be actually in it.

So, Wilcox had a point, and it wasn't a point Esther liked very much. She needed to counter it, and should have at the briefing session. She hadn't known how, though, and so, hoist the drawbridge to impose a sudden ending to the session: talk him down, silence him, devise an escape.

She loitered near one of the ex-warehouses, now an apartment block, and enjoyed feeling dwarfed by it, her rank and importance of no account. This towering bricks and mortar job couldn't be more substantial and actual, could it? There was underground parking and for a while she watched the cars entering and leaving, that busyness another glimpse of ordinary, workaday life – perhaps off to the supermarket, or to fetch kids at the end of the school day. Routines. Reassuring routines: or this was how she'd regarded them.

The old, modelled alderman couldn't be 'actual' in that sense, of course. He was a piece of municipal art, a replica. He looked stony solid though and had a printed, enduring, capitalized name on a plaque: 'RICHARD ROBERT LAUCENSTON, 1847–1899'. Perhaps she was standing where the carts used to stand in his time, loading or unloading. She felt herself to be part of a continuing, checkable, worthwhile community history. She could manage an inner glow.

But not for long. Even at the time, and certainly today on her lounger, she decided her reactions there were absolute bullshit. She just happened to be a cop posted to these parts for a while and had next to no connection with its history. In any case, she knew it was barmy to believe she could get herself further into the blood and guts of a coming hairy operation by strolling near some statue. Yet she'd permitted herself the limited spell of fantasizing. She needed that. And sod Wilcox.

She'd considered it best not to mention this snatched, woman-of-the-people sojourn to Gerald. He'd regard her as nuts and would tell her so, more than once. And he'd see this dreamy stuff as a preposterous attempt by her to get into the imaginative world that he, as an *artiste*, would claim as exclusively his and his bassoon's. Her job, he would argue, was in the banal and workaday, and should stay stuck in the banal and workaday.

And perhaps he would be right. There *was* something lunatic, and something perverse, about coming here. Wilcox and those damn see-all, scare-all glasses had shoved her reasoning askew. The police presence at Mondial-Trave was supposed to be secret. This location had been named confidentially by an informant. She'd ordered hidden cameras into place to record who might be showing a special interest in this corner spot and the nearby streets. And now, look at her – yes, she thought, look at her, the mad, maundering bitch – here she was, strolling very visibly, flagrantly, about, more or less proclaiming that the police had this area marked and watched. All right, she was in civilians clothes. But anyone in either of the firms would recognize her. Of course they would. It was a basic of their careers to identify top law people, however they were dressed.

She could excuse herself a little with the argument that both firms had already done their inspections by Vauxhall and Mazda, so the risk of her getting spotted now was not serious. No? She imagined the people on the cameras here, in one of the flats and a store room above the minimarket in Trave, amazed to see her in daylight and taking her time. She glanced up to a window on the fourth floor of one of the apartment blocks in case she could glimpse the photographer. No. These people knew how to stay out of sight. She ought to learn from them. She gave a sort of token wave and smile towards the window, anyway. *Hello there, lads, lasses. OK, I shouldn't be here. You're right. But I am. I needed a refresher – a cosying up to the real and actual. Soft and pathetic, isn't it?*

# Thirteen

Ralph finished that unhurried but edgy tour of the club and sat down again behind the bar. His recollections still gave him the gripes, but maybe not quite so badly now. After all, here he indisputably was, in his own club, at its, as it were, nerve centre, and as well protected as anyone could be in his kind of immense, brilliantly developing, shoot-first occupation. He felt that a stranger observing the present scene would sense a holy aptness: the generous spread and fitments of the club itself, and he, its proprietor, very much at the strategic nub – alert, capable and, at this time of day, on bottled water only, to fend off dehydration.

With all his usual fine, spontaneous, warm friendliness he smiled to welcome a group of members just arrived. This fucking lot were exactly the squalid, dud, *hoi polloi* sort he'd joyfully kick out, and keep out permanently, the moment he'd got The Monty's social, intellectual, tailoring and odorous tone up a milli-fraction to Athenaeum level.

It would be a true kindness to give this crew and similar the everlasting heave-ho because they'd feel pathetically crude and alien in the new classy atmosphere, like sneeze-snot on caviar. Soon, Ralph wanted to see the club's special functions announced in *The Times*, such as lectures by distinguished business chiefs on Nigerian fiscal policy; or a professor from some very valid university discussing with screen illustrations ancient monastery manuscripts where later writing in Latin had been put over the original to cut stationery costs for monks.

But, until then, he believed in limited, though proper, landlordly politeness to most members, regardless of sleaze level and 'Dearest Mother o' mine' vermilion wrist tattoos; though, obviously, not to that drunken arsehole who berserked and opened unfriendly fire on William Blake. Afterwards, clamouring in his dismal style for forgiveness, he'd argued that the damage was *only* to the beard of someone starkers on all fours.' Only! He'd had the neck to emphasize that word. The dim, disrespectful prick couldn't see the wider significance, the artistic, literary, mythological oomph behind that beard, very much a typical part of *The Marriage of Heaven and Hell* as a complete work, and, also, therefore, so meaningful on the custom-made, metal-hanging rampart with its Blakean decor.

It had been an attack not just on a beard but on a whole life system. It was Hunnish. It made Ralph think of a notorious air raid on a defenceless town in the Spanish civil war – Guernica. The artist, Picasso, had done a pretty weird picture of it, but he undoubtedly meant well. And he would condemn, also, the blitzing of another work of art, the William Blake at The Monty. Although Ralph didn't object to the occasional, well-judged use of slang, what that cretin with the gun in the club referred slightingly to as 'starkers' was, in fact, the naked primitive state for all humanity pre-garments; and 'on all fours' – as he'd contemptuously said – because knees hadn't really got going in those early days, enabling people to stand and walk. The song, *Knees Up Mother Brown (Knees Up, Knees Up, Never Get The Breeze Up)*, couldn't have been composed in that period, 'up' being beyond the range of knees then. The development of human knees would have a terrific amount to do with that great but controversial discovery, 'survival of the fittest.' The word 'fittest' there referred partly and importantly to knees.

It had to be admitted, though, that not just this slob but most of The Monty membership would miss the full significance of the Blake pictures. Ralph saw these people as tied to painfully narrow, miserably basic attitudes, unable to deal with symbolism and/or overtones. 'You bloody what?' they'd reply if Ralph spoke of somebody or something having an emblematic quality. They understood about guns, bullets, morning-after pills, tattoos, farcically grandiose wreaths for slaughtered turf-war colleagues, shivs, grievous bodily harm, girls and/or boys, probation, menaces, money, more money, substances, sweeteners, defence lawyers, plea bargaining, finks, and that was it.

On the other hand, and very much on the other hand, Ralph had come across a phrase that fitted himself exactly – 'renaissance man.' This referred to history, renaissance meaning rebirth, and indicating a time when all sorts of knowledge became available again after a long, very dud period.

86

Ralph took the words 'renaissance man' to mean someone with plenty of culture from many directions – knowing poetry, music, painting, algebra. You name it, the renaissance man had it. He might even take in funk and country.

Although Ralph would not expect to find many renaissance men among Monty memberships, yes, he did think of himself as in this category. And he realized that the true renaissance man could never be content with the culture he already had but must ceaselessly try to expand. He saw his bond with the William Blake as a definite part of the Ember renaissance man profile. But he did not intend the montage to be for ever *The Marriage of Heaven and Hell*. Expand! Seek new horizons! This was why he had become interested in the Dickens film poster from Hull. As he'd already realized, that *Great Expectations* illustration would have a practical meaning for people in the club, because most of them possessed their own great expectations, imagining that one day they'd have something so brilliant that even a grasping, two-timing fence would feel he had to give a decent price. But, at the same time, this move into something different from the Blake would show that Ralph had an appetite for worthwhile creative works, never mind where they came from. Ralph felt sorry for most Monty people with their utterly unspiritual existence, but not sorry enough to put up with their company if he didn't have to. For the present, he fucking well did have to, or The Monty would go under.

However, Ralph would prefer to reminisce than involve himself in anything beyond basic pleasantries with a bunch like this loutish group now buying drinks. But it irritated him to find that his recollection of what happened straight after the Vauxhall sightseeing expedition had faded. Somewhere, he'd read how occasionally the memory could apply a humane touch and blur unpleasant flashbacks, or even edit them out altogether. Ralph didn't want that kind of deceptive, soft-soap tenderness, though, thanks very much. He despised people who were 'in denial', as it was known – clinging to a pathetic, self-fooling pretence that what had taken place hadn't, and therefore couldn't have any effect on now. Ralph would prefer absolute accuracy, no matter how agonizing. He, Ralph Ember, could take it. This unflinching attitude he regarded as the essence of manliness. And he saw himself as a devoted, resourceful custodian of such manliness.

Not long ago he'd been reading about the Great War of 1914–18 and came across a proclamation by Britain's top soldier, Earl Haig, in April 1918, when things looked very dark: 'With our backs to the wall we must fight on to the end.' Ralph had noted that 'must': no option existed; resistance was natural, inevitable. This was the kind of bold, face-up-to-it attitude Ralph admired. He aimed to find why he had ever come to be called 'Panicking Ralph' or, so much sickeningly worse, 'Panicking Ralphy'. When he'd achieved this he felt sure he could show that those stinking names arose from foul, malevolent, slanderous misrepresentation, based almost certainly on envy.

Some envy of himself he could accept as

harmless and inevitable. It might become excessive, though, and lead to vindictiveness. A quest – that's what Ralph was on: a mission to reclaim his dignity, yes, his genuine staunch, unique selfhood from twisted, lying creeps; and from those who delightedly passed on the behind-his-back scoffing to him, such as Assistant Chief Fuckface Iles.

# Fourteen

To some extent Ember understood why sections of his recall should be misty. They had to do with his thinking then, his attitudes, ideas, brain-stuff, rather than actual events, and they were bound to be a bit woolly and vague so long afterwards. However, some moves following the Vauxhall ride he could certainly remember well and exactly.

First: he'd decided he must return very soon to the Mondial-Trave location, though entirely alone this time; an unaccompanied, private, excursion in his Volvo, not the Vauxhall.

Second: at this spot he'd witnessed something – through, as it happened, two panes of glass – witnessed something he certainly did *not* feel at all unclear about. How could he? No blurring of this was possible.

But what he couldn't fully explain to himself was why he'd chosen to make such an urgent, personal revisit to that patch when only recently he'd taken two very good pathfinder scans of it with Gladhand and the others.

'Very good scans.' Were they *really* this, he'd wondered. That's what the *intention* had been, certainly. But did these motorized exercises get his concentrated, eager attention? Maybe not. That vicious jerk, Quentin Stayley, had hugely enraged him, and so perhaps distracted Ralph from a thorough inspection of the likely battle terrain. He needed a fresh look at that parcel of ground, undistracted by bloody Quent.

Ralph, seated at the Monty bar, found his mind uncontrollably jumping about. It would amble off, dwelling on the miserable hints and insults that had come from Quent Stayley in the Vauxhall. But those chewy, wandering recollections would suddenly get interrupted by other recollections much more precise and sharp. It was as though they came at him like capital letters on a vivid red banner with white lettering, terse, emphatic, anxious messages he'd seemed to see, momentarily re-running questions he'd put to himself on that second survey trip, that unaccompanied, second survey trip to Mondial-Trave. So, he had two very different kind of memories of the journeys into that elected battle region. They could be labelled 'Vauxhall' and 'Solo'.

Vauxhall: In his damn fluting, know-all, pony-tailed, varsity voice Stayley had seemed to suggest that Ralph would have no hope of pulling women; or no hope of pulling women except for leathery elderlies like Mimi Apertine, who'd, admittedly, shown flagrant, unwavering hots for Ralph: embarrassing, but Ralph was extremely accustomed to this kind of thing and would not let it derail him.

Solo: WOULD THIS HAIRDRESSER'S SHOP PORCH GIVE HIM ADEQUATE COVER?

Vauxhall: Ralph had certainly never thought ill of women unable to conceal – or subdue, come to that – a fierce desire for him. It was their nature, their unbidden but unstoppable emotional and physical response to him. In some ways it

91

was to their credit. They didn't bottle up this yearning. They made it apparent. They were unashamed. They were entitled to be unashamed. He'd always shown toleration. He'd always put up with it. He'd always treated such situations light-heartedly so that no woman should feel snubbed and hurt by rejection, if he did reject. Arrogance, unkindness, he'd hated then and still did. Renaissance men had a very humane and kindly side to their personalities. They recognized that as long as there was pussy some women would be pussy-driven, especially if they met someone like Ralph.

Solo: WHAT THE HELL WAS THIS COP DOING DOWN HERE, ANYWAY?

Vauxhall: Mimi he'd regarded as a great, talented operator with a terrific CV, no question, but getting on a bit, and short of half an ear after that Israeli army shooting-range accident; probably – more than probably – no fault of her own, but still leaving her lobeless on the left. Ralph hadn't liked to think of the bullet with this authentic piece of her stuck to its nose rushing on perhaps towards the wrong end, the non-target end, of the range, so that this small blob of her flesh whacked into who knew what or where and remained uselessly there, separated from the body – Mimi's – where it previously fulfilled a good role alongside her neck, even if only ornamental: lobes had nothing to do with actual hearing.

She had never spoken of this range incident, but Ralph thought he could visualize the sequence. As a combat veteran she would have been instructing novice personnel in the use of small-arms and standing behind one of them as she or he fired at a target, offering advice after volleys. '*Squeeze* the trigger, not pull.' 'Fill your lungs before you fire. Breathing can cause a body tremor and mess up aim.' Ralph himself had received that kind of coaching on a private range, as a vital preliminary to his preferred vocation in the substances; the way a priest or rabbi would have to go for training at a seminary before taking over a church or synagogue.

Perhaps the automatic pistol of Mimi's trainee had jammed. He or she possibly turned, flustered, to ask Mimi for help, and at that moment the pistol cleared itself and started firing. Mimi, alert, experienced, would drop to the ground out of the way when under attack, but, possibly not quite fast enough, even for someone militarily so clued up. A bullet shaved the left side of her face, taking the lobe with it. Maybe she'd been lucky the damage wasn't worse.

Ralph could imagine the error causing serious confusion. Blood should never be seen on a range, a place of strictly imitation warfare; but an ear lobe, due to fleshy plumpness, could produce plenty. Also, other recruits, hearing the shouting and even possible screaming, might themselves instinctively turn to see what was going on, fingers still on the trigger, and further accidental shots could fly, oblivious to the official targets.

Solo: HE COULD VIEW FROM HERE AS THROUGH TWO WINDOW PANES, THE GLASS SIDE WALL OF THE ENTRANCE AND THE MAIN FRONT DISPLAY PLATE, COULDN'T HE?

93

Vauxhall: Mimi's injury had caused a marked imbalance to her appearance. He'd realized some men might find this pleasantly quaint and extra sexy. Possibly this kind of perverse thinking was what had made Quent speak about her as he had in the car. Few could boast of having had a woman showing that kind of unilateral lack. Probably, some would have wondered whether there had been over-enthusiastic, passionate ear-nibbling during a past session of foreplay, and maybe this prospect thrilled them, there still being one lobe to dally with, of course; perhaps the solitariness making it prized all the more. A man on top might have noticed he could see more of the pillow to one side of her than the other, but this would be a minor factor and needn't at all spoil the evening.

Solo: WAS SHE WRITING IN A JOTTER? WHAT, FOR GOD'S SAKE?

Vauxhall: Ralph, though, had considered Mimi's loss unnerving. He'd felt that to suggest she should get the remaining lobe taken off to even things up would have been heartless and offensive. Also, that could lead to problems with her passport photo, which might have been taken when she had one lobe. Perhaps border officials somewhere would claim she wasn't who she said she was. A diplomatic incident might result, with publicity. Pasque Uno naturally avoided all publicity if it could and Gladhand certainly would not want involvement in controversy about an ear.

In Ralph's opinion, many women suffered a dire life, and he hadn't wanted to cause any of

94

them more discomfort, by, for instance, speaking tactlessly about the torn-off lobe. Another point concerning men on top was that some liked to grip the woman's ears to aid forward bodily propulsion during bonking upthrust. Ralph had considered that enough of the left ear was still OK to offer this facility.

Solo: DID SHE WAVE AT SOMEONE IN THE APARTMENT BLOCK?

Vauxhall: And then, as well as Quent's cheap hints about Mimi, there'd been all his miserable talk forecasting disaster in the scheduled shoot-out with Opal Render. That also had gravely distracted Ralph. Stayley had taken the front seat alongside Gladhand as if plainly entitled to the nearness and princely status, and then had wilfully abused that position. He'd seemed to regard it as an appointed duty to highlight the idea of catastrophe. Morale? He sabotaged it, but apparently didn't care. He loved yakking and yakking that craven bilge. It had made Ralph wonder what would have happened if Winston Churchill had spoken like that, rather than rallying Britain with his oratory in 1940: capitulation instead of magnificent resistance. Haig, Churchill, the same resolve.

Stayley's performance had contained, of course, a definite hint that Gladhand was short of the generalship needed to make a triumph of this coming conflict. And Ralph had detected another hint – that he, Stayley, would do it better if he had charge: Oxford, age and the greying ponytail turned him into Genghis fucking Kahn, did they?

So, there'd been at least a pair of influences

that might have unsettled Ralph and, yes, possibly made him less attentive to the serious work they were on – that work closely to study a vital slice of townscape. It could be called No-Man's Land, and therefore Every-Man's Land, though Dale Hoskins had meant to put an end to that by eliminating Opal Render. Then, it wouldn't quite be every man's, just Pasque Uno's. Yes, Uno, Uno, Uno, and not the United Nations Organization, either! One gorgeous, prevailing flower would bloom on this turf: Pasque. It had been a bright and necessary ambition.

As Gladhand mentioned, the words 'cleanse' and 'cleansing' had taken on a dark significance after some of those Balkans incidents. But they also kept their original sense – to purify, to decontaminate. Gladhand had simply wanted to cleanse the city by once and for all killing off Opal Render.

Solo: HADN'T SHE ENGAGED IN SOME KIND OF DAFT PRETEND LOVE AFFAIR WITH THE ALDERMAN?

Vauxhall: Of course, Ralph realized that, when he considered those two types of gross behaviour by Stayley, the one that had especially infuriated him was not Quent's blandly commandeering the front seat, and persistently mouthing his palsied, alarmist defeatism, but the vile slur about Ralph's negligible prospects with women. Stayley's malign suggestion that Ralph couldn't attract younger, double-lobed, tastier lovelies than Mimi had blatantly ignored his widely noted resemblance to the young Charlton Heston. Chuck, as he was fondly called, had performed impressively not just as El Cid, but also Moses, Ben Hur, Mark Antony and Heathcliff, the wildly romantic character out on the moors in a classic love tale, regardless of harsh weather. As Moses, Chuck had brought the Ten Commandments down from a mountain inscribed on stone tablets. Ralph considered several of the commandments quite sensible and worth the effort.

He'd reckoned that some years ago many a bedroom wall of young girls in the United States, and possibly in Britain, too, would be decorated with a poster picture of Chuck, possibly stripped to the waist in *Ben Hur.* But Stayley behaved as if none of this had any relevance to Ember. Ralph reacted with a mixture of anger, injury and disappointment. He wasn't sure which had been the strongest element – anger, injury or disappointment – but each very justified, he believed. Any one of them could have unforgivably preoccupied him. Ralph had felt more hostility to Stayley than to any of the Opal Render personnel. This was a dreadfully sad outcome of the Vauxhall operation.

Looking back now from his Monty perch, Ember recognized that the only comparable insolence to Stayley's during Ralph's classic business career would, yes, come from the brass-necked, braying sod of sods, Assistant Chief Constable Desmond Iles, though, of course, Ralph hadn't met him or even heard of him at the period of Mondial-Trave, south-east London. Such a treat for the future! Iles and his sidekick, Detective Chief Superintendent Colin Harpur, often looked in at The Monty for free drinks, and so that Iles could mock and rubbish Ralph – 'Someone asked me the other day how dear Panicking Ralphy was getting along, Ember. "Exemplarily," I at once and gladly replied. Could any other term suit?'

Iles also liked to terrorize all club members present for being the kind of crooks or fellow-travellers that Ralph would admit most of them were, at this merely pending stage in The Monty's development. Ralph had recently come across another interesting phrase, 'Rome wasn't built in a day,' and he'd adapted this to, 'The Monty can't get into The Athenaeum or Garrick class in a day, either.'

Solo: BUT HAD THERE BEEN ANY RETURN WAVE FROM WHAT SEEMED TO BE FLOOR FOUR?

Thinking of Iles, Ralph's brain moved off on a completely new route, not Vauxhall or Solo. He recalled a film entitled *Planet of the Apes*. Chuck Heston had starred as a space traveller who returns to earth after a bit of a sci-fi time-jump and finds civilization as he'd known it a couple of aeons ago completely obliterated and apes running the shop instead. These turned out to be good apes, though, possibly superior to humans, especially as humans had suckled and raised Iles. It would take more than aeons to civilize that dung-beetle.

If Iles heard now about the bullet hole in *The Marriage of Heaven and Hell,* most likely his first reaction would be to guffaw and/or whoop with callous, indecently prolonged merriment. He'd make it prolonged to show he regarded the damaged Blake as typical of disasters certain to

98

fuck up Ralph's life continually; and, therefore, the cackling at this specific Blake episode should be enlarged, expanded, to cover a whole context of hilarious pain, bound to have come Ralph's way already, or sweetly ready to scrag him rotten in the future. There might also be bodily convulsions to accompany the laughter, as though the joke was so enormous it had twanged all his ligaments, tendons, muscles and vertebrae, getting him very close to helplessness and collapse.

Then Iles would probably invite more detail so he could really wallow in the vast distress and humiliation the potshotting was bound to have caused Ralph, and treat himself to further cruel, booming, wet-his-pants chortles. From years of studying Iles, Ember reckoned he could itemize the ACC's rub-Ralph's-nose-in-it demands now.

He'd want Ralph to repeat, as if on oath, a full narrative description of events, starting with:

(i) The drawing and flourishing of the .38 Smith and Wesson, and noisy, rat-arsed encouragement from his friends to fire.

(ii) Holster or pocket?

(iii) The cocking of the .38, if a .38 S. and W. had a cocking device.

(iv) The aiming up at the art, perhaps only a daft, pistol-waving threat at first.

(v) Any hate-words, philistinisms, curses, jokes, warnings, obscenities, commiserations, yelled by the gunman at the Blake figures such as, 'It's a marriage, is it? Well, here's a hallmarked lead wedding pressie!'

99

(vi) One-handed or two-handed grip on the .38?
(vii) Firing from stiff-armed shoulder height or at Jesse James hip level?
(viii) An account of the shots and the clang of bullets on bonny, life-protecting steel, followed, possibly, by a liberated screech of ricochets.
(ix) Flying glass spears from the Worcester-shire sauce bottle.
(x) T-shirt and pool table staining.
(xi) Thuds as the bounce-off bullets reached a wall and had finally to quit circulating.

Most probably, he'd require Ralph to imitate these later sounds, particularly the sauce bottle frag-menting and the brief, busy, sharp hullabaloo of the gadabout ricochets. He'd listen, grinning, until the performance finished and then gleefully call for an encore, or more than one, the grin in place throughout but occasionally developing into a guffaw re-run and bodily jackknifing, especially at the disintegration of the sauce bottle and piquant drenching of a customer's upper body. He might cry out in a kind of evil ecstasy, 'Brilliant!' 'So, Monty!' 'So *Ralphy's* Monty!' 'Trim your whiskers, sir?' That's the kind of flip-pant bastard he was.

Of course, Ember saw the resemblance between the two uncongenial shooting episodes and thanked God Mimi and her lobe were from a different time, a different place, or Iles would have demanded a comparison with that gunplay and require Ralph to do a careful inventory check on all ears present, right as well as left, although

100

Mimi's lobe loss had been left only. Iles would put on a special caring thoroughness about lobes so as to feed his mickey-taking, mischievous programme. Decorum? He'd piss on it, if he knew what it meant. He'd find fucking comedy where others would see only suffering, sadness and devastation. Very possibly he'd point out that Mimi could economize fifty per cent by buying only single earrings, perhaps advertising online for anyone who'd lost one to get in touch for possible purchase by her of the other.

Everybody else, thinking of those sharp, glass missiles roving at devilish speed, would recognize the acute, doodlebug hazard they caused. For Iles they were just something to get a reverberating, vandal chuckle from. Ralph imagined him telling his wife or colleagues: 'And then, guess what, one of the bouncing bullets smacks into a Lea and Perrins bottle and tasty, jagged fragments go whizzing around the bar looking for a throat to cut! Such sauciness!'

# Fifteen

That was Iles, and before him came Stayley. Perhaps the disgusting malice from Quent on the day hadn't greatly mattered. What *had* mattered was that soon after the Vauxhall trip Ralph decided he'd seriously skimped his examinations of the likely combat zone, pushed them down to second or third priority. This shortfall badly troubled him. He'd judged it an unforgivable, treasonous failure. Gladhand had considerately laid on an instructive sortie, yet Ralph's response was disgracefully poor, inadequate, severely divided. Although he heartily despised ingratitude, this was what he had shown at Mondial-Trave in the Vauxhall. He'd needed to get back there confidentially and remedy these shameful omissions.

Although, quite probably, Gladhand Hoskins would never have discovered Ralph's appalling, vanity-based slackness on the Vauxhall trek, it didn't matter: his return had not been meant to satisfy Gladhand, but chiefly to appease Ralph's personal, sensitive, wakeful conscience. He loathed the notion that he might have put his own concerns above those of Gladhand and the firm. This would be intolerable egomania, and, yes, a kind of treachery. The lovely wholeness and continuing health of Pasque Uno, that noble, emblematic flower, counted for more than a quibble about whether Stayley provocatively ignored Ralph's glorious Chuck aspects. The solo pilgrimage to Mondial-Trave had represented a kind of penance and recompense, a session of self-scourging.

He'd parked in a side street and then gone on foot towards the converted warehouse and the statue of the alderman. At once he'd felt terrific relief. It was a plain, wonderfully physical matter. The pavement relayed a signal of welcome, and of commendation, up through the soles of his trainers and his patterned socks. 'You've done very well, Ralph, to make this corrective, compensating second look-around.' That had seemed to be the comforting message now, not via a red and white banner, but as if from the trodden-on, confederate concrete. He'd sensed in it the suggestion that this additional, private call had been expected, because Ralph's uprightness and honesty were famous, and uncontaminated yet by the obstreperous snidery of those nicknames, sick-names, fuck-you-Ember names. His slovenly behaviour in the Vauxhall was not forgotten, but had been at least filed away.

He would do some proper research and make notes, so that his walkabout was more than simply a gesture of respect for Gladhand, though it certainly *was* that; primarily was that. Didn't Dale deserve this? Merit – he had it by the skipful. The so-called, extremely exclusive, 'Order of Merit', for being pretty OK at something, such as theatricals or getting jungle creatures on to TV, was in the private gift of the monarch, and Ralph could remember thinking that, although Gladhand would probably never get one of those, owing to his modesty and reluctance to push forward for recognition, it was the Queen's loss, not Dale's. All who knew him closest, day-to-day, could observe his merit for themselves, in what was often very tricky commerce, and benefit from it: Buck House endorsement superfluous.

So, as well as making this heartfelt tribute to Gladhand, Ralph had determined to secure practical gains. He wanted to think of himself as a professional, and a professional had to deal in data as well as feelings. That 'confederate concrete', eloquent under his feet, must get accurately charted: potholes, camber, paving section-lengths before broken by a street junction, width from shopfronts to kerb. He'd pace out distances, assess shooting angles, note traffic density, though this, of course, might differ on the day; but he'd have a reasonable estimate.

Ember had calculated that Scumbag Stayley was going to be mortified when Ralph came up with plentiful, credible, deeply relevant statistics. Stayley wouldn't understand how Ralph could have amassed them all on brief there-and-back viewings in the Vauxhall, and, naturally, Ralph wasn't going to tell him about the me-alone, on-the-hoof, supplementary survey. *Very uneven flagstones for three metres here, and part obstruction by newsagent's advertising boards outside shop.* Ember speculated that Stayley might be forced to regard Ralph's findings as a kind of supremely assured visual and mental skill, not very far from magic, and less far from genius, though, obviously Quent would never admit this. It had been time for Stayley to discover not just that Ralph excited deep and accommodating interest from a swathe of discriminating women, but that he could also reliably deduce the shape and stages of an impending battle, despite Stayley's morbid chatter.

Because of that surly, jealous prat's architectured indifference to the Chuck resemblance, Ralph had been particularly geared up that day on his own, walking at Mondial-Trave, to get his perfect facsimile of the star acknowledged, and he keenly watched other folk for signs of shock and delighted wonderment. Over the years, Ralph had often noticed, while out on a stroll, some other pedestrian glance at his face, as in the ordinary way people did exchange looks, but then refocus, this time intently. Ralph could see what was happening and it amused him. The person he'd encountered would be saying to herself or himself, 'That chap reminds me of someone, but who? Who? Cinema? TV? Celebrity? Movie Channel? Ah! Of course, he's the image of a great Hollywood actor. Which, though? Oh, which? What was his name? Yes, got it, got it! Charlton Heston, yes Charlton Heston.' Now and then there'd be a sudden grin and a nod, as though to reassure Ralph the likeness had been registered. It was a kind of congratulation for so brilliantly cloning Heston at his zenith. Most probably they'd thought he could do a similar job tomorrow and emerge as Humphrey Bogart!

At Mondial-Trave, during his new exploration, there had seemed few people about, as a matter of fact. He could see a woman ahead having a long stare at the alderman, and at the base he stood on. A fan of cubes? Could she get off on old stone worthies? '*My dear, he's so constant, so there-when-you-want-him.*' She'd appeared very aware of her surroundings and therefore might instantly spot Ralph's distinctiveness; ironically, however, distinctiveness as a kind of twin: Chuck twice! He was never altogether sure which he preferred – the instant appreciation by some stranger that here was an amazingly accurate image of Heston; or, alternatively, that two-stage, double-take process: the first a normal, casual exchange of squints, passer-by to passer-by, then, though, signs of the astonished realization in the other that Ralph might be a splendid reissue of Heston in his magnificently wholesome, heroic, leader-of-men days.

It could be argued that the second of these responses was the more authentic and substantial because of the extra consideration given, not just a sudden eye-opener. But the 'sudden eye-opener' also had worth. In it lay the power of a glorious, undeniable revelation. Ralph had wondered which camp the woman near the alderman would be in, immediate or delayed. Something about her movements made him think she'd go for the more or less instinctive and instant and intuitive, the boisterously hormonal. Ralph had realized his next thought might be regarded as fanciful, but he'd sensed she'd feel cheated he wasn't stripped to the waist like Ben in some shots. He didn't object to that kind of yearning in a woman. In fact, it could be regarded as what made a woman a woman, this all-powerful, shameless urge in their very blood.

# Sixteen

And then, as Ralph studied the woman thoroughly, trying to characterize her, gauge her impulses, on the admittedly slight evidence, he'd suffered a hellish, almost disabling, shock. Oh, God, why did he dream and kid himself that everyone was fascinated by Ralph W. Ember? His breathing had grown difficult for a moment, and he swayed where he stood, nearly staggered: it had struck him that he shouldn't be speculating about what *she'd* make of *him*, but instead, worry about what *he,* damn late in the day, made of *her.*

Christ, this was that police chief wasn't it – Superintendent Esther Davidson, top detective at the nick, and, naturally, known and recognized by everyone seriously dedicated to the trafficking art: fresh skin, strong jaw; familiar, and classified as formidable and dangerous?

Would this hairdresser's shop porch give him adequate cover? He'd moved into the deep doorway next to a news-agent's. What the hell was this cop doing down here, anyway? He could view from here, as through two window panes, the glass side wall of the entrance and the main front display plate, couldn't he? She put a chummy, grateful hand on the alderman's plinth, possibly groping his feet. It had been as if she took some kind of pleasure or reassurance in the solidity. He could part understand a need to do

107

this. These feet weren't made for walking, but they had given the alderman his sure and steady foundation for more than a century He stood – yes, stood! – for civic pride and fruitful industry: an inspiring example, Ralph thought. He decided again that he wouldn't mind having a statue to himself like that at the end of a notable life. But – also again – he realized prejudice might prevent this. And, even if it did get commissioned by grateful authorities and built, some shit might come along with one of those spray cans – or the equivalent decades ahead – and overlay 'Ralph W. Ember' on the name plate with 'Panicking Ralphy Ember,' just as the monks used to overlay previous writing on parchment, but in this later case from malice, not economy.

Davidson had on a dark blue or navy business suit, the skirt to her knees, medium black heels, a handbag on a strap from her left shoulder, a trilby-style cotton hat, also navy or black. He'd decided she didn't look police, but legalistic, say a bailiff or court usher. There'd been a story around that she and her husband, Gerald, a professional bassoon musician, were sometimes erotically, and/or spitefully, violent with each other, and she might appear in public with sticking plasters, shiners and bruising on her face. Ember didn't make out anything like that now. She was tall, nimble, slightly aquiline, with auburn hair worn long enough for a little of it to be visible from under the hat. Was she writing in a jotter? What, for God's sake? She'd have been in her early thirties, he'd guessed, a 1960s baby, young for a Super. Her teeth had seemed all her own and unchipped, somehow intact despite years of matrimony.

She'd turned and stared up for a few moments at one of the apartment blocks. But, no – that didn't describe things properly. He'd adjusted the thought. He had the feeling her viewing was more specific than this, more focused; more meaningful, not just the building as a nice, imposing piece of conversion skill: commercial heritage, yet acceptably modernized. The changeover was completed years ago and she must have seen it many times before today; wouldn't be gazing at it as if in awed admiration now. That might have been like a socialite New York drunk in a story Ralph had read who'd gone on a ten-year bender and was astounded when he dried out and rejoined the world to find the Empire State skyscraper in place on his regular playground.

It had looked to Ralph that Esther Davidson was aiming her gaze towards a particular apartment window, perhaps four floors up. She didn't seem totally sure which at first and her search took in two or three, but then, after a while, she'd appeared to fix on one.

Did she wave at somebody in the apartment block? From her spot near the alderman, she seemed to give a very brief, crooked-arm wave in the direction of that selected window. Or he'd thought that's what it amounted to. The movement looked tentative, ambiguous, and was certainly very quickly over, no semaphore, as though she'd felt bound to acknowledge somebody in the chosen flat but feared she might draw the attention of others to the window. Well, she *had* drawn attention to the window – Ralph's.

He couldn't be totally sure which apartment, but he narrowed the likelies to two. He'd glanced at both of them in turn and then re-glanced in reverse order but made out nothing in either. They didn't need net curtains at fourth-floor level and anyone standing at the window looking out would be very visible. But no. Not for Ralph. Had someone been visible to Davidson, though – a momentary sighting, then withdrawal?

As well as the slight wave there had also been a slight smile up to the window from her. It gave Ralph his glimpse of her teeth, seemingly her own and perfect. She was a long way off, so, again, there had to be uncertainty – about the teeth, and even uncertainty that she'd smiled. But definitely there'd been some communication in her momentary change of expression – smile, wince, grimace – evidence one way or the other of some sort of relationship. He'd settle for smile.

So, if he settled for it, how did he settle what it meant? Why would she be giving a smile to an acquaintance, or more than an acquaintance, momentarily at the window, someone, or more than one, who dodged back and away once the basic rendezvous formalities had been done? It had obviously proved she knew a contact would be up there, watching. Davidson was more or less checking in: *all present and correct, plinth examination proceeding, as per schedule.* Checking in, who to? Ember had known that she and her husband didn't live in one of these blocks. They had a house in Bromley, at the eastern edge of the Met's ground. It wasn't Gerald she'd waved to and smiled at. He might be touring with his bassoon, anyway.

Did she have an affair going with an occupant on the fourth floor? Had the rough-house sessions with Gerald lost their giddy, rupturing charm for her? Maybe she'd found someone who could punch, elbow and kick better, and/or could *take* a punch, elbow and kick better and retaliate, so the bouts would last longer, involve considerably more delicious abuse. Might that explain the attempt at secrecy, he'd wondered. But, if so, why didn't she get to him, not mess about with the monument's granite feet, et cetera? Hadn't she engaged in some kind of daft, pretend love affair with the alderman?

She'd moved out from near the monument and wrote and/or sketched for a few moments in her jotter. She seemed to have switched off her interest in the apartment window; no further minimal dispatches. But had there been any return wave from what seemed to be floor four? Instead of maintaining contact with the window, she appeared to continue what he had been intending to do himself. Standing on the pavement, she'd begun to gaze systematically about and to make more notes of what she saw, a kind of fervent busyness.

He'd felt certain she was describing features in the layout – shops, the alderman and his plinth, anti-parking bollards, street junctions, pavements, kerbs, the pub, a post office, perhaps this hairdresser's, the newsagent's – and measuring distances with her eye and recording them: not a bailiff or usher or cop now but an estate agent. Did she have someone like Stayley who needed to be persuaded of her abilities? It had scared him to discover they chose such similar approaches to Mondial-Trave. Bloody eerie. Character overlap? He was the budding Charlton one moment, Davidson CID, the next.

More than eerie? That was an emotional, impractical kind of reaction, and Ralph had been concentrating hard lately on developing his business practicality: very necessary if he wanted progress within the firm's corporate structure. And he *had* wanted progress within the firm's corporate structure. Craved it. One of his cousins, an army officer, always spoke of promotion as 'a step'. Ralph wanted a lot of steps. He'd recently come across the phrase 'career path'. This was the kind of path that interested him. It could lead on and on. He knew that if he'd decided on joining the government Foreign Service, instead of Pasque Uno and the substances enterprise, he would have expected to get to an ambassador's post in a major country, such as the U.S.A. or Russia, not some little bit of nowhere riddled with corruption and Aids. He'd tried to cool his brain and get it to interpret what the arrival and actions of Superintendent Davidson meant.

He'd keep an eye on those actions for a while yet, but would have to get out from the cover of this shop entrance soon, or he'd become noticeable to the staff inside; maybe already was. He'd realized that could be a problem later – after the gunplay with Opal Render, and likely injuries and deaths: what point in the shooting if it *didn't* produce injuries and deaths; Opal Render injuries and deaths: extinction of Opal Render in the interests of civic hygiene, and other interests, such as Gladhand's and Pasque Uno's? That was a practical summary of coming events.

Police investigating – fishing for identities – would call on all these shops, the pub, the post office, the newsagent's and the hairdresser's, to ask about any unusual behaviour they'd seen recently. He, Ralph, had been unusual behaviour, had been until he could bugger off from the doorway. *'Yes, officer, a man, twenties, lurking about in the salon entrance – "lurking's" not too strong a term, I feel – lurking for quite a stretch gazing towards the alderman through the glass side wall of the porch, across the customer waiting area, and then through the front window. Something seemed to startle him.'*

The detectives were sure to like this, and ask for a description. Ralph would figure big on their list. He could imagine some replies:

*'He looked like one of those old film stars, officer.'*

*'Which old film star? Lassie?'*

*'Big, bony faced. Was El Cid. TV re-shows it every Easter, strapped dead on his horse so the troops won't know they're short of a chief.'*

*'So we search for a replica Charlton Heston, do we? Not many of them about.'*

*'Heston, yes, that's it. Dead spit. Called "Chuck?" Gun enthusiast? Thought every American householder should be able to defend himself. In one film, he brought the*

113

*commandments down from Mount Sinai, including "Thou shalt not steal." But he reasoned some wouldn't take any notice and still try to steal. The commandments definitely were on the side of goodness or it wouldn't have been worth carrying them down the mountain. But there could be no guarantee they'd always work, and he knew it. So you should be able to shoot burglars' heads off. This was part of the U.S. constitution. If his parents went to the trouble of calling him "Charlton" they wouldn't be pleased to hear it devalued to "Chuck", especially when that's got alternative meanings such as upchuck. But possibly "Charlton Heston" was only a concocted stage name.'*

For a few minutes more Ralph had watched Davidson through the two windows. He remembered dredging up a quote, probably from the Bible, about looking through a glass darkly, then, later, getting face to face. This was a double glass, but the view didn't seem darkened as a result; and neither had he wanted to see Davidson face to face, nor, more important, *her* to see *him* face to face: the dangerously memorable, bony, strong, Heston-type face. It wasn't always a plus. She continued to gaze about and make notes, flipping over the jotter pages rather faster now. He'd guessed she might be sketching some of what she regarded as key spots. What made them key, though? Would *her* key spots match *his*? It surprised him that she didn't produce a mobile phone and take photographs. Ralph had brought one. Of course, relaxing in The Monty bar now he knew the answers to many of the conundrums that baffled him at Mondial-Trave. Hindsighting reigned!

Davidson had finished with the alderman and his feet and custom-made platform and walked towards the corner of Mondial, the jotter still ready in her hand. She turned into Trave Square and went out of sight. She did seem concerned with exactly the adjoining slices of terrain that Ralph was concerned with, that Gladhand was concerned with, and that Opal Render would be concerned with. At once, Ralph left the doorway and made for his car, briskly, but not at a noticeable, jittery scamper. Chuck would never get jittery, would never scamper. He could move and move fast when necessary, but with unostentatious, decisive power. Ralph had decided there was no need to follow Davidson. She would probably only do in the Square what he had seen her do here, geography research. Her failure to use a camera still puzzled him. By then, most people had a mobile. A police superintendent would certainly have one.

But then, as he reached his Volvo, a frightening thought had clobbered him: of course, of fucking blatant course, she might not *need* to take photographs because that was already being done, secretly from a high spot in the apartment block, *de haut en bloody bas*. Could this explain the gesture and the smile up towards that fourth-floor flat? '*Hi, kids, surprise, surprise, yes, it's your boss taking a personal shufti around the area and making notes to caption and augment your pix. No reflections on the quality of your work – always excellent – just a humble attempt to add an explanatory footnote or two.*'

Ralph hadn't been able to make out anything unusual at either of the windows he'd concentrated on, but these might be clever, experienced operators, their work 'always excellent'. They knew how to conceal themselves and their long lenses: basic to their training. Would any further photos by Davidson be redundant? Did she and her people have this ground under continuous, undisclosed surveillance, a confidential renting of an empty flat? Perhaps there was something similar in Trave Square. She might have to do another couple of discreet greetings signals there, *de bas en haut.*

These photographers would be in addition to the normal CCTV coverage of Mondial-Trave. CCTV was just becoming commonplace. Gladhand's stolen Vauxhall might be on film, which was why only a vehicle untraceable to Pasque Uno had been necessary. And Ralph had expected that the street battle, when it came, would probably require balaclavas or proper masks. Davidson and her officers, though, might want more particular subjects than CCTV could offer – precise, persistently tracked targets, recorded by official police cameras. But if there'd been photographers installed up there for God knew how long, why should Esther Davidson feel she had to carry out her own, on-foot scrutiny – a superintendent doing a dogsbody job? Ralph had failed to fathom this. For those jottered captions and footnotes? Again he'd wondered whether her motives might be similar to his – some very personal wish to correct or amend a previous error or deficiency.

He didn't regard her motives as especially important, though. What *had* been important, terrifyingly important, and to the point, was the possibility that the police knew about the oncoming Opal Render/Pasque Uno confrontation from somewhere, and would be present in tooled-up, gun-trained numbers, ready to blast both sides if required, and on ground nicely pre-charted via expertly placed hidden cameras, and by Esther Davidson on a ramble, a wide-awake, carefully written-up and sketch-rich ramble. That 'from somewhere' meant from an informant, or informants, and what seemed to be a very capable informant, or very capable informants.

Possibly, Davidson also knew from this super-crafty spy system who had been here to brush up their close, tactical knowledge of the area, for instance four men, on a day-trip in the Vauxhall: Dale (Gladhand) Hoskins at the wheel, Stayley, gob ever-open and poisonous, next to him, two others in the rear, possibly also identifiable, Greg Mace and himself. The very capable informant, or informants, had possibly provided a bundle of names, as well as the land guide. This would be four men on a round trip, one way past the prom-ised battle site, and then past it again on the return. If they sent the registration details to the police computer and discovered the car had been taken away, interest in the four men would soar. Of course they *would* send the details to the computer, a more or less instant procedure.

And Davidson might learn from the latest length of nosy filming that someone astonishingly like the younger Charlton Heston had hung about

117

in Mondial, using a unisex hairdressing premises as a hide from which to observe her and the alderman and jotter. Ralph recalled some doggerel he'd made up later in the Volvo when slightly less skew-whiffed by the afternoon's rough surprises:

*I spy,*
*from on high,*
*with my fine Leica eye*
*someone beginning*
*with C,*
*for Chuck.*
*But, fuck,*
*it's not Chuck;*
*not C,*
*but E,*
*for Ember:*
*Remember.*

All this, he'd realized, might be confirmed by post-battle interviews with some of the shop people and so on. Ralph had felt how wise he'd been to come and see what was what. What to do about what was what, though, was what he'd call problematical. Deeply.

# Seventeen

Of course, seated with his recollections near the William Blake dangling slab at The Monty, Ralph realized it could guard him from only one very simple kind of attack. Besides, the high shield had become so famous now that anyone wanting to target him would carefully, craftily, hatch an attack plan to bypass it. People all over the city, and probably beyond, would hear about some loony piss-artist who, utterly unprovoked, shot at The Monty's ornate, aerial barrier: the result, exceptionally unpleasant staining and grave hazard from a fragmented sauce bottle. Iles wasn't the only one who'd regard this disgraceful incident as wondrously comic, though he'd definitely be far and away the fucking noisiest, and the most likely to get sent into convulsions by his uncontrollable, profoundly antisocial and anti-cultural laughter. And he'd mouth his descriptions everywhere. Thanks, Iles.

Ralph had picked up a rumour that some members no longer referred to the club as The Monty but called it The Flak-Jacket, suggesting this was necessary kit if members and their guests wanted to stay unspeared by flying glass shards. *See you at the Flak, nine-ish, OK?* That seemed to Ralph appallingly disrespectful to the club, and, perhaps much more importantly, to William Blake, who must have put a terrific amount of work and imagination into his creations; for instance, a tyger spelt with a 'y' and glowing at night, as well as *The Marriage of Heaven and Hell* and other very significant items, both art and writing; so versatile! He was surely due proper deference, not stinko violence. And this stinko violence could send a suggestion to anyone wanting to open fire on Ralph at The Monty that a slightly more devious approach than would have been available before the new fitment was now essential.

Ralph had been afraid that somebody could take a couple of paces through the club's main door and get a direct, straight-ahead view of him at his miniature accounting desk behind the bar, more or less asking to be done. The gunman would finish him with half a dozen rapid rounds – classic, double-handed, anti-recoil, stiff-arm aiming stance. Then he'd turn to disappear fast, probably into a waiting escape car, and speed off to collect the second half of his honorarium on completion, plus expenses for the ammunition and for travel, if he'd been hired in from elsewhere.

Originally, Ralph had assumed the metal bulwark would give effective protection from that category of uncomplicated, easy, attempted hit. And it might have. But, these days, a marksman who'd done just a minor bit of research about The Monty and Ralph, would factor in the disguised steel canopy. He'd pick his sniping spot a little to the right or left, and fire around the obstruction, the way German tanks notoriously outflanked the Maginot Line at the beginning of the Second World War, and took Belgium and France.

And there might be more than one marksman, able to riddle Ralph from several angles. As well as The Monty, he had that high-earning, tax-exempt, expanding, recreational commodities business, and so, very naturally, he also had envious, scheming, dog-eat-dog enemies. But, added to these routine perils of the substances profession, he knew there were still people who remembered what had happened at Mondial-Trave in London and stupidly blamed him even so long after: stupidly and outrageously and murderously.

He suspected the Mondial-Trave episode was where those insulting nicknames – Panicking Ralph and/or Panicking Ralphy – had their rotten, unjust start. So, yes, there might once have been a motive for that, though totally mistaken. But why had those odious descriptions stuck so long after? Did he detect more envy here? Oh, yes: despite Quent Stayley's rabid insults back then, most men saw the splendid, women-wowing, desire-fanning Chuck Heston element in Ralph's looks and decided they had to negative it, smash it, reduce him to somewhere lower than their own low selves via these vicious, destructive, belittling insignia. He had children. Wouldn't it be awful if they found out that their father had been given extra titles that made him sound like a poltroon?

He reckoned that this dismal group who'd just come into the club would be the kind who'd call him Panicking Ralph or Panicking Ralphy when he wasn't present, although they'd go all bum-sucking and smarmy when talking to him face to face. *How we love The Monty, Ralph! The warm mahogany panelling and beautifully polished brass fittings. A living credit to you!*

It was on account of such possible two-timing

spiel that he tried to avoid conversation with loutish lots like these. Until The Monty was gloriously relaunched in its new, exclusive, intellectually glittering form, Ralph would accept all sorts of crud as paid-up members. Come the rebirth, though, he'd apply the old heave-ho to all who didn't fit. He wanted people he could genuinely respond to at a select social level, and who could genuinely respond to him at that level. In Ralph's view this was how a club should be: a comfortable meeting spot for members of similar tastes, brainpower, courteousness and sensitivity.

Sensitivity in particular: for example, would this oafish crew at the bar now understand, empathize with, the bewilderingly painful pressures that suddenly came on him at Mondial-Trave? Answer? No. And no again. They'd be too thick and self-obsessed to recognize the problems beating so hard on Ralph there, let alone have any notion how to solve them. As he'd driven back that day, thinking about the probable police cameras taking a constant, recorded peep at the area, he'd had to think also about what he should do with the new information he'd harvested – harvested by accident.

But, hang on, was there more to it than that? Might it be only *seeming* accident? Great artists, such as, for instance, William Blake, sometimes received inspiration they could not rationally account for. It invited itself, arrived unexplained, and unexplainable, as if from a sublime but hidden store. They were vastly privileged to receive it, and acknowledged this, felt their work take from it uniquely energizing nourishment. It was what made them great. They happily, grate-fully, accepted its brilliant influence. It estab-lished their genius.

Ralph wondered if, perhaps, *he* had been guided in the same supernatural way with *his* work – that Volvo visit to Mondial-Trave. Obviously, a project to shoot dead or maim as many Opal Render people as possible didn't involve identical artistic considerations as, say, the tyger poem or *The Marriage Of Heaven And Hell.* But it was the machinery of the two differing kinds of inspir-ation that interested Ralph. An impulse had taken him there on the same morning chosen by the chief of detectives. Remarkable? He'd thought so. Amazing? Yes. Beyond remarkable and amazing? Possibly. Anyway, no matter how he'd gathered these revelations, he had to ask himself now *why* she'd picked that day and time and, in fact, why she was there at all, as though she and Ralph were in some totally baffling, yet obviously valid, way unbreakably linked.

And – crux of crux questions – he had to ask himself, also, whether he should tell Gladhand and the other Pasque Uno folk what he'd seen, and what he made of it. This dilemma could not be more severe. Such a report could end all pros-pects of a battle encounter with Opal Render at Mondial-Trave. The planning would have been an absolute waste. That mature and noble hope of purifying the trade scene by morgueing the bulk of Opal Render's people, and giving complete, unrivalled, deserved dominance to Pasque Uno, would fizzle out.

# Eighteen

Esther, in her garden, remembered herself remembering – went back to the past and then, in the past, went back to the past of *that* past. She had set up those three secret filming posts at Mondial-Trave, two in apartment blocks, one in an attic over a confectionery shop: very pricey coverage, what with rent payments and the photographers' special, long-shift subsistence allowance, and, eventually, domestic cleaners. The outlay and effort showed she'd given the informant's forecast of a street battle high credibility. Well, he'd been brilliant earlier, and she had to believe in form. Police did. They called it 'previous', meaning someone had a convicted crooked history, and most likely had a similar crooked present, due another conviction.

The informant's previous was different, though. He had a record, but a record for accurate, helpful, very confidential, clairvoyant, paid-for whispers, not lawlessness. The law, in fact, needed him (or her) and those like him (or her). Detectives detecting often depended on someone like him (or her) and dished out variable fees from an official but secret fund for insights.

She'd given the camera positions operational names, pinched from a theatre farce about someone relentlessly nosy, the way photography was relentlessly nosy: Paul Pry One, Two and

Three. Paul Pry Two produced the most valuable film clips. These included the Pasque Uno (Vauxhall) and Opal Render (Mazda) reconnaissance visits that Esther had shown in her briefing of the ambush party. Sergeant Fiona Hive-Knight had charge of Two. Esther thought that perhaps the code name of her post should have been gender-aware: Paul*ine* Pry.

She was mid-thirties, fair hair tuft-cut into a miniature field of stooks, round, cheerful, conspiratorial face, dark blue eyes, large, parade-ground voice, twice divorced. Hive-Knight and her two children – one from each former husband – lived with a widower house decorator and *his* two children. She revered film and photography. Fiona was the past and the bits of film she'd show were a move into that deeper past.

Fiona felt the camera could get at crux qualities hidden away not just in people but in things. She had a fancy for the term 'innate'. When, a week ago, she'd screened the Vauxhall clip for Esther, Hive-Knight had said: 'Here's an interesting vehicle, ma'am.' Then she'd explained why. Esther remembered some of Fiona's keywords: 'purposeful', 'innate', 'designated', 'environs', 'mull', 'trundle', 'intent', 'obliterated', 'doggedness'. Esther used this string of prompts to recall the full lecturette, more or less verbatim.

It had gone something like: 'This is a purposeful car with an obvious, innate, designated, single task. Low speed, so time for crew to observe environs and mull prospects. The car trundles. It trundles with visualizing intent. It's as if it has been waiting for a call to this role and has stood ready, happy to be conscripted for such a vital, scrutinizing service, willing to have its identity speculated upon and traced, because the tracing couldn't really hurt anyone. The lines of this car betoken doggedness and responsibility.' She'd paused. The Vauxhall disappeared as they watched and then came back, but moving in the opposite direction, and travelling just as slowly as earlier. 'And now, here it returns. Did I speak of doggedness? Yes, oh yes, Persistence. Thoroughness. Anything that's worth doing is worth doing twice. A second trundle. Identical intent – casing the district, possibly seeing different angles because it's at a different angle to the surrounds itself, of course. We think four people aboard, though the back seat is problematical. It's Gladhand and Quentin Stayley in the front, people we know, naturally. Rear, it could be Greg Mace, also known to us, and he might be obscuring someone else, not identifiable.'

'Our tipster names someone new to PU called Ralph Ember,' Esther had said.

'Well, he could be a possible,' Fiona said. She'd sounded peeved that Esther might be ahead of her.

'Very little known of him,' Esther replied.

'Right.'

Altogether, Esther could recollect three sessions in the projection room: first, when Fiona did her inane, not innate, humanizing Vauxhall character sketch – the car's delighted, no doubt smiling, acceptance of its there-and-back trundling destiny; second, the gun-group briefing, with troublesome, almost insubordinate, jabber from Wilcox; the third had come a couple of days afterwards when Esther viewed some later Mondial-Trave film, again with Fiona. Past of the past again, but a more recent past of the past now. Parts of this clip actually featured Esther. Inevitably. And, as she'd watched, she remembered behaving as these new pictures on the screen showed her behaving.

There'd been a small, would-be secret grin and a mini-wave up towards Paul Pry Two in a hired fourth-floor flat; a touchy-feely few moments at the plinth and shoes of the historic alderman, taking reassurance and pleasure from their serious, inflexible, supremely authentic stoniness; some writing and sketching activity with a Biro and jotter.

Then: 'Now, here, ma'am, look at this, please,' Fiona Hive-Knight had ordered, with tremendous echoing emphasis on the 'Now': something vital upcoming. The camera swung away from Esther. 'It's the porch to a hairdresser's salon,' Fiona had said. They'd been filming through two sheets of glass, she explained, the front window and the side pane of the porch. These blurred focus slightly. She thought the deep entrance to the place made a kind of protected hidey-hole for anyone standing there to scan the street. And the film showed a man *was* standing there: mid- or late-twenties, tall, well-built, non-fleshy face, jeans, long-sleeved V-neck tan sweater, red-trimmed training shoes.

Hive-Knight said he seemed to be gazing up towards the monument, and therefore up towards Esther, and gazing very fixedly, perhaps surprised

127

and bewildered. Esther had agreed. It couldn't be the alderman that fascinated him, Fiona argued, no matter how splendid the alderman's civic and charity work had been a century or so ago. Esther was unnerved. The camera had shifted away from her and on to the man, so she didn't appear on this section of film; yet he was apparently observing her, staring at her. It shook Esther's sense of self. It was as though she existed only in his eyes and consciousness. She'd come here today looking for the nitty-gritty, the concrete, the real. But, for a dazing moment she had seemed reduced to a figment. She thought of the two evil night visitors in a famous novel, *The Turn of the Screw.* You didn't know whether they were real or the overheated imaginings of a governess. Esther had struggled to get out of that kind of limbo land and in a while managed it. She felt this tumble into sudden gibbering fantasy was as daft as Fiona's goofy humanizing ramblings about the Vauxhall.

Then the camera went briefly on to Esther again and showed her rounding the corner into Trave, and out of Paul Pry Two's ambit. Abrupt change of shot once more: back to the hairdresser's. The man left the porch at once, as if he no longer needed to hang about spying. He'd seen enough? Job done. He didn't walk towards the junction with Trave to follow Esther, but in the opposite direction, until he, too, passed from range. Fiona said he'd possibly been making for a car parked a discreet distance away. She'd given no reason for that guess but Esther thought it could be right. Fiona didn't offer a personality analysis of this other, supposed vehicle – its patience and knack of being in the right place while it waited for the driver.

As he'd stepped out from the doorway, and was no longer behind the two layers of glass, it had become suddenly possible for the lens to get a square-on, clear look at his face. 'God, he reminds me of someone,' Esther recalled saying.

She recalled Hive-Knight's reply, too: 'El Cid? Ben Hur?'

'We have Ralph W. Ember's appearance as matching the young Charlton Heston's.'

'Bingo, if I may say, ma'am!' Fiona replied.

# Nineteen

The Monty began to get busy. It was the run-up to Christmas, and people were feeling festive and in a drinks-all-round spending mood. They seemed to see a joyful link between the club and the nativity story. And they came wishing to celebrate that link, something like the three kings.

But Ralph himself didn't care for Christmas, although he had nothing against the nativity. He believed it the time when he was most likely to get shot and killed, probably on his own premises, The Monty. He recognized, of course, that his feelings about the festival might seem odd, a paradox. After all, as so many of the members seemed to realize, it should be a season of happiness, goodwill and liquored-up merrymaking, this merrymaking not necessarily causing damage to The Monty or any of its staff or membership. Yet the Christmas period brought Ralph thoughts of violent death. His. Those worries were eternally with him, but at Yule they boomed.

He had to try to be festive, though, or, at least, to *seem* festive. There was a saying among actors and theatre producers, 'the show must go on,' and Ralph applied this brave slogan to the club, and to his own role. The Monty brought responsibilities. Ralph could not shirk them. It was not in his nature to. He was host and seasonal affability, or, *apparent* affability was required. People in a celebratory state would expect him to be celebratory, too. Although the recession meant a very severe tightening of budget for many families, not all Monty members had suffered an income drop; for some, the glorious, interesting reverse, in fact. The obvious point was that the downturn squeezed businesses as well as ordinary people and a lot of companies had been forced to cut back on hired security personnel, leaving their premises tastily vulnerable.

Because of this, that political phrase 'the feel-good factor' was exceptionally robust among Monty members. The state of the British economy impacted positively and encouragingly on the careers of quite a few club regulars. Possibly they'd have an even better Christmas than usual because of the slump, their cash flow in brilliant spate. London clubs, such as The Athenaeum and The Carlton, could never match this. Simply, they seriously lacked memberships ready to balaclava up and jemmy warehouses and stores whose watchman patrols had been overhastily slashed to reduce costs. Some of *their* members might actually own the kind of business properties now more than usually liable to get done over big because of stupid skimping on guards.

Of course, Ralph wished The Monty didn't have its crummy special distinction as a depot for villains, and he still hoped to make enormous changes soon. He'd already made a kind of start. For instance, he did his best to stop people automatically rendezvousing at the club for the profits share-out ceremonies after selling stuff to their receivers of acquired goods. That type of fiscal get-together could end in curse-rich yelling and/ or multi-participant violence, if someone suspected there'd already been skimming off the top of the 'overs', as their loot total was fondly known; exactly the kind of very unpleasant, raucous atmosphere Ralph struggled to exclude from The Monty, thanks very much. A good deal of champagne and rum and blackcurrant might be bought for these distribution sessions, so by barring them Ralph was doing himself out of good business. But put a couple of bottles of champagne plus rum and blacks inside some of these people and you couldn't be sure how the rest of the evening would turn out. Ralph loathed disorder, whatever the season.

Even when these divvying up occasions went off peacefully, Ralph did not find them acceptable or wholesome. No, no, no. He remembered comic-paper strip cartoons enjoyed as a kid where robbers would be portrayed with a sack on their back marked 'SWAG'. He hated to have The Monty blatantly associated with swag. It grieved and disgusted him to see piles of twenties and even fifties laid out on a bar-room table in front of four or five smug, gloating members. They'd make a disgraceful, smirking mini-drama out of totting up their cut and of checking for the water-mark and special thread in the fifties by holding the notes one by one up to the light to confirm them genuine, not forged. They had no thought of The Monty's reputation as a social centre, nor of the club's possible fine, elegant future.

Perhaps, though, Ralph could sympathize a little with their disregard for The Monty's future because they would be no fucking part of it, the uncultured, mercenary sods, though they wouldn't know it, not yet. Out, and stay out! Flap your trade fifties about somewhere else. Ralph detested vulgar display. Endlessly he sought decorum, and couldn't always rely on finding it at the current Monty.

Also, Ember objected to the choice of the Monty for meetings to shortlist forthcoming targets and discuss the details of forced entry methods, muting of alarms systems, CCTV coverage, category of goods to be taken, freighting requirements. But he couldn't supervise every corner of the club during all its opening hours.

Actually, he had an irritating idea that, despite his well-known disapproval, more, not fewer, income-allotting rituals and planning conferences took place in The Monty now, because of those increased project opportunities. These were sensitive, grab-all folk whose instincts or genes told them conditions wouldn't always be so splendidly bonny, and they should seize the day, meaning, mainly, the night.

Ralph thought he could stay seated at his desk reminiscing for another few minutes, and then he'd help the bar staff serve drinks. He didn't mind 'mucking in', as he called it. He regarded himself as a 'hands-on' licensee – another of Ralph's personal phrases – not someone who stayed detached and aloof. Ralph abhorred snobbery along with vulgarity and a failure of decorum. Yes, he regarded many of those he would one day kick out as gutter filth. But this was only because they *were* gutter filth and any other way of regarding them would be evasive and false. And 'hands-on' as regards his work among the club staff had no groping overtone when he mucked in enthusiastically and graciously with female employees. Ralph found all that *droit de seigneur* stuff – entitlement of the master to access in-house girls – ignoble and unnecessary for someone like himself, rather hounded by opportunities.

Margaret would look in a little later and she and Ralph could have a ploughman's lunch. He liked the sound of that – 'ploughman's lunch'. It suggested tradition and fundamental, honest quality, the kind of attributes he sought for The Monty. Margaret didn't often come to the club these days – possibly saw it as slightly uncouth, maybe massively uncouth – but she was shopping for Christmas presents this morning and would need a break before going to collect the children from ski lessons at the artificial slope.

Margaret, yes. At the time of his supplementary gawp trip in the Volvo to Mondial-Trave during the early PU days she and he were living near King's Cross station in London, not a bad district, and had two daughters, Venetia and Fay. The family remained the same. She didn't know then the kind of career he was starting – hoping to start – with Pasque Uno and Gladhand. There'd been no need for a full prospectus right away. When she'd asked he'd said, 'Marketing', which, to a degree, was true. He realized she knew, and/or guessed a good deal more about his businesses now, of course. She put up with them. He thought this was probably how she'd describe her attitude if they ever spoke frankly about it. They didn't. She'd see there was a household to be financed, daughters to be privately educated, ski-tripped and ponied, a country house, 'Low Pastures', to be heated, lit and kept up to standard.

Plainly, she'd had relationships before Ralph, but he'd prided himself on not being the sort to get nosy, prudish and unforgiving about that, and he'd felt totally sure she was spruce, although, clearly, you could never tell what previous men had brought to bed with them from other heartfelt, ardent connections. This might put the potential infection range on to infinity. And infinity added up to one hell of a number. Ralph had believed then, and believed now, that a vast amount of interlocking occurred in the world, making vigilant hygiene essential for both parties. And three-somes or more than three would send the mathematical calculation of risk into millions, even billions. Men travelled abroad to Africa and/or Canada, for instance. There might be imports.

Health was not something you could ask a woman about, though, pre-closeness. That would be hurtful and insulting. Condoms possibly reduced the dangers but made things unspontaneous, and, in any case, might burst. But, of course, he knew now that his decent faith in Margaret, and in the type of partners she had picked prior to Ralph, proved to be wholly and characteristically OK.

He recalled that he would have liked to talk to her immediately after the Mondial-Trave episode about the arrival of Superintendent Davidson, the apparent contact with someone

in an apartment, the jotter, and the grim likelihood – certainty – that Pasque Uno or Opal
Render contained a well-informed fink who
talked prospects and locations to the police;
talked so convincingly to the police that Davidson
had to come for a renewed dekko. Margaret
possessed a good brain. He'd have valued her
take on this situation. But he'd decided it was
unnecessary to disclose that much to her. How
would he have worded it, for God's sake? He
tried to imagine the kind of oh-by-the-way,
chatty, conversational approach about a potential
massacre:

'*Margaret, could I put a bit of a problem to
you? I'd be grateful for fresh thoughts on it. You
might have heard of two drugs firms, Pasque Uno
and Opal Render. Me, I'm in Pasque Uno – new
laddy, at the indentured apprentice stage, but
getting ahead, I believe. They spot a true flair
for the trade in me, I think. For a while both
sides have been preparing for a final, winner-
takes-the-lot battle. The victors would secure
permanently the Mondial-Trave slice of desirable
commercial territory. We in PU have been confident that we could annihilate OR in any gun
scrap. For us, it's nothing like, say, the Battle of
the Ardennes in the Second World War, but just
a normal, routine instance of healthy business
competition; healthy for those who survive, and
with all their limbs and faculties, that is,
obviously.*

'*This morning I went down to take a further
gander at the ground because previously I was
distracted by abominable slurs from another*

*member of PU, wilfully ignoring what many are kind enough to observe in me – you among them – the young Charlton Heston resemblance. A remarkable fluke ensued. I don't think I exaggerate. The detective chief of the borough, Superintendent Esther Davidson, was also there, apparently to do her own survey of the area and record her findings in a jotter: that is, the same sort of mission as my own. I watched her from a hairdresser's porch which gave some concealment but also allowed good vision through two panes of window glass.*

*'We have to ask, haven't we, what are the implications of this visit by her? As I see it – and I'd value your view of my view, yes yours of mine, in a moment, please – as I see it, the implications are:*

*'(One): The police know something special is due at Mondial-Trave. The ground needs charting, perhaps re-charting.*

*'(Two): This suggests they have an informant in one of the companies, PU or OR.*

*'(Three): We can't tell how much this informant, and, therefore, Davidson, know about what is scheduled for Mondial-Trave, but the informant and she are aware that something is planned for there. She'll probably decide she must make preparations.*

*'(Four): Some of these preparations might already have been undertaken. She appeared to signal a greeting to a contact/contacts, on the fourth floor of an apartment block. This apartment could be regarded as what is known as 'a vantage point', and there might be others. A vantage point*

137

is a point that offers someone, or more than one, the advantage of a vantage or view.

'(Five): We might ask who is/who are this contact/these contacts?

'(Six): The fourth-floor apartments have a wide vision field. I think an intelligent assumption as to its occupants – temporary, ad hoc *occupants* – would be that he or she or they is/are a camera crew conducting a continuous snoop on one major section of Mondial-Trave.

'(Seven): It would also be an intelligent assumption to expect there are other camera positions covering the rest of Mondial-Trave.

'(Eight): She might know from her informant, or deduce from her police experience and police intuition, that what is to happen at Mondial-Trave is a turf shoot-out. Her jotter activity – words and/or sketches – could be to do with noting possible battleground features and their potential use.

'(Nine): If this is so, she will arrange for a tooled-up, sizeable police group to be present, probably concealed, ready to blast PU and OR, ostensibly for putting uninvolved citizens at risk through gunfire on the streets, but, really, because it's a sweet chance to annihilate the two companies, as if in a praiseworthy operation to protect the public.

'(Ten): Instead of a one-to-one confrontation of the two firms, there will be a third party presence, a police contingent including marksmen, markswomen, better trained than any of us, possibly better armed, and numerically superior to the units from both firms added together.

'Now, Margaret, you will ask – and are absolutely entitled to ask – "What, then, is the problem – the central, core problem – that you wish me to comment on, Ralph, dear?" My answer is easily put, Margaret: do I tell the head of PU, Dale Hoskins, what I have seen and what I suspect? Ah, but I can tell you are surprised. You feel, do you, that there is no problem here? You consider it obvious that I must tell Dale and colleagues. You may say that my discoveries have changed the whole nature of the Mondial-Trave situation and that Dale Hoskins and the rest of PU will be deeply thankful for my individual enterprise and tactical skills, such as spotting the suitability as a nook of the hairdresser's porch.

'You may well explain: "Your intervention, Ralph, will save lives, possibly including your own, but also those of PU members in general. It's true your brilliant coup will most likely also save Opal Render lives, which you might regard as a hugely unfortunate snag. If, because of what you have revealed, Dale Hoskins decides to abandon the Mondial-Trave project, there will be no street fight and the police party will have no cause, no pretext, for using their weapons on the Opal Render party, suppose they turned up, ready to do battle, but unaware that PU won't show.

'"OR will have committed no offence simply by arriving ready for a shoot-out, and so the superintendent cannot give her unit the order to attack." You'll say, Margaret, that this is admittedly a drawback because none of the opposition will get killed or even profoundly maimed, but

139

there will surely be further opportunities to stage the decisive challenge."'

But, supposing that little chat had taken place, Ralph realized he would have had to make certain points in response.

'Thank you, Margaret. That is a really well thought-out, clear verdict. I have to draw your attention, though, to some special factors:

'(One): I do not know as a certainty why Davidson was there.

'(Two): I have no proper evidence regarding her jotter entries.

'(Three): Nor have I any proper evidence that there is a camera crew in a fourth-floor flat and elsewhere. Now, Margaret, I have at least one enemy in PU who might be glad of a chance to accuse me of panic and alarmism because I am afraid to take part in the planned battle. He might say I have concocted those speculations about Davidson's reasons for the Mondial-Trave visit so as to get the operation cancelled by Dale Hoskins.

'(Four): I see a further damaging point that could be exploited by someone hostile to me: my observation of Superintendent Davidson took place only because I behaved in a blatantly maverick, grossly undisciplined fashion. Dale Hoskins had arranged a discreet, motorized inspection of the Mondial-Trave site so as not to give any sign of an impending clash bringing trouble to the district. By going alone and openly to Mondial-Trave, I have shown a wholesale disregard for all the care and subtlety exercised via a pinched Vauxhall. I could be accused of

140

*either deliberately or thoughtlessly destroying the prospect of a Mondial-Trave triumph by PU.*

*(Five): Whichever way my report was received I would not come out of it well. I might not come out of it alive. Again I say, I do not exaggerate. My career with Pasque Uno could be in enormous peril. And my personal safety might be, too.'*

More people arrived at the club and Ralph left his seat at the desk and went to act as assistant barman. He enjoyed buckling down occasionally to this kind of basic duty. It entailed one-to-one, face-to-face contact with some of the members, but nothing too intimate or personal. There was a tipple connection, and no more than that. When a customer gave his or her order Ralph would repeat it back to them before pouring and serving. He wanted to create the illusion that his life was devoted to getting things exactly right for Monty clientele. *'Two double vodka and tonics with ice, two glasses of red, large, a large Tia Maria, two pints of Abbot Ale. Coming up!'* They were words without any particular magical quality, but Ralph believed people felt honoured to have their wants so graciously and accurately provided by the proprietor himself, Milord Monty, as some affectionately called him.

Tomorrow, he'd get the Christmas tree and decorations in place. There was always anxiety concerning the tree. If Ralph chose a comparatively small, manageable one, say four or five feet high, a member, pissed out of his or her skull on booze one festive night might pull it and all the lights and wiring from the tub and use it as a weapon against someone who'd upset him or her; or against almost anyone, just for the Yule joy of wielding it and knocking people over, like with a halberd or jousting staff. Ralph had discovered that people's understanding of the word 'Merry', as in 'Merry Christmas', varied a great deal and, for some, would include whacking bystanders with a conifer.

On the other hand, if Ralph brought in a much taller tree – too big to be swung about like that – someone might do notable harm to other members and/or the furnishings just by pushing it over, maybe jocosely crying out the lumberjack warning, 'Timber!' Ralph had thought of stripping the insulating rubber off the fairy-lights wire. Anyone handling the tree would suffer a grand, momentarily paralysing, possibly fatal, shock, like cows touching an electrified fence. But bare wires meant fire risk. Those insurance bandits would say the disaster had been self-induced if The Monty burned down, and refuse to cough. A pity, this: Ralph might have been able to give the club a completely fresh identity if the building were new: a step on the way to catching up on The Athenaeum for class.

As well as this chanciness, Ralph had to take into account that, although Margaret was not keen on the club, she did bring the children to a party for members' families and Ralph wouldn't expose them to that sort of blaze hazard. He'd decided to go for the *smaller* tree type this year. He might cement it into the tub, though if that block were pulled out with the tree it might make it an even more hurtful item. Sometimes, ownership of the club seemed to Ralph not worth the constant difficulties. But these were minor worries compared to the fears for his safety.

Occasionally he thought of The Monty as a kind of social symbol. He tried to bring order and harmony to the club, just as Harpur and Iles tried to bring order and harmony to their manor, but all the time they were beset by those bringing only trouble, lawlessness, and defiance. It depressed Ralph to recognize that when he looked at a Christmas tree, with all its holy significance, he had to consider it above all as a potential destructive menace.

But, of course, there'd been a time way back when he felt himself threatened by a much larger destructive menace.

# Twenty

He served a few more drinks then went upstairs
to the club office, dishing out additional smiles
and minor nods to patron slobs and slobesses *en
route*. It was the least he could do, so he did it.
The smiles were what he would regard as manly
smiles, not sickeningly full and lavish, not love-
me-do-I'm-harmless, but brief, brisk and better
than nothing.

He reckoned that if you'd discovered some
people called you 'Panicking Ralph' or 'Panicking
Ralphy' behind your back you'd need to be
guarded with your smiles in case you were
smiling at some of the people who actually called
you 'Panicking Ralph' or 'Panicking Ralphy'
behind your back. These smiles had to be formal,
of no deep worth. They were conditional smiles
and did not suggest buddydom or fondness or
forgiveness. When people took out membership
of The Monty they didn't also take out a right
to unlimited geniality from The Monty's owner.

In the office, he opened the safe and produced
a blue-covered, foolscap ring-binder. It contained
four pages of handwritten, pencilled notes, each
page roman-numbered top left – i, ii, iii, iv – the
dots very strongly applied, as if to confirm the
complete reliability of whatever was said on each
sheet. Ralph believed you would never get dots
like that on rubbish. Poor material would be a

betrayal of the dots. These dots had chutzpah but also robustness and dignity.

He hated sloppiness in anything written down. He liked stuff to look as authoritative as a legal document, even if done by hand and in pencil. Good presentation cost nothing except, possibly, a few extra moments of carefulness. It showed respect for the reader. In this case, because the pages were usually locked up, the only reader would be Ralph, but he considered that as a quibble and believed the principle should operate generally. Everybody recognized that one of the great things about the Roman Empire was the quality of what would be called now its civil service. This had been based on that special numerals system, though Ralph realized it wouldn't have seemed special to them at the time, just everyday, and the only numbers around. It was quite a while before Arab figures took over. That didn't mean he disdained Arab numerals, or regarded them as *iii*rd rate. After all, he used them, not roman, when totting up profits from both his businesses, and Arabic coped OK with these totals: no shortage of noughts to give the thousands, ten thousands and hundreds of thousands. It was merely that he would prefer some documents to have the dynamism given by roman. In Ralph's view, everybody needed certain themes and/or missions in their life, and this occasional use of roman figures was one of his, or, as he sometimes waggishly thought of it, *i* of his.

The notes were an account of a conversation with Dale Hoskins following that extraordinary vigil in the hairdresser's porch. Well, he reckoned it could even be termed a 'unique vigil'. Few, if any, people would have watched from a unisex hairdresser's deep doorway a detective superintendent of the Metropolitan Police seemingly flirt with a statue of an alderman. Gladhand had owned a tall house in Cheyne Walk, Chelsea, not far from where Sir Mick Jagger once lived, and not far, either, from the house where Gerry Adams and Martin McGuinness had secret peace talks with the British government in the 1970s about the troubles in Ireland.

When Ralph telephoned to say he had something urgent to discuss, Gladhand invited him over. Dale appreciated that kind of glossy street. It gave him what he called 'a suitable background'. It had what he described as 'an aura'. Although you never saw auras mentioned in property For Sale bills, an aura might be present owing to history and setting. Auras cost, but could be vital to someone like Gladhand. He'd come on extremely fast in the substances craft but Ralph knew he didn't want to appear as just a remarkable very sudden success. There'd be something fragile and short-term spectacular about that. He needed strong auras and backgrounds to give him true, lasting stature, not the stony kind of the alderman, of course, but a living resoluteness and durability. Everyone knew the story of that young man who made himself wings, stuck them on his body and flew very impressively up and up until he got too near the sun and the inferior wax he'd used melted, so the wings came off and he dropped down into the sea faster than he'd climbed. This was an old Greek tale and it disappointed Ralph that the expensive school his daughters went to did this type of yarn in English, instead of teaching the proper classical language. Ralph would guard against that kind of catastrophic tumble.

It certainly hadn't been usual for Ralph to write summaries of Pasque Uno matters. Words on paper could be turned against you as evidence if things went rough, just as words on tape did for Nixon. But Ralph had sensed ahead of the meeting with Dale at his home that this was going to be a very cruxy kind of occasion, and should get properly minuted. It would most likely involve a major strategy survey, even though Ralph had been only a raw starter in the Pasque Uno company, nowhere near policy-making level. When a school kid, he and his pals used to call birds just out of the nest 'yuckers'. He had been a Pasque Uno yucker.

At that stage, he'd been proud to serve in PU at all, even as a yucker, or less than that if required. He'd revered Gladhand and the firm. In case any decisions should change this relationship, Ralph had wanted permanent, written testimony to prove he'd done nothing stupid or cowardly or careless that might have spoiled, even destroyed, his esteem for PU and its chief. Or, to give the positive side, he'd felt he needed an honest schedule of events preserved, to reassure himself in the future that he had behaved properly, loyally, intelligently, although a yucker.

Ralph had been to the Cheyne Walk house several times before. He liked the butler, Pedro, from abroad somewhere, but able to fit in, as certain overseas people could: think of William the Conqueror. Pedro preferred to keep his automatic at waistband level, rather than in a shoulder holster. Most of the domestic staff were foreign. Probably Pedro was wanted by the police in his own country, so Gladhand had given him a niche. That would be typical of Gladhand. Practical. Quite often humane as long as it wasn't inconvenient. He objected to immigration, but if immigration happened on quite a scale, anyway, he'd want to get a plus or two out of it, such as more customers for coke, et cetera, and Pedro. Gladhand believed in making unfavourable conditions favourable. This was the new alchemy. This was leadership. Very few houses in Cheyne Walk would be without a butler. Gladhand was sure to want at least parity. That was part of the required background and aura.

Within a couple of hours of the meeting with Gladhand there, Ralph had set down his recollections of it thoroughly and, he'd swear, accurately. He'd heard of *aide memoires* – written accounts of recent verbal agreements or discussions. Ralph had intended his *aide memoire* to prove he'd acted only and entirely for the good of Dale and PU – possibly for the safety and survival of Dale and PU. He'd guessed this might be disputed by evil, scheming maniacs like Quent Stayley. Ember would need to see off these doubters and the *aide* could get itself translated and aid him with that.

Also, looking at these foolscap sheets now, in The Monty office, Ralph had an idea that one day, because of a very worthwhile, interesting life on a number of social, commercial and intellectual levels, he might wish to write his memoirs, or even a full autobiography, especially after he'd moved the club up to Athenaeum status, or above. The notes would be such a help then. He understood there was a good market for the life stories of celebrities told by themselves. Although he did not consider himself a full-scale celebrity at present, there might be enormous developments over the next few years. It wouldn't be necessary to put in anything about the shot William Blake, nor the ruined Worcestershire sauce bottle. These were demeaning incidents, not flattering to Ralph or the club, or English literature. But, by then, The Monty would have been transformed, and that unhelpful episode of no account.

Ralph had viewed Pasque Uno as similar to one of those professional livery companies, or a Masonic lodge, which demanded, and deserved, a member's absolute commitment. But he'd feared his beautiful bond with Pasque Uno could come under massive strain because of what he would reveal about the Davidson sighting. He had hinted at that strain in the imaginary, flashback talk with Margaret. The talk might have been imaginary, the strain wasn't.

Of course, he did not know then that the nicknames 'Panicking Ralph' and 'Panicking Ralphy' could result from what was to happen concerning Mondial-Trave. But he had wanted no self-blame if big upsets came. And they did. He knew that now. Ralph often put himself – his actions and motives – under unsparing examination. He didn't assume he was entitled to an easy time.

He'd admit he had dazzlingly fine, Hollywood-standard looks and brilliant business flair. How could he deny it? These would take him only so far, though.

He believed that until this point the names 'Panicking Ralph' and 'Panicking Ralphy' had not existed, not even secretly, behind his back. And he believed now that they still should not exist, not even secretly, behind his back, or at all. They seemed to Ralph most likely concocted back then by Stayley, and also deliberately spread by him, the pony-tailed scheming fucker, M.A. (Oxon). No, not just 'most likely'. Definitely. Mr Stab-in-the-back. Mr Envy. Mr Shit-stirrer. Mr Malign. Mr Man-who-would-be-king, Mr Denier-of-the-Chuck retread.

*'Ralph Ember? Oh, you mean Panicking Ralph, do you? Or Panicking Ralphy. Yes, I know him. I always wonder how he got those nicknames.'* No, you didn't always wonder, or ever wonder, you glib prick. You made them up for no reason except spite and then broadcast them. He'd had business cards with that 'M.A. (Oxon)' after his name. He was the sort who would. He had explained to Ralph that the 'Oxon' came from the old Latin name of the university. Thanks ever so! Ralph wondered whether he'd have been able to get through life without knowing that.

Pedro, Gladhand's butler, had spotted Ember's Charlton Heston *doppelgängerism* immediately – had mentioned it, when he first saw Ralph, in an amazed, congratulatory tone, not foolishly jokey, by calling Ralph 'El Cid' or 'Ben Hur'. Pedro had obviously known he should treat

Gladhand's business associates with maximum regard, even a novice like Ralph.

Hoskins had told Ralph that Pedro was a wonderful shot with a handgun, no matter what model, single- or double-hand stance, recoil totally catered for. He could give someone a new hair parting at fifty metres. And, Hoskins said very warmly, Pedro also possessed every other talent traditionally required in a top-class English butler. When on household duty he wore a standard, faultless, definitely made-to-measure morning suit – black single-breasted jacket, black waistcoat, silver striped black trousers, and kept the Sig automatic at his midriff level. Most of Ralph's friends and colleagues went for a shoulder harness these days, to avoid the crude, melodramatic cowboy look. But Pedro said he felt more prepared with the gun at the top of his striped trousers, even though, as he'd remarked to Ralph earlier, with a big, very unBritish sort of chuckle, he might accidentally shoot his dick off, owing to the barrel pointing down towards that area.

Pedro could do humour but not too much of it, Gladhand had said. A limit was vital. Ralph agreed. Nobody wanted a butler who constantly acted the stand-up comic, spouting one-liners at a significant dinner function, with tureens and so on. Moderation. Knowing his place: not always to be relied on in foreigners. His accent when using the coarse, slang word 'dick' made the moment of fun even more amusing. It came out as 'deek'. Ralph thought that if Pedro had said, 'Shoot his cock off,' instead, it would have sounded much graver, less droll, endangering the source of new generations. 'Dick' seemed child-like and humorously disrespectful, almost. The 'ock' of cock had a beefier, more masculine resonance than the 'ick' of dick, the 'eek' of deek.

Ralph had rated resonances as worth some study. Words and their distinctive tones interested him. He thought the flavour of 'shoot my dick off' indicated plenty re Pedro's character. The 'dick' showed him to be of a playful, light-hearted nature; perhaps owing to earlier life in a sunny climate with orange groves and brightly coloured parasols. 'Shoot my penis off' would have come over as quite different: use of that accurate anatomical term could take away all the jokiness. There was, of course, an undoubted dark aspect, whether the term employed was 'dick' or 'penis': that loaded Sig automatic aspect, and a possible groin injury inflicted from extremely close range with a workmanlike nine mm bullet; or more than one if all control of the gun was lost. This contrast seemed to Ralph on a par with Pedro's very conventional butler's garments, but also his probably unlicensed gun, ready behind the side pocket of the flunkey jacket for whatever it needed to be ready for. You could call it cocked. Ralph thought that, although most of the properties in Cheyne Walk would have butlers, very few, if any, would carry a handgun as part of their usual occupational gear.

Gladhand had several times fumed about the very high council tax, or rates, on his type of large, expensive house – worth then, Ralph reckoned, at least four million pounds. Of course, Dale wasn't a halfwit and knew there had to be charges and taxes to keep the district and country running. But Gladhand argued in quite a passionate style that he, personally, had already contributed massively to well-being, whether national or local. He said he provided, at a very fair, even bargain, price, substances to help people relax and refresh themselves. They, therefore, become all the more ready to go to work later and so help swell the gross domestic product; if only to earn enough to buy more of the habit commodity tomorrow or next week.

Obviously, the PU business never paid any corporation tax because, officially, there was no corporation. How could there be, officially? For a quiet, internal laugh, Ralph would now and then imagine somebody going to Companies House and requesting details of the firm – capital basis, board of management, dividend payment dates. The clerk would ask what type of business it was. Answer – 'Gear.' End of inquiry.

Gladhand's house contained an indoor pool, a cinema, meditation suite and gym. He'd heard several celebrities had that kind of set-up, and he kept pace. Gladhand had said he liked to get out of bed and spend some dawns prone on an unvivid Turkish rug in the meditation suite, if punishment beatings or beyond were planned for the coming day because dealers had been over-mixing and pocketing the extra purchase cash.

'Quentin's here, as a matter of fact,' Gladhand had said on the phone when Ember called after the Davidson episode. 'If you're concerned about company business the more voices the better. The

Pasque might be Uno but its members like to be companionable, don't you think, Ralph?'

Ember remembered he'd longed to have shouted an answer: No, fucking NO, I don't think it, not if one of the members is that sphincterless arsehole, Quent. 'Well, yes, probably, Dale,' Ralph had actually, tactfully, replied. So, why was this slippery goon at Gladhand's home? 'As a matter of fact,' Gladhand had said, 'Quentin's here, as a matter of fact' – oh, so by-the-way and chatty. How lucky! How fortunate! Did Dale have any real notion of what the devious sod was like, as a matter of fucking fact? Ralph reckoned that, as a matter of fact, if he hadn't phoned Gladhand post-hairdresser's porch Quent's visit might never have been mentioned – Ralph bypassed, Ralph de-looped? Ralph too new to the firm to be treated as an insider? Ralph no Oxon M.A.

And, now, when he opened the office safe, thinking the pencilled notes would bring an exhaustive, comforting, roman-numbered report of his parley with Gladhand, he meant, really – disgustingly – a parley with Gladhand *and* Quent. It hurt and sickened him, though, to admit Stayley had been part of it, too. And a big part. The malicious, mouthy, educated, snide, elderly jerk had probably talked more than Gladhand, and nearly all of it negative, toxic. Stayley hadn't known how to be anything *but* negative and toxic. On his health file with the G.P. his physical state would be described as 'negative and toxic'. Yet Dale put up with him and his bolshy niggling. Not just put up with him, invited him to his property on the quiet. Why?

Quent might look around this ducky villa and resent that it belonged to someone as young as Gladhand without an Oxon. degree. Quent would wonder how to kick Dale out and move in himself. Likewise with the chiefdom of PU. Leadership of the firm would be Quent's first target. Once Dale had lost that position and the money that went with it, Gladhand would be unable to keep up a house like this, nor afford a butler-minder like Pedro. Stayley probably calculated that he could get the house at a knock-down price.

That day, Pedro had taken Ralph's overcoat and said: 'The master and his colleague are in the black and white room, sir.' Pedro kept his voice pretty neutral on that word, 'colleague' – no merry sneer, or lavatory chain miming – though Ralph had wanted to laugh. He'd felt almost certain Pedro was not one to go through a guest's pockets, either on Gladhand's orders, or as a personal eccentricity, but Ralph made sure he left nothing important in them. Pedro hung the coat in a cloakroom off the big hall, then went ahead of Ralph to the door of the black and white lounge, opened it and announced him: 'Mr Ralph Ember.' Again, Pedro had spoken this deadpan, no piss-taking, bellowed flourish as if Ralph were a duke or TV chef.

The black and white gave another example of Gladhand's determination to be in vogue, and possibly even in *Vogue*. He had mentioned to Ralph on an earlier visit that he'd been impressed by a magazine article about the ex-politician Lord Mandelson's home, where the theme was minimalist. Dale had said anyone could see why such policy makers wanted a sense of space around them. It was a kind of encouragement to them to let their minds roam widely, as if in the inviting emptiness of their study or lounge.

Such an uncluttered domestic setting spoke to them of opportunity and of creative potential. Gladhand needed similar conditions for his own thinking about business and PU. He had adopted the same style of furnishing and, as a consequence, could bring opportunities and creative thinking to the firm. Ralph had thought that he, too, might follow Gladhand's domestic scheme.

In Gladhand's lounge the walls and ceiling were radiantly white and the few chairs steel-framed in black with plump, black cushions. By contrast, in the meditation suite, which Dale had twice shown him earlier, khaki hessian covered all the walls to suggest a serious, non-gaudy approach to things. Gladhand had said an interior decorator advised him that meditation and hessian were made for each other.

In the lounge, there was a small, low glass table on curved, black metal legs. Gladhand and Quent were seated near it, Gladhand in a heavy beige cardigan, check shirt and matching cravat, tan slacks and brogues: fogey-at-home style. Stayley had on jeans and a denim waistcoat over a dark red, open-necked shirt. The red rubber band holding his ponytail looked thicker than usual, as though he considered his hair had become especially vibrant and required more severe restraint, for its own good, like, you could say, an unbroken-in pony.

Hoskins had stood at once and came forward to shake Ralph's hand and, with maximum enthusiasm, point him to one of the chairs. As to nicknames, anyone could see how he got his. 'Celeste and the children are out visiting my sister, I'm afraid. They'd have loved to see you, Ralph, I know. Melanie's home for Christmas after her first term at boarding school. A teenager now! We started young!' A teapot, milk jug and sugar basin stood on the table, and a plate of oatmeal biscuits, plus a couple of china cups and saucers. The china looked almost transparent and good, decorated with pale flowers and berry illustrations.

Ralph wanted to learn about china. He'd do some research on the various makes and marks when he had time. It surprised him that Dale had obviously developed a hefty knowledge of fine products and the funds to buy them, although still young. He started everything young – not just a family! Ember aimed for this kind of swift career advance himself, which was why he valued his post with such a strong, growing firm as PU.

Pedro had withdrawn after showing Ralph into the room, but now reappeared briefly carrying a silver tray with another cup and saucer of the same design as the others. He placed these on the table and left again, without making any humorous remark. Ralph had thought of the underlying Sig when Pedro bent over the table to put the cup and saucer there, but that movement didn't seem to send unhelpful pressure to the trigger, and the delivery went along OK. Gladhand wouldn't want that kind of injury in

157

such a neighbourhood. The word was sure to get around. Neighbours would wonder what kind of butler it could be who carried a pistol while setting up afternoon tea. The media would spell out the accident with some bluntness.

He poured for all of them, asking about milk and sugar, put a biscuit on each saucer, and resumed his seat. Dale had something deeply unimpoverished-looking about him. He was square-built, not fat, but his face and neck had a smoothness and a slightly bulging quality, seeming to suggest this might be only the surface and that there was plenty beneath, like an iceberg, where what's on show is only a fraction of its mass. He'd possibly found a diet that really packed the stuff in tight and solid, yet it remained ready – and even keen – for reinforcement.

After a little general chit-chat things had become serious. Now, at The Monty office, Ralph sat down in the big old leather arm chair he kept there and began to read from page i of his pains-taking notes.

# Twenty-One

*Q spoke first – to be expected. He said Dale thought I had sounded 'sort of alarmed' on the phone. Quent put on a lovely, caring voice, caring and superior. So, why couldn't Gladhand himself tell me I'd sounded 'sort of alarmed'? Had Stayley been appointed Personnel Director of PU and IC members' welfare? I thought this was a bit shifty of Dale.*

*'Something had disturbed you, Ralph?' Quent said this last bit like it wouldn't take much to do that as I was already a nervous wreck. I let it go. I had decided to keep things sweet as far as I could. This, after all, was about people's lives and the future, or not, of a fine, gold-chip business.*

*So, I replied, mild and reasonable, that I wouldn't say alarmed or disturbed, although, of course, I had been alarmed and disturbed. Still was. Gladhand and Q would find out soon that it was right to feel alarmed and disturbed, and barmy and stubborn not to feel alarmed and disturbed.*

*'What would you say you were, then, Ralph?' Stayley asked.*

*'Perhaps "troubled",' I said. 'Perhaps very aware of change, Quentin.'*

*'"Troubled" on what account, Ralph?'*

159

Stayley said. '"Aware of change" in which respect?' It was spoken gently, invitingly, like a teacher trying to get an answer out of some blockhead kid, such as, 'What number is one more than two?'

'Fortuitous,' I replied.

'Ah,' Stayley said.

'Yes,' I said. 'Fortuitous.'

'But fortuitous in what particular?' Stayley said.

Dale sipped his tea and took a bite of the biscuit. He seemed relaxed. There came a stage, though, when 'relaxed' meant dozy, slack. Well, all right it was part of leadership: you showed you were not perturbed so you didn't perturb others, especially didn't perturb someone who had already sounded 'alarmed' on the phone. But I had to make him understand that he shouldn't feel relaxed. Relaxed was ridiculous. Relaxed wasn't cool. Relaxed was smug. Relaxed was blind. Why I'd said 'change'. 'I'm sure Ralph wouldn't be one to call this special mini-conference about something trivial,' Dale said. 'He is, as he has mentioned, troubled and this means we have to get to the root of that trouble.'

I thanked him for this. I said I was grateful for his trust in me, and what I meant was it seemed quite a bit different from that twat Quent's attitude. Of course, this wouldn't bother Quent. He had such an ego he didn't care much what others thought of him and his behaviour, not even Dale. Someone of Quent's age flourishing a mangy ponytail

*obviously didn't give a toss about others'*
*opinions. 'Pray, take me as you find me.'*
*'Thanks, but no.'*
   *'Although Ralph hasn't been with us long,*
*he has learned the basics very fast,' Dale said.*

For his note Ralph remembered he'd tidied up
some of Gladhand's grammar. It would have
seemed a mockery always to put things down
exactly as he said them. Dale had never sorted
out the difference between 'hasn't' and 'haven't'
or 'he's' and 'he've', and he liked 'got to' for
'have to'. He had still been calling the street
'Chain' Walk, not Cheyne, pronounced Cheynee.
That hadn't mattered much. It didn't stop him
buying the house full price, cheque up front, no
mortgage. He said the estate agent almost fainted.
London had a 'Fetter Lane', so maybe there could
have been a Chain Walk, too.

*'To do with what, then, Ralphy, the "trouble"?'*
*Quent said.*
   *He knew sticking the 'y' on would irritate,*
*but I made myself stay calm. He stared at my*
*face to see if I rage-twitched. He'd enjoy that.*
*I didn't. This situation should not be made*
*even worse by objections to a 'y'. It would*
*be out of proportion. I said: 'There's a leak.'*
   *Dale stopped chewing for a second. He'd*
*had a shock. Although this was a minimalist*
*room, he could still get a rough, maxi surprise*
*in it. But then, he resumed his work on the*
*biscuit. He had to look steady, unshaken, even*
*if he wasn't. He had to seem that kind of*

man. *This could make everything tricky later in the meeting.*

'Leaks from where?' *Stayley said.*

*Me:* 'I don't know.'

*Q.* 'You do know there's a leak but you can't tell us where it's coming from?' *(Satirical – very.)*

*Me:* 'No, I can't. I've seen the result, but I can't tell how it happened.'

*Stayley shrugged. It meant,* 'Hark at him! He brings us a rumour, or half a rumour, and expects us to get the jitters.' *But Q said:* 'A leak as to what, Ralph?'

*Me:* 'Mondial-Trave.'

*D:* 'What about it, Ralph?'

*Me:* 'The police. That's why I said fortuitous.'

*Q.* 'Maybe, but fortuitous how? What *was* fortuitous?'

*Me:* 'Davidson.'

*Dale:* 'The dame detective?'

*That was his phrase,* 'the dame detective'. *This worried me. If it had been Quent who said it, I wouldn't have been bothered. It was the kind of sniping disrespect he specialized in. But this was Gladhand. It sounded like he wanted to make her seem slightly comical, not a difficulty they needed to fret about: think of a pantomime dame; or sex items as in that song,* 'There is nothing like a dame.' *Maybe he really didn't think much of her, which might be a mistake, an underestimate. This was a woman, acting head of the C.I.D. while the Chief Super was off sick. She must have some*

162

*brain, some toughness. Perhaps she offered a real threat. It could be foolish to ignore that. Remember Adolf and the Russian winter. Or perhaps Gladhand didn't really discount her but was trying to keep his confidence up, and Quent's and mine. Leadership. Either way, he made me anxious: she could be a danger he didn't recognize or a danger he did recognize but pretended he didn't. Leadership?*

*Q. 'What about her?'*
*Me: 'Why I said a leak.'*
*D: 'I'm not clear what you're getting at, Ralph.'*
*Q: 'No, Ralph.'*
*Me: 'At Mondial-Trave.'*
*D: 'At Mondial-Trave when?'*
*Me: 'Today.'*
*Q: 'She was? How do you know?'*
*Me: 'I saw her.'*
*'Q: 'You saw her at Mondial-Trave?'*
*'Me: 'Yes.' It was like a police interrogation. 'Near the monument and so on.'*

Ralph hadn't recorded descriptions of his state of mind, but he could recall that, as he'd feared, the atmosphere became hostile at around this stage in the conversations – hostile even from Dale, very hostile from that prat, Q.

*D: 'When did you see her?*
*Me: 'This morning. A few hours ago.'*
*Q: 'You were at Mondial-Trave this morning?'*

163

*Me: 'Yes. A couple of hours ago.'*

*Q: 'Alone?'*

*Me: 'Yes.'*

*Q: 'But why?'*

*Me: 'I wanted to remind myself of the terrain.'*

*Q: 'Why?'*

*Me: 'In case the clash with Opal Render takes place.'*

*Quent had to jump in with his Educated Evans impersonation then. He asked why I had to go into the 'subjunctive mood'. Obviously, the smart, college-boy sod expected me to say 'The what?' and gasp in admiration at his way with the dictionary. I wasn't going to fall for that one, though. I just stayed quiet, like I hadn't heard this. Silence – quite a weapon.*

Naturally, Ralph knew what the subjunctive mood was now. He'd done a Foundation Year towards a mature student degree. But back then, maybe not.

*Q: 'The subjunctive. Expressing doubt. Why do you talk as if the rumble at Mondial-Trave were uncertain?'*

*That 'were' instead of 'was' would most probably be part of the subjunctivitus.*

*Me: 'Why do you say I sound uncertain, Quent?'*

*Q: 'Your words – "in case" the clash takes place, like it might not.'*

*Well, of course in bloody case. The detective*

164

*dame and her wandering put everything into
the subjunctive mood, didn't they? Only an
imbecile would fail to express doubt now.*

*D: 'Davidson alone there?'*

*Me: 'Note taking. A jotter.'*

*Q: 'Note taking as to what?'*

*Me: 'Terrain.'*

*Q: 'Like you?'*

*Me: 'Possibly signalled to colleagues in
one of the flats.'*

*Q: 'Which colleagues?'*

*Me: 'I don't know.'*

*Q: 'Did you see anyone?'*

*Me: 'No.'*

*Q: 'Signalled how?'*

*Me: 'Perhaps a small wave. A smile.'*

*Q: '"Perhaps"?'*

*Me: 'She'd be careful, discreet.'*

*Q: 'Why?'*

*Me: 'The person, persons, in the flat might
be on secret surveillance. She wouldn't want
to point them out.'*

*Q: 'Surveillance of what?'*

*Me: 'Like I said, terrain. The Mondial-
Trave area. They're in an upper floor. They
could have a whole stretch of ground in view
along Mondial and to the Trave junction.'*

*Q: 'Why would they be watching?'*

*Me: 'On account of the leak.'*

*Q: 'The supposed leak. And what is the
supposed leak supposed to say, Ralph?'
(Further rotten satire.)*

*D: 'Well, it's obvious what Ralph thinks,
isn't it?'*

165

*Q: 'I'd just like to hear it from him, Dale, that's all.' He sounded ratty because Dale had interrupted the questioning.'*

*Me: 'The confrontation.'*

*D: 'You believe someone's whispered to Esther Davidson that there's going to be a fight with Opal Render?'*

*Me: 'At Mondial-Trave.'*

*D: 'By surveillance you mean a camera?'*

*Me: 'Possibly a camera, yes.'*

*Q: 'You didn't see one, though?'*

*Me: 'No.'*

*Q: 'A camera for what purpose?'*

*Me: 'To record any activity.'*

*Q: 'You'd be activity, wouldn't you?'*

*Me: 'I tried to keep out of sight. A hair-dresser's porch.'*

*Q; 'You hung about, drawing attention, in a hairdresser's porch?'*

*Me: 'I watched through two panes of glass. I don't think I could have been observed.'*

*Q: 'But the people in the hairdresser's – customers, staff? They'll remember, won't they? After the battle police will swamp the shops and so on, asking their questions. This could give them a lead.'*

*Me: 'They looked too busy in the hairdresser's to notice me.'*

*Q: 'No customers waiting? Gazing about?'*

*Me: 'I didn't notice any.'*

*Q: 'But you'd be looking the other way, wouldn't you, Ralph – not into the salon? You're watching Davidson. How long were you standing there on show?'*

166

*Me: 'Say ten minutes, maybe less. Possibly they'd think I'd arranged to meet someone there.'*

*Q: 'Maybe. But nobody else arrived.'*

*Me: 'I'd been stood up!'*

Ralph went on to page ii.

*D: 'Why would Davidson make notes, Ralph, if she had a camera showing the scene for her?'*

*Me: 'I don't know. Some people are brought up on paper and handwritten stuff. They're never totally happy with visuals.'*

*Q: 'We'd been to see the terrain, as you call it, nice and anonymously in the stolen Vauxhall, yet you go down there in full view, I can't understand that.'*

*Me: 'Not in full view. I've said I used the hairdresser's.'*

*Q. 'But you had to get to the hairdresser's. You'd be walking on the pavement in the open for a while, wouldn't you, right in front of the camera, if there was a camera?'*

*Me: 'I'd be exposed a short while.'*

*Q: 'You were at Mondial-Trave to no real purpose, because you'd already had a double chance to view the ground. There and back in the Vauxhall. That had been the specific aim of the trip.'*

*Me: But I couldn't concentrate on it because of you and your fucking gob. I didn't say that, though. 'Just to confirm a few things, Quent,' I replied.*

167

*Dale stays quiet for a while, finishes off his tea, pours himself another, then tops up for Q and me. Now, Dale asks the big question, the very big question – what did I make of it all – what did I make of Davidson being there and the camera – if one existed? He'd slapped Quent down by saying what I was thinking. Now, though, like Q, he wanted me to speak my thoughts. He seemed confused, off balance.*

*What I wanted to say was simple. It would explain why I had telephoned and why I had come to Chelsea so fast. I believed I'd been watching preparations for a police hit on the firms. Plainly Davidson knew that famous bit of military teaching: 'Time spent on reconnaissance is never wasted.' I could have developed this: 'Time spent on reconnaissance is never wasted, even if a camera was doing the same job, and even if, for me, I'd been there in a Vauxhall.' But I saw it would be stupid to rush in and blurt this at them. It might sound like panic. I don't want that foul reputation.*

These two sentences in the notes always gave Ralph on re-readings a tremor. The word, 'panic' had a touch of chilling clairvoyance to it. Out of those circumstances would come his stinking nicknames. But these notes said he must avoid seeming to panic. He'd failed?

He continued his reading: the paragraph that came next was a kind of concession. It backed up the case against him, didn't it?

*A woman had strolled in Mondial-Trave, possibly making notes about the area, possibly sending a tiny wave and a momentary smile to an apartment block window. OK, it wasn't just a woman but an important woman detective. All the same, he'd admit that a lot of imagination – maybe scaredy-cat imagination – would be needed to make these glimpses add up to warnings of a police surprise welcome party. 'I was shocked to see her there,' I said. (God, so feeble, so evasive.)*

*'Right, you were shocked. What of it?' Quentin said. (Satirical.)*

*'We can understand your shock,' Dale said. 'It's natural. But that shock will pass. Maybe it's already starting to pass.'*

*I wanted to shout, 'No, it bloody isn't. This was a shocking shock, and it sticks. It would be dozy to ignore and forget this shock.' But I didn't.*

*D: 'There could be many harmless explanations why Davidson went there.'*

*'Many,' Quent said. 'Mondial-Trave is part of her patch. Familiarization could be routine. Perhaps tomorrow she'll be doing an inspection somewhere else – jottering.' (Satirical.) 'Hands on.'*

*Me: 'But the camera?' I knew it was a fat and flaring mistake as soon as I said it – a gift opening to Quent. Does the bugger have that effect on me – the rabbit in headlights, asking for doom?*

*Q: 'What camera?'*

*Me: 'The camera in—'*

169

*Q: 'But you hadn't seen a camera – you've told us that.'*

*Me: 'I felt that for sure there was—'*

*Q: 'Policy can't be changed because you had a feeling, a feeling born from a figment, Ralphy.'*

*Most probably they had courses in alliteration at Oxford and Stayley got a First Class Honours in it. I was surprised he didn't say 'a feeling formed from a fucking figment, friend.'*

*D: 'Naturally, we'll keep alert, Ralph.' Gladhand seemed to know how much I hated the Ralphy label, and he deliberately corrected that disrespectful swine, Quent. 'And we'll have the possibilities you've raised continuously in our minds.'*

*Q: 'Oh, Certainly.'*

Page iii.

*Dale came out then with the bluntest inquiry, the most obvious inquiry. He asked, did I expect a trap, an ambush?*

*Me: That's what we'd been talking about, wasn't it, for God's sake? If a big-wheel detective is examining the landscape it's not because she's thinking of where to site traffic lights. It's about suitable attack spots. 'I wondered, Dale, if she was looking for locations where she could hide her assault crew.'*

*Q: 'Is there evidence for that?'*

*Me: 'The note taking. The research.'*

*Q: 'The jotter?' (Sarcasm.)*

*Me:* 'Well, yes, the jotter.'

*Q:* 'We don't know what was in *the jotter*.'

*Me:* 'We can make a reasonable guess. This kind of situation – there has to be some guessing, some speculation.'

*Q:* 'Dale doesn't act on guesswork, however reasonable it might seem.' (*Pious. Bum-sucking.*)

Of course Dale acted sometimes on guesswork. Every leader did. But it would be called something else – 'assessment', 'anticipation', 'vision', 'investment boldness'.

*D:* 'It might seem reasonable from one point of view, such as yours, Ralph, but we have to consider other possibilities. This is good business rigmarole, nothing more than that, but it has to be followed.' (*Polite.*)

*Q:* 'Superintendents don't go on ambushes.' (*Fuck politeness.*)

*Me:* 'But she could be in charge. She'd do it from one of those Control Unit vehicles, in touch by radio or phone; one-way windows and screens to take film.'

*Q:* 'You see this woman dawdling around and from that you deduce a battlefield.' (*Satirical.*)

I said she wasn't just 'this woman', was she?

*Q:* 'Isn't she?'

I reminded him that she was a high-rank, powerful cop. And he replied I must be a feminist. 'Well, well, I do believe you're a feminist, Ralphy,' was how he phrased it. Maximum offensiveness. But then he did a rewording,

171

*made a kind of apology* – his *kind, which didn't add up to much.*

*Q: 'All right, all right, let's amend: you see a woman cop dawdling around and from that you deduce a battlefield.'*

*So, obviously, I could get back at him again. I said, 'No, I didn't have to deduce a battlefield, did I? It existed, had been selected. Very much so. Hadn't we Vauxhalled there and back to chart it? The plan is to clash with Opal Render on that stretch of ground. I didn't invent the battle `site. It's already invented.'*

*Q: 'Fair point: let's amend once more.' (Appeasing, bogus-considerate.)*

*A slab of smart-arse repetition came next, which I think I can do verbatim:*

*Q: 'You deduce she knows it's to be a battlefield and is therefore getting ready to take part, and take part in a winning, overwhelming style. From that deduction you deduce Dale should abandon the confrontation plan. That's why you said "in case" the fight took place. "In case" is doubt. "In case" suggests a possibility, not a likelihood, and definitely not a certainty. There's no "in case" about it, Ralph. It will happen. You don't believe it will or should, do you, Ralphy? But where's the real evidence to back your deductions? It's all so thin. It's a theory built on nothing. "My God! A woman near the memorial alderman. Catastrophe!" Possibly you were already in an anti-view as to the PU-OR settlement, and this could make you see things*

172

*that appear to back your standpoint. That kind of thing can happen. Someone's mind is already made up, possibly without the someone being aware of it, and automatically, subconsciously translates subsequent events into confirmations of what's already a fixed idea. Nothing to feel guilt about, Ralph. It's a commonplace psychological condition.'*

*'Condition' made it sound like the pox or lunacy.*

*D: 'Yes, your argument is slightly thin, Ralph.' I could tell he wanted to be kindly, though – not like Stayley. All Quent aimed to do was knock, mock and belittle. If you were his age, educated up to your eyebrows and still in only a middling job, paying just enough to buy new double-strength rubber bands for your pigtail, you were almost sure to be bitter.*

*Dale said he and Quent appreciated greatly that I had come so swiftly to tell them what I had seen during the skilled tracking of Davidson. That shite, Quent, added with total, thoroughbred phoniness, 'Oh, absolutely.' But he could gush it because Dale was obviously going to tell me that what I'd seen would not change the confrontation plans. He'd already said it, more or less. Hadn't he latched on to that slimy put-down from Quent – 'thin'? Now, I could feel the full rejection on the way and of course, Stayley could as well – so he'd make a show of thanks and matey warmth, the false, graduate git. 'We'll proceed, regardless,' Dale said. I wondered, regardless of*

173

*what – sanity? Was Gladhand afraid to show caution and wisdom – so necessary in a leader – afraid because Quent would see them as timorousness, as cue for a top job grab?*

That was the end of the notes on page iii. Ralph had used page iv to expand on his reactions to the response from Quent and Gladhand. He read from there now:

*Listening to them I felt it was as if the Pasque Uno/Opal Render culminating battle had been pre-scheduled by Fate and was therefore bound to happen, was destined to happen. Nothing could stop it, not even my certainty that the police knew of the plan and intended to be present, armed, numerous and delighted by the chance to massacre members of both firms legally, for the sake of peace and safety on the streets. I considered Davidson's little comradely smile to the camera crew as the equivalent of licking her lips at the prospect of such delicious, judicial slaughter.*

*OR and PU had agreed the location. Of course they had: the location was the conflict. Each company wanted permanently to clear the other out of Mondial Street, Trave Square and Dorothea Gardens district. The winner would hold complete commercial control of the ground. But that was only the banal, mater ialistic reason behind the war. Their approaching gunfight was as much to do with vague, almost mystical, factors: self-respect and pride. Neither honcho would back down.*

*Neither honcho* could *back down. They were dragooned by their power.*

*The terrible dishonour and loss of face would be worse than defeat in battle. Both businesses probably contained lurking wannabes, like Quent, eager to get rid of the potentate and replace him. They'd watch for evidence of dithering and general weakness, ready to move and try their takeover; a customary business putsch; one of those so-called palace revolutions. Dale Hoskins, as chief of Pasque Uno would have realized this, and so would Piers Elroy Stanton, his opposite at the head of Opal Render. They lived non-stop with that sort of menace. Now, their dispute has become dangerously, idiotically, perhaps, a contest of gladiators.*

Ralph had hated that determinism, found it incomprehensible, despised it. Madness had taken over. The two leaders had allowed themselves to become captives of their own stupid vanity, and for ever nervous about scheming, bolshy subordinates. The chiefs promoted people like Quent to make them grateful and contented and manageable, but it didn't always work. Because they'd been given *a* top job they thought they could and should get *the* top job. They became more ambitious, more ruthless. 'I'm the king of the castle, get down you dirty rascal.' But some dirty rascals kept trying, pushing, scheming. Were your ears burning, Stayley? Someone was talking about you.

Ralph was only young then, though, and a new

boy in the PU firm, a yucker, and not ready to question Gladhand hard, not capable of questioning Gladhand hard, advising him to be on guard against Quent. But he hadn't been prepared to share that eyes-shut, mind-shut craziness, either. A yucker, yes. A sucker, no, a lemming no: not willing to join a daft, corporate rush to disaster. He put the foolscap notes back in the safe, but didn't re-lock it yet.

On the shelf above the notes lay some cuttings from the local newspaper, *The South East,* meaning south-east London, but to add *London* to the title would have made it less universal and less snappy. He realized that to keep cuttings in the safe could appear in some ways absurd. After all, they were the opposite of secret. They had been published. But he kept them locked up because he didn't want to reveal an interest in what they reported; a painful but obsessive interest, a kind of ritual penance.

He took one cutting out now and went back to his chair and, starting a little way down the column, scanned it – as he had scanned it and the other cuttings often before. He could manage a dozen or so sentences before horror and depression hit him, and he'd have to give up. But he felt obliged to look back periodically to events on that day, because those events might have a bearing on why the atrocious nicknames, 'Panicking Ralph', 'Panicking Ralphy', had been hatched for him. He believed in facing up to unpleasantness, no matter how dire. He felt that not to face up would indicate a sort of panic: in other words, would confirm the rightness of those insulting, wholly unwarranted stigma. Read. Digest. Regret.

*What came to be called 'the pillar-box death' occurred at 11.05, ten metres south from the junction of Mondial Street and Trave Square, on a broad stretch of pavement outside the local post office. Its doors had been closed and locked at the first sound of gunfire. Terrified customers huddled well back against the counter, away from the windows. They were shocked at the intensity, the quantity, of the shooting. 'The battle for Stalingrad had nothing on this,' one elderly post office customer said afterwards.*

*Outside, Clive Palgrave of Pasque Uno was hit by three bullets, two in the chest, puncturing the heart, one in the neck. He had apparently become isolated from the main Pasque Uno group. Palgrave, known as 'Aftermath', had been holding a nine mm, fully loaded pistol. He dropped the gun now, though. He needed both hands free. He tried to support himself by clinging to the post office street pillar box in a frantic embrace. But, life and strength were leaving him. He swayed clear of the pillar box like a drunk. His fingers grabbed at air as he tried to get a grip on the metal again and stay propped upright. He lost his hold and folded down against the pillar box, though. This had been very high grade marksmanship.*

There was a photograph of the pillar box – a dull

picture, hardly worth the space – with the front
window of the post office behind. Ralph decided
that would be enough for the time being. He'd
had his quota of self-punishment. He put the
newsprint back into the safe, locked it and went
down to the bar.

Margaret, small, blonde, confident, navy
woollen greatcoat, amber scarf, desert boots,
came into the club soon after. He knew she didn't
much like spending time at The Monty – 'louche'
her word for it sometimes, and sometimes 'a
menagerie' or 'cesspit' – but she'd needed a break
after shopping and before she went to pick up
the children from ski practice. She took off the
greatcoat and scarf, and they'd settled at a table
with their meal. Ralph said in an intimate, significant, now-hear-this sort of tone: 'I've been
thinking quite a bit about the past today, Maggie.'

'Oh, all that,' she said, her mouth full.

'Yes, all that,' Ralph said. He gave a real rasp
to the final 't' in 'that', to show he regarded this
topic as serious. He wanted the emphatic 't' to
take the same kind of persuasive role as the dots
on some roman numerals.

'That's the thing about the past, isn't it?' she
said.

'What?'

'It's the past. I got a very pretty Etruscan replica
vase for my sister,' Margaret replied, Double
Gloucester shreds like pale bunting across a
couple of her front teeth.

'Yes, the past,' Ralph said. 'There were things
I couldn't talk to you about then, although I'd
wanted to.'

'We were both very busy, I suppose, me with the kids, you with trying to get yourself a place with Hoskins. But, I'd have listened, Ralph. It's one of the marriage vows, isn't it?'

'What?'

'Love, honour, obey and listen to.'

'I know you would have listened, and I knew at the time. But it was impossible. Occasionally – this morning, as a matter of fact – I make up the kind of talk I might have had with you, though without ever actually saying it.'

She nodded, but didn't seem keen on this kind of conversation. He felt there were things she'd prefer were not spelled out now: too much clarity could be painful. Her attitude might be self-protection. He understood her need for that. 'Oh, yes, yes, I think I sensed you were holding back,' she said, in her do-bears-shit-in-the-woods voice.

'Did you?' Ralph felt resentful. She was doing some hindsight on him. He thought he'd been quite skilled at concealment.

'"Marketing." You told me your work was marketing. Remember? But you never said *what* you marketed, so, naturally, I thought it must be something . . . something, well, sensitive. Not something to boast about, or be frank about. You obviously weren't marketing breakfast cereals or mountain bikes. I considered you might be entitled to the secrecy.'

'I didn't want secrecy from you,' he said. 'No, indeed.' Ralph regarded lies as OK when the objective was kindness. He thought of himself as always kind except, obviously, when it didn't suit.

She put her fork down on the plate and took a gentle hold on his arm for a moment. It was affectionate, but also a signal that enough had been said about those dubious things from their history. Older, Etruscan history, either actual or imitation, might be more comfortable.

He wasn't sure whether he liked her gripping his sleeve like that when Monty members and staff would be watching, and getting a giggle out of it later. *'Did you see them? A pair of ageing love birds.'* But he tried to push on: 'I longed to be frank then.'

'Something from those days bothers you now?' she replied.

Yes, something from those days bothered him. Major bother. Margaret had spotted this. She'd always been quick at reading him, up to a point; up to the point that he permitted. Her tone changed suddenly. Ralph thought she sounded concerned, not bored or indifferent or flippant any longer despite that inadequate word, 'bothers'. She must know there might be dangers to him from the kind of business he ran, and possibly dangers to the family. There'd been a time when she left him briefly, because he refused to quit the substances vocation, and the stress had got too much for her.[1] Perhaps she feared that kind of stress and what caused it could return.

He would have liked to answer her question: 'Yes, something from those days does bother me. For instance, you may remember a *South East* report about death alongside a pillar box. I dodged out of a situation because I thought it completely

[1] See *The Girl With The Long Back*

nuts. Others didn't think it nuts. *They* thought it an unavoidable, holy commitment. It *was* nuts. And doomed. But there are people who don't forgive me. They think I helped bring their defeat by my desertion. That's why we went to live in Portugal for a while. They might even think I leaked the fight details to a woman cop.'

To explain like that would increase her fears, though; might make her consider another walkout with the children. And perhaps it wouldn't be brief this time, but final. He couldn't face that. So once again he stayed silent. Or, rather, he did some dutiful talk about the shopping and his recurrent Christmas tree teaser. He guessed she'd notice how he'd switched the conversation away from the past, and its influences on the present, and she'd decide this must be another of those 'sensitive' topics, too sensitive for Margaret to be told what it was. She reached up and with her finger unhurriedly de-smeared her Double Gloucestered teeth. Then, with the same finger, she pointed towards the bar. 'I see you've got replacement Worcestershire sauce,' she said. 'Is that wise, Ralph?' He drew back slightly in case she gripped his arm again and put her all-purpose finger on his jacket sleeve. Someone in his position mustn't be seen in smeared clothing. He had a responsibility as club owner, even if the club was the unreconstructed Monty.

# Twenty-Two

*What came to be called 'the pillar-box death'
occurred at 11.05, ten metres south from the
junction of Mondial Street and Trave Square,
on a broad stretch of pavement outside the
local post office. Its doors had been closed
and locked at the first sound of gunfire.
Terrified customers huddled well back against
the counter, away from the windows. They
were shocked at the intensity, the quantity, of
the shooting. 'The battle for Stalingrad had
nothing on this,' one elderly post office
customer said afterwards.*

As well as her notes and tapes, Esther kept a
scrapbook where she'd pasted some cuttings from
the local newspaper, *The South East,* and from the
Sunday national press. These reports covered
the Mondial-Trave incident. In the conservatory
now, she'd skipped the introductory paragraphs
explaining the firms' names and other basics and
was reading from a little way down *The South
East's* page-one piece. A footnote said it continued
on pages six and seven. Across three columns a
photograph headed 'One of the five death sites'
showed a pillar box with the post office frontage
behind. She read on:

*Outside, Clive Palgrave, of Pasque Uno was*

*hit by three bullets, two in the chest, punc-*
*turing the heart, one in the neck. He had*
*apparently become isolated from the main*
*Pasque Uno group. Palgrave, known as*
*'Aftermath', had been holding a nine mm,*
*fully loaded pistol. He dropped the gun now,*
*though. He needed both hands free. He tried*
*to support himself by clinging to the post*
*office street pillar box in a frantic embrace.*
*But, life and strength were leaving him. He*
*swayed clear of the pillar box like a drunk.*
*His fingers grabbed at air as he tried to get*
*a grip on the metal again and stay propped*
*upright. He lost his hold and folded down*
*against the pillar box, though. This had been*
*very high grade marksmanship.*

Even without the picture and commentary, Esther
could recall that pillar box. She'd wondered
during her private visit to Mondial-Trave whether
it would figure somehow in the coming action,
that stubby, red, ordinariness recruited into havoc.
She hadn't visualized anything quite as grim as
what did happen there, though. She'd gone to
Mondial-Trave alone to remind herself of the
solid, hard actualities of the place – to get rid of
woolly, almost mystical, thoughts about it that
had gripped her for a while. The pillar box had
been one of the solid actualities she'd noticed.
And Clive Palgrave had found it solid, too, solid
enough to help him stay on his feet for possibly
thirty seconds more than if it hadn't been there
for him to get his arms around and try to hang
on to. Someone at the time had said Palgrave

died at his post. When falling he scraped against the pillar box and his blood smeared the white plate giving collection times, as though to wipe out its orderliness.

She turned up the gas heater. Esther loved the conservatory, even in winter. Gerald didn't use it much. It was hexagonal and he said hexagons always seemed to him like failed octagons and this made him uneasy: he had so many commitments that he couldn't spare pity for hexagons. She was able to think of the conservatory as *her* domain. She would sneak out to a lounger here and enjoy some tranquillity when not in the mood for violence with him: unwillingness did come over her occasionally. Like most couples they weren't perfectly attuned in their tastes, and, on the whole, Gerald seemed slightly keener on brutality sessions than she was. He accepted responsibility for making sure the first aid box always had enough plasters, painkillers and bandages, and seemed to feel this entitled him to as many jousts with her as he wanted. 'Tourniquets need tourneys,' he used to snarl if she seemed unenthusiastic now and then.

But people living at the back of the Davidson house could see into the glass-walled conservatory, and this put restraint on Gerald, inhibited him. Although an artist, and in some senses bohemian, he had a conventional element and might have been affected by that Girls Aloud pop group release, *What will the neighbours say?* Big blood deposits on the side of the conservatory would look especially unpleasant and tell-tale, whether hers or his or theirs. These might be much larger

184

stains than Aftermath Palgrave's blood on the pillar box plate. Gerald had mentioned to Esther that blood smudging two of the sides, rather than just one, would appear really bad, affecting a third of the available surfaces, instead of merely a quarter, if only it had been an octagon. He felt octagons had a kind of worldliness and tolerance missing in hexagons.

An actual shattering of the glass during these erotic ructions because she or he were flung against it and out into the garden could be quite embarrassing, like a boxer hammered through the ropes and falling among ringsiders. Most probably it would be Gerald. He half-liked getting flung. He found this passage through the air what he termed 'linnet-like'. He'd never wanted to work out a defence against it. Never mind the linnet – those ghastly bow-ties he wore looked like propellers of an old-fashioned aircraft when she threw him somewhere. All the same, he probably wouldn't care for the flight to happen through a smithereened window pane.

Altogether, the conservatory bothered him. It wasn't just the congenital aversion to hexagons. He was afraid somebody nosey-parkering from one of the other houses might ring the police about a fracas, even though they'd probably know Esther was herself the police, and very well placed in it. People who hated the police on principle might like the chance to tell the emergency services that a superintendent and her husband were destroying the social tone of the area by trying to kill each other, and not with kindness, but kidney punches.

He thought he might get arrested and charged with assaulting an officer. Maybe Esther would be summonsed to give evidence against him, even if he himself possibly had visible wounds and bruising where *she* had savaged *him,* and could plead self-defence. This kind of public humiliation would not be good for a marriage, and so the conservatory had come to be regarded as neutral ground, an acknowledged, cherished sanctuary – cherished by her.

Of course, should Gerald feel cheated out of an episode of romantic thuggery he might try to get her to come back into the house for concealment and muffling of his shouts and screams, which he regarded as a crucial part of the carry-on, comparable with the yell and/or ecstatic groan of orgasm. But when she didn't fancy it she wouldn't. He could not risk attempting to frog-march or drag her by hand or an unyielding bite into her cheek or neck because that might be observed. He wasn't strong enough, anyway. She could terrace him if it became for the best, 'for the best' meaning when she felt he was trying to bully.

Playing in an orchestra didn't build muscle or hone fight skills. He frequently left himself very open to heavy, dazing elbow jabs in the face, though she took care not to damage his mouth: it had to be OK for the bassoon. He found works by Hindemith and Danzi very lip challenging. 'That fucking Op Forty-Seven by Danzi,' as Gerald sometimes complained. His skills and puff had begun to fade as he grew older, and work became less easy to get.

He was away at present helping to coach a youth orchestra but her habit of withdrawing to the conservatory when she required uninterrupted solitariness was strong, and she'd brought the Mondial-Trave material here today more or less automatically, not because she needed to avoid him in the house. Gerald had composed a gavotte piece for the culminating performance of the youth orchestra at the weekend, and she'd promised to drive over and be in the audience. This wasn't a decision that came easily. Apart from the foul music she'd have to sit through, an ACC called Desmond Iles operated in that region. She'd met him now and then at chief police officer conferences; and she'd had some fairly close dealings with him on a case not long ago.[2] Perhaps she'd bump into him on this trip. She found she didn't really want that, though. She'd been thinking lately about applying for Chief Constable jobs, and it was vital no complexities got in her way. Desmond Iles could be a complexity.

The music – Gerald's and the rest of it – would undoubtedly nauseate her, but they believed in mutual support when not trying to take each other apart physically in the interests of pepping up sex and crossing what Gerald called 'nude frontiers'.

But for now she read on about the past:

*Although the shooting continued around them, two paramedics answering 999 calls reached Palgrave within ten minutes, but*

[2] See *In The Absence of Iles*

187

*found him already dead. Doctors said later that either of the heart wounds would have killed him instantly. Repeat, high grade marksmanship.*

*Aftermath Palgrave, aged thirty-four, married with a stepson in infant school, had survived turf battles in Manchester and Liverpool previously, which brought him his nickname. However, he did not live into aftermath yesterday. He claimed to be a descendant of Francis Turner Palgrave, who produced the famous Golden Treasury poetry anthology in 1861, still published in updated forms under the Palgrave name.*

*Some saw this relationship – if, in fact, it existed – as typifying Britain's moral disintegration during the last century and a half: in Victorian times this family produced an esteemed literary scholar, familiar with the poetic works of all sorts, including William Shakespeare and Alfred Lord Tennyson; when it came to the contemporary Clive Palgrave, though, the name belonged to a convicted small-time pusher and occasional foot-soldier, ordered into the Mondial-Trave combat for Pasque Uno. And not much of a foot-soldier, either: he had discarded his gun; was apparently incapable of maintaining cover; and, so, had presented a perfect target.*

*Witnesses told* The South East *that the gun parties from each firm seemed to arrive in the Mondial-Trave stretch of ground at more or less the same time, as if there had been an agreement to meet and fight it out, 'a kind*

188

*of* High Noon *situation,' one witness said, referring to the Gary Cooper film, often re-shown on TV. A resident in one of the apartment blocks that overlook the area, and who did not wish to be named, said: 'I had glanced out of the window at about ten fifty-five and everything at street level was normal – people and traffic moving about as on any other day. But then when I looked out again a few minutes later there'd been a tremendous change. I saw people hurrying, even scurrying, to get off the pavement and into shelter somewhere. The traffic had speeded up, as if drivers wanted to leave Mondial Street quickly – and safely. I had been drawn back to the window by what I now know to be sounds of gunfire. Perhaps I did suspect this at the time. Mondial Street and Trave Square, plus the Gardens, are all well known as drug dealing centres and we continually expect serious trouble*

*'I didn't understand at first what was happening. But then I saw three men running towards the Mondial-Trave junction. Each of them was masked, each carried a pistol, openly carried a pistol. For a moment I thought it must be some kind of stunt – perhaps filming, or an advertising or publicity ploy. Then the three of them stopped, though, and got down into what I regarded as a sniper's crouch, their pistols in two-handed grips pointing towards the post office. A robbery? However, in a little while I saw they weren't interested in the post office, but the pillar box*

*standing outside. There was another man there, sort of half shielding himself and pointing a handgun down the street towards the three. I think the three fired first, though. I heard a lot of shots. The man at the pillar box staggered. He dropped his gun and then fell himself.*

'*My wife and I had wondered earlier in the week whether something unusual was happening, or was going to happen, in the street because we'd seen a camera crew in the corridor, a woman apparently in charge. They went into a flat two along from us. I thought they might be filming the street for some reason. We didn't know who they were. They wore civilian clothes but we both had the impression they might be police, the woman with quite a loud voice and a jolly but clever sort of face, as if she was used to plotting things.*' *Malone and Pearson, estate agents who manage the apartment block for Corbett, Fallows and Parker Ltd., owners, told* The South East *that they could not comment on individual tenancies.*

And how correct in their response had Malone and Pearson been! And how correct in their speculating the couple in number eight had been! Always when she read this interview Esther thought those two were exceptionally wise, and careful with it: he'd talk, but not disclose his name. They'd identified the camera crew as police, and guessed their purpose: to film the street below ahead of some expected operation.

They had picked out Sergeant Fiona Hive-Knight as boss of the camera party and noted her boom-boom voice and general air of subterfuge. For several days in the projection room before the Mondial-Trave climax Esther had studied film clips with Fiona, mostly from the police camera, some from CCTV.

Esther turned to the inside pages, six and seven, of *The South East. Page six* contained three more death location pictures, with short biographies of each victim. The statue of alderman Laucenston figured in two of these photographs, and there was a general view of one side of Trave Square. Piers Elroy Stanton had been killed close to the 'Gleam And Smile' dental practice in Trave. One of his aides, Luke Byfort, was arrested there. *Piers Stanton, aged thirty, married, was the leader of the Opal Render firm,* the report said. *He created Opal Render and profited greatly from it.* Then came a list of his properties and a mention for the two racehorses, Dombey And Some and Colonel Jackeen, plus their track triumphs.

Gregory Mace, of Pasque Uno, also killed in Trave, was described as prominent in a gay rights movement, and an accomplished ice-skater. The fourth photograph, on the opposite page, showed a smart gift shop in Trave Square near where Mace died. It sold expensive handbags, costume jewellery, fashion belts, gloves, scarves, and was called 'La Brouette – The Wheelbarrow' – to suggest charming higgledy-piggledyness, though the prices were calculated enough. Gerald had occasionally bought her presents from there when they lived in London. He liked choosing stuff from a shop with a French name. He was entirely in favour of the continent and adored the French composer, Poulenc, who did some nice shorter bassoon pieces.

He always spoke the name with explosive emphasis on the first and last consonants as if to assert his loyalty and rout anyone who said Poulenc was piss. Gerald told her he could hear Poulenc's trio for oboe, bassoon and piano companionably in his head sometimes when trying to get her in an arm lock behind her back and up towards her shoulder for maximum pain. Gerald believed in the complex merging of musical beauty with his addiction to putting arm joints, and sometimes leg joints, to the extreme test. He found a satisfying fullness in the mixing of such different experiences, like sweet and sour sauce in a Chinese restaurant or that strange stuff, hot ice.

*Dale Hoskins, aged thirty-six, of Cheyne Walk, Chelsea, known as 'Gladhand' because of his ability to suggest friendliness and generosity, leader of Pasque Uno, was shot and killed by a single Thirty-Eight Smith and Wesson bullet in the head in Trave Square. This is not a type of gun normally used by police, who prefer Glocks. Hoskins was married with a teenage daughter away at boarding school and twin infant sons. The* report said there had been seven arrests, including two treated in hospital for gunshot wounds. No names were given. *It appears that the intention of Hoskins and Pasque Uno*

*was to drive the Opal Render contingent
down to the enclosed car park of the Red
Letter public house where survivors of the
initial battle phases could be eliminated.
Because of the unexpected police participa-
tion, though, this objective had to be reduced
in scope and only two OR personnel reached
there.*

Esther turned the scrapbook page to a Sunday
paper cutting that gave a more detailed analysis
of what came to be called 'The Mondial-Trave
Inferno'. The Sunday press usually had the leisure
to work some implied comment, some editorial
slant into the bare recounting of incident. One
double-page article carried a two-decker head-
line: 'REVEALED – THE NEW GUN-BASED
POLICE POLICY! MAY WE PLEASE JOIN IN
YOUR TURF WAR?' Didn't the press love that
'Revealed' as a starter to one of their headlines?
And didn't the press love to harass the police?

Was that jokey, impudent slice of weekend jour-
nalism a true and fair way to sum up police
intervention in the half-hour of shooting and
urban slaughter? Esther had wondered this when
she first read the long slab of Sunday attitudi-
nizing; and still wondered, looking back from
her winter-conservatory afternoon years later. It
was why she occasionally revisited those historic
episodes with the help of her tapes and cuttings.
History could have a big bearing on the present.

Did the way she'd handled the Mondial-Trave
situation change permanently how criminal firms
were dealt with – that is, they were allowed to

prepare for a battle and then get wiped out in a surprise police attack when the battle took place? And would the present scene, the today scene, also require major altered thinking? According to that sniggering press article, police tactics had been amended at Mondial-Trave to contain and counter the armed threat from two powerful, entrenched gangs scrapping for ascendancy. Well, yes, conditions in the illegal drugs business would always be developing, switching, adjusting to new pressures. Policing had to keep pace.

And what interested Esther was the possibility that, if there'd been changes then, there would be changes here, now. No business could stand still. Which fresh, unfamiliar factors could be found in the drugs trade today? How would she defeat them? She'd moved up to a higher rank and weightier responsibilities. She was expected to get ahead of the dirty game and stay there, rightly expected to. That is, if the game continued to be regarded as dirty. There were increasing, closely argued demands for legalization of recreational drugs. Or of *some* recreational drugs. Desmond Iles thought that way. So did that heavyweight magazine, *The Economist,* calling legalization 'the least bad solution' to the drugs problem. Several top flight medics agreed. Federal law in America declared all drugs illegal, but the states of Washington and Colorado had decriminalized cannabis and there was apparently a movement called 'Grass For Grannies' in Illinois, Ohio and Missouri.

But legalization in Britain hadn't happened so far and, although she'd been promoted out of

London and the Metropolitan force, and operated far from Mondial-Trave and Dorothea Gardens, the basic aim stayed pretty much the same: to spot what kind of modernized business plans the gangs here worked to currently; to combat these; and to forecast what might come next and see those off, too.

So, the conservatory interlude with her assisted recollections was not *altogether* an idling spell. Maybe the past could tell her something about what she might expect in the here and now, and – much trickier – what she might expect to follow. She read some more from a Sunday broadsheet:

*The police are certain to face accusations that they knew of the doomed drift towards gun-based street trouble but did nothing to prevent it. Rather, a decision was taken at some high level – undisclosed at this stage – a decision to permit the violence, or, at least, to let it start. Crooks eliminating crooks would do law and order a favour. Even if neither firm completely destroyed the other, an armed police squad could deal effectively with the outnumbered, outgunned fragments left. It is clear that two sizeable police units – at least fifteen officers in each by our reckoning – were in place at the site and ready to dispose of any survivors – to arrest, or quell in a firearms exchange. Almost certainly the area had been under surveillance for some while, possibly by hidden camera teams. Mondial-Trave became a sophisticated trap and a zap, prime setting for an ambush.*

# PART TWO

The now and the near future

# Twenty-Three

Chief Superintendent Colin Harpur had heard a whisper that Ralph Ember might be in special danger this Christmas. Of course, because of his glorious trading status, Ralph was always in danger from the envious and acquisitive. But, apparently, during this particular, approaching holiday period the risks would be exceptional, unparalleled.

The tip-off came from someone Harpur graded as the most talented informant he'd ever dealt with; perhaps the most talented informant any detective anywhere had ever dealt with. It was difficult to know this for sure: informants didn't have a merit league with someone at the top on highest points and entitled to a silver cup and medal. Informants preferred obscurity, concealment, no general recognition. They tended to whisper, not shout. General recognition would be perilous, and, in any case, was bound to make the informant useless: once recognized, his, or her, urge to leak secrets could be guarded against. And punished, perhaps fatally. Informants liked to deliver information, but didn't like *being* information.

There'd been, as there quite frequently was, a telephone call to Harpur at home in Arthur Street. His daughter, Jill, aged thirteen, picked up the receiver first. 'Dad, it's for you,' she yelled.

'OK,' Harpur said.

'I think it's your stool pigeon,' Jill said, without covering the mouthpiece or pressing the Secrecy button. 'That shady, finky sort of voice?'

Harpur took the phone. 'Was that the younger one, Col?' the shady, finky sort of voice asked pleasantly.

'Sorry about the crude language. She watches a lot of telly crime, talks Detroit sometimes.'

'Can you make it to Number Three soonest?'

'I'll be there,' Harpur said. He put the phone down.

'Was I right, Dad?' Jill asked, awarding herself a thumbs-up sign.

'I have to go out,' Harpur replied.

'It's late,' Jill said.

'He's an adult,' Hazel, her sister, said. 'He's not afraid of the dark.' Hazel was nearly sixteen, old enough to be left in charge. Jill often got a snub from her. They were in the big sitting room of Harpur's house, the girls playing some computer game. The three of them had put up Christmas decorations earlier in the day. Harpur enjoyed that kind of joint family project. He was a single parent now, after the death of their mother. He tried to keep things reasonably peaceful between the children. Tricky.

'Will you be tooled up? Are you stepping into unknown territory? Police often have to step into unknown territory. Is it urgent?' Jill said. 'Will he make disclosures? That's what finks do, isn't it – make *disclosures*?' She gave that word real punch.

'Routine,' Harpur said.

'These *disclosures* wouldn't be available to police otherwise,' Jill said. She put on a deep, harsh, muted tone: '"For your beautiful ears only, Mr Harpur." These *disclosures* come from someone able to get stuff from inside a crooked firm, having done observation out of the corner of his eye so as not to be noticed observing.'

'He couldn't have said much,' Hazel replied. 'So brief.'

'Security,' Jill said. 'Kept short because phone lines could be listened in to by all sorts. Coded, I expect. Was it, Dad? Sort of sounding harmless, but meaning something else. Like *The Eagle Has Landed* on the movie channel, not to do with an eagle, really, but a plot to capture Mr Churchill by Nazis in the war.'

'Oh, God,' Hazel said, 'we're into German Secret Service stuff now, are we?'

But, yes, perhaps there had been a kind of elementary code. Number Three was a concrete defence post on the foreshore, as a matter of fact left over from that war, a kind of museum piece now. After all those years it didn't smell too good, but was used as a shelter by fishermen if the weather turned rough, by unwealthy lovers who wanted privacy, and by Harpur and possessor of that shady, finky kind of voice, Jack Lamb. They, also, wanted privacy. They had other meeting spots and rotated them, so each needed a number.

Jack adored the military touch given by this little, redundant, circa-1940, anti-invasion fortress and, to harmonize, would turn up at Number Three in historic clothes bought at an army surplus store. Tonight he had on one of those hip-length, khaki overcoats – bum-freezers, as they were known – that British cavalry officers used to wear when in the saddle; and a French kepi-style soldier's peaked cap. Although Jack liked discreetness and codes he went in for this kind of conspicuous, warpath gear. But he would be getting on for 260 pounds and was six feet five inches tall, so perhaps he reasoned he'd be noticed whatever he wore. Harpur was hefty – some said like a fair-haired Rocky Marciano, undefeated world champion heavyweight – but Jack dwarfed him. People thought of informants as slinky and furtive, like Toothpick Charlie in *Some Like It Hot,* twitchily trying to hide behind his upturned coat collar. Jack wasn't slinky or furtive and didn't twitch.

He would have found it contemptible to take money for his *disclosures,* but it was understood by both men that Harpur shouldn't look too closely into the splendidly profitable, infinitely dodgy art business Jack ran, selling great works by renowned painters, many of them genuine, apparently. Lamb said it would be tedious and irksome and such a bore for Harpur if he thought he should check how certain of these priceless items got into Jack's hands, and had a magnificent purchase price put on them by him, although they were priceless.

Jack stood massive and wholly undaunted at a loophole now, gazing out into the darkness, ready, eager to repel solo any seaborne, landing-craft attack, the kepi to the side of his head, making him look devil-may-care and gallantly unfazed/unfazable. 'Ralph Ember, Col,' he said, over his shoulder. 'Or "Panicking Ralph", as he's called.' He spoke quietly, but in this enclosed, thick-walled pillbox the words got a crackling, nearly raucous, echo. They seemed to break up into strange, eerie, black-magic chant combinations: 'Ral Fembercol; Ralph Embercle; Orpar Nicking Ralfasi Scald.'

'People don't call him "Panicking" to his face,' Harpur said.

'No, not to his face, but by competitors in the great druggy game, and by villains generally. He's in jeopardy, Col, in serious jeopardy. Naturally, he attracts the normal territorial jealousy but I hear, too, there's something unforgiven, unforgivable, in his past – something not defined so far. London, possibly? Is south-east London in his background? Maybe a moment of cowardice in a gang fight – how he got the nickname? Because of his failure, perhaps people were killed, or injured, and/or locked up. It's a while ago but isn't it conceivable that someone's out of jail now and still aggrieved? Releases speed up for Yule. Maybe a relative or chum of one of those killed or permanently disabled has let resentment fester and now wants to do payback.'

'You know this?' Harpur asked. 'How, Jack?' It was the kind of question any detective would ask an informant, and the kind of question no informant would answer. Sources had to be protected or the informant would get no more information to inform with, and could even get killed or permanently disabled himself for gab.

Jack said: 'There might be trouble aimed at

Panicking around Christmas time. Opportunities. Good King Wenceslas looked out, and Ralph should look out, too.'

'What type of trouble, Jack?'

'Kill-Ralph type,' Jack replied. 'I don't like it.' As an informant, Lamb was very selective. He didn't betray willy-nilly for reward. There had to be what he considered a decent purpose. To safeguard from outside attack a considerable local figure like Ralph Wyvern Ember would amount to a decent purpose. If Jack could be called a fink, his finkdom was of a noble, protective kind. 'I think Ralph started his career up in the capital, didn't he, Colin? Do I recall reading of a major street imbroglio somewhere near Peckham?'

'Do you?'

'I read a lot. Five pavement deaths, much blood, much trauma, much jail?'

'Were there?'

'A pillar box prominent.'

'Was there?'

'Also a statue.'

'Yes?'

'Two firms and an armed police party involved. Some controversial behaviour by Ralph on that occasion?'

'Was there? What kind of controversial?'

'The panicking kind? Or possibly not something *he* would regard as panic. Perhaps to him it seemed only wise caution. Others might demur. A lot of demurring goes on in the substances realm.'

'How did the panic, or whatever it was, show itself?'

'Goodbye, Col.' Lamb obviously believed bum freezer officers and kepi troops would be terse. He had to behave in character. He turned from his sentry duty at the loophole, his vigil over, and sort of sidled towards the door and then his car. But it was difficult for someone built like Jack to sidle. He surged. Harpur waited a few minutes and then himself left: unwise for a cop to be seen with his talebearer-in-chief at a place like this and at a time like this.

In the morning, at breakfast, Jill said: 'Did he disclose, Dad – cough some good stuff? "Strictly restricted"?' Harpur had cooked the breakfast himself today. He saw this as obligatory for a single parent. Or obligatory when his girlfriend, Denise, hadn't slept over. She did great breakfasts and the children loved it when she stayed. Denise was an undergraduate at the university up the road and had gone home to Stafford for the early part of the Christmas vacation. That, too, amounted to an obligation, though not one Harpur rejoiced in.

'Do you like dealing with squealers, Dad?' Hazel said. 'Don't they give you the creeps?'

'I don't think of them as squealers,' he said.

'No? What then – narks, touts, snoops?'

'He *has* to deal with them,' Jill said. 'It's what detectives are for. You think it's all magnifying glasses and DNA, Haze. It's not like Shylock Holmes any longer. There have to be finks.'

'Sherlock,' Hazel replied. 'Shylock's someone else. "You spat on me on Wednesday last."'

'I wouldn't ever, Haze,' Jill said.

'And Sherlock Holmes was before DNA.'

'Well, anyway,' Jill said. She'd always defend Harpur from Hazel's digs. He was grateful.

Of course, he would never tell his boss, Assistant Chief Constable (Operations) Desmond Iles, about any insights that came to Harpur from Jack Lamb. Iles believed he should already know everything, and would get deeply ratty if Harpur suggested he didn't. And – another factor, more important – no detective was supposed to have a one-to-one, exclusive arrangement with an informant. A rule laid down that an informant belonged not to an individual officer but to the whole detection force. So, informants had to be officially registered. It was a categorical, virtually even absolute, command, to prevent corruption. And to prevent a reversal of the arrangement when an informant might take over a detective rather than the other way about. But – obviously – Jack would never have let anyone officially register him, so Harpur ignored the categorical, even absolute command, and would have ignored it if it were even more categorical and absolute.

Mid-afternoon at headquarters today the ACC knocked at Harpur's office door and walked in, leaving it ajar. He had on his magnificent pale-blue, high-quality dress uniform. Most probably he'd been at some formal, festive, civic luncheon, offering good chances for him to give offence. He seemed unhappy. 'This Counties Youth Orchestra, Col, that I read of. Why does it have to come here, for God's sake?'

'A short stay.'

'Why at all?

'I gather that gifted youngsters are picked to

go on a brief, concentrated course where they're coached by expert instrumentalists. It happens every year in the days just before Christmas when kids are on holiday. They assemble in a different city each time, with a concert at the end to show what they've learned. Our turn to accommodate them. A privilege.'

'Greasy old pros in cardigans encouraging girls, and maybe boys, to get their lips right to do blow-jobs.'

'Yes, brass and woodwind.'

'What I said – blow jobs. Haven't we got enough problems on our patch already, Col, some unseen as yet but definitely there? They'll all be heated up by toccatas and fucking fugues. Orchestrated lust, Col. Scandals in our bailiwick. I worry, Harpur.'

'In which respect, sir, other than the youth orchestra?'

'Christmas,' Iles said. 'The whole caboodle. People think we're off guard. Carols and mince pies and goodwill to all men.'

'Which people?'

'They make their moves,' Iles replied.

'Which moves, sir?'

Iles took a seat. For a while he gazed down to admire the slimness of his legs as nicely swathed by the fine material. His hair was quite long again now, after a spell when he had it cut close to capture the Jean Gabin style he'd seen on old films. 'They're out there all the time, Harpur.'

'Who, sir?'

'Take my word for it. I sense things. It's a unique flair. Yet I hope I'm not one to boast, Col.'

'Few would accuse you of that, sir.'

'Which fucking few, Harpur?'

'Many's the person I've heard exclaim after meeting you, "That Assistant Chief Constable Iles – he's not one to boast. Boasting and ACC Iles could not be further apart." Then they'll mention chalk and cheese – very different commodities. Likewise you and boastfulness. Or, another way of putting it, there's clear blue water between boastfulness and you.'

'I get feelings, Col. I get sort of hints about the future, and about hidden elements in the present.'

And it was true. Harpur had long ago recognized that Iles's mind could sometimes leave Harpur's own far behind. Chalk and cheese. Clear blue water. 'Hints from where, sir?'

'Oh, yes,' Iles replied. 'Intimations, Col, in the fullest reach of that term.'

'But from where, sir?'

'Who knows? They simply arrive. I am their, as it were, passive but deeply thankful receptacle.'

'Wonderful. Mysterious, sir. Like the Book of Revelation in the Bible. If there was a racing card for the four horsemen of the apocalypse you'd have picked the winner, even if an apparent outsider.'

Iles's voice began to go high and screamwards, and a light, purest white froth flecked with jostling, tiny bubbles coated his lips. Harpur quickly stood and hurried to close the door properly. 'So, you'll ask, won't you, Harpur, how come, if I get these sort of supernatural promptings, one of these supernatural promptings didn't supernaturally tell me you were disgracefully banging my wife in flophouse beds, *al fresco* under hydrangea bushes in public parks during daylight, even on the back seat of marked police patrol vehicles, despite your undeniably inferior rank to mine?'

All that with Sarah Iles was a while ago now, but the Assistant Chief still had loud, famous fits of agonizing. Harpur always kept himself ready to check the door was shut when Iles dropped by for a chat because the ACC's contribution to the chats could get noisy and hysterical, occasionally howlingly tearful. People would loiter in the corridor outside hoping to hear another repeat of the Assistant Chief's performance. This brand of in-house entertainment wasn't usual from ACCs. It helped to make the day interesting for some. Harpur took his chair again. 'Exactly what intimations, sir?' he said.

Iles did another admiring inspection of his legs and this seemed to comfort him. The rage passed. 'Something, somewhere on our ground, Col,' he said.

'I'll keep an eye,' Harpur said.

'I know I can half trust you, Col. On some things.' His voice seemed about to soar and sharpen again.

Harpur said: 'I'll tell everyone in the Department to keep awake, sir. Thanks for the early warning.'

Iles, in that uncharming, telepathic, yes, mystical way of his, stared at Harpur. 'Oh, you already knew from one of your damned hidden contacts that catastrophe was on the Christmas menu, did you, you eternally sly bugger?' he said. 'To do with Ember? Or, maybe, Manse Shale? What form will it come in, Col?'

'Talking of music and specifically carols, I'd certainly be interested to know your favourite, sir,' Harpur replied.

When he set Iles's vague, inspired unease alongside Lamb's warning about Ralph and the Christmas 'opportunities' Harpur thought it might be sensible to speak a word to Ember, put him on guard. Harpur drove down towards The Monty. Ralph should be there now, getting the club ready for another festive night's business. Harpur felt what could be jargonized as 'a duty of care'. And it would be bad, wouldn't it, if some trouble came to Ralph after that quite particular warning from Jack Lamb; and a sort of general alert from Iles, though the ACC couldn't say where exactly the danger might strike. He had mentioned Ember's business associate, Mansel Shale, as well as Ralph himself. Harpur's concern grew and he'd left headquarters immediately after the talk with Iles.

Despite Ember's high position in the substances trade, Harpur felt a kind of affection for him. He saw absurd, floundering nobility in Ralph. It came from his daft, dogged, utterly impossible efforts to achieve a refined, cultured, intellectually distinguished status for his backstreet, thieves-kitchen club. Even Iles occasionally showed some fondness for Ralph, although the Assistant Chief would mock and ridicule him when they met. Ember probably realized Iles mocked and ridiculed almost everybody, so Ralph needn't take the insults too personally.

He could voyage on in his doomed search for The Monty's new, cleansed, glittering identity, still fiercely powered by that barmy, constant ambition. A poem Jill studied lately for homework contained what seemed to Harpur like an exact reference to Ralph. Jill had asked Harpur what 'inviolable' meant. It came in the lines about a gypsy who was also a scholar. He'd given himself a mission to search non-stop for some special truth not far from Oxford. Harpur could recall the words: 'Still nursing the unconquerable hope, Still clutching the inviolable shade.' Harpur had needed to look up what 'inviolable' meant: 'never to be broken or dishonoured.' That description fitted absolutely Ralph W. Ember's plans for his club. Surely, there was something crazily, admirably epic about such useless determination in Ralph? Harpur mentioned to Jill this resemblance between Ember and the gypsy and she'd wanted to put Ralph and The Monty into the composition she had to write about the poem. 'This would perk it up, Dad,' she said, 'by proving that an old poem with whiskers on could still be about matters today, such as The Monty.' Harpur persuaded her against, though.

Yes, he sympathized with Ember but, just the same, realized he mustn't get too close. As he slowed and signalled now and was about to pull into The Monty's car park, he decided this visit would probably be wrong. Instead, he resumed his straight-ahead course and normal speed and went back to his office. If he'd gone to talk about these rumours it might have looked to others as though he and Ember were buddies, had some sort of alliance, a secret, illicit partnership. Club staff would observe the hush-hush conversation and make their assumptions. They might also talk outside to pals, relatives, of their assumptions. This was a senior police officer apparently in cahoots with a very major drugs tycoon. Harpur didn't fancy that kind of slur.

In any case, the information Harpur had . . . well, it could hardly be called information. Although he still valued Lamb as a marvellous font of reliable 'disclosures' in Number Three he'd not gone much beyond that short, imprecise promise of 'serious jeopardy' for Ralph; and Iles could only come up with his spooky, undefined 'intimations'. Iles was exceptionally brilliant at intimations, but they still amounted to intimations only. Harpur thought he might have seemed panicky if he'd gone to Ralph with these flimsy hints. And it was Ember who'd somehow earned the nickname 'Panicking', not himself, thank you very much.

# Twenty-Four

After Margaret left, Ralph put on an overcoat, scarf, gloves and navy, woollen bobble hat and did one of his customary, random-timed tours around the outside of the club. He was looking for arson devices secretly planted by playful trade colleagues wishing to torch the building whether occupied or not. Ralph thought that, because of the scarf enclosing his chin, and the way the hat covered quite a depth of his forehead, people would not pick up the resemblance to Charlton Heston as quickly as normal – if there had been people about. But it was very cold in the club yard and car park and he considered winter clothing wise.

The point was, he, personally, knew of his resemblance to the young Chuck, was confident in it, and didn't need constant reaffirmations from others. Some might consider it sad and wasteful for him to cover up his features, but he knew that as soon as he took the scarf off everything would be there as always, visible and intact, a dead spit. He despised vanity – the kind of vanity that would wish to dictate constant flourishing of his face. Normally, he would have gone home to 'Low Pastures' between his morning and night stints at the club, but over the Christmas weeks he had to put in a good deal of extra time.

When he'd done about half the survey, he glanced away from his search for a moment, and towards the road. He glimpsed Harpur at the wheel of an unmarked Peugeot near The Monty car park, as if about to drive in. He didn't appear to spot Ralph, who was part hidden by a delivery truck.

Ralph could put up all right with Harpur on a solo call. He sometimes talked reasonable, unabusive sense. Harpur recognized the importance of community spirit, and knew Ralph possessed a true slice of that. It was only when Assistant Chief Iles and his damn mockery accompanied Harpur that things generally turned foul, sarky and barbaric.

Of course, one way to shut Iles up was to remind him that not so long ago his supposed colleague, Col Harpur, had been giving it on a regular, but very unofficial, basis to Iles's wife, Sarah. Ralph always regarded this as an extreme reaction, though, and would only use it if Iles kept on and on with his damn merrymaking viciousness. Ralph considered that a woman's reputation and dignity should be very carefully protected, even a policeman's woman, unless, obviously, it became necessary to slag her off as a way of flooring her loathsome husband.

Ralph's mother would often quote a saying to him when he was growing up, 'Manners maketh man.' Ralph still regarded this as very worthwhile teaching, unless you were dealing with someone like Iles, who didn't know what the fucking word 'manners' meant and whose only delight was to kick shit out of people. If you tried to treat him with respectful manners he'd see this as a pathetic weakness and would kick you even harder.

Whatever Harpur wished to discuss today, Ralph would gladly go along with. For Ralph civility rated high. Manners were what made man different from animals. Manners were what a laughing hyena like Iles was completely short of.

But then Harpur's Peugeot straightened, moved past the car park entrance and went on. He seemed to have been hit by sudden second thoughts. Ralph wondered what the first thoughts were, but couldn't get far with that. Although the prospect of a visit by Harpur hadn't disturbed him, this sudden uncertainty did. It magnified Ember's suspicion that, behind the surface jollity of Christmas time, hovered some menace aimed specifically at him.

It wasn't only the possible fire bombs. That threat existed permanently; could be considered routine, a standard part of business success. Now, Ralph sensed special, so-far undefined perils. Possibly Harpur also registered this increased danger and had come to check Ember was OK. Yes, for a cop, Harpur had some quite decent aspects, though his boss, Iles, despised these and tried to eliminate them, of course. Ralph's car stood parked in its reserved spot and this might have reassured Harpur all was well, and so he hadn't bothered to stop.

Disappointment struck Ralph. Besides being willing to listen to whatever Harpur might have wanted to say, Ralph, himself, had something genuinely interesting to speak about, something that would impress Harpur, and which he could pass on to that brass-necked egomaniac, Iles. It might help bring even him to a proper respect,

215

perhaps outright admiration, for Ralph. This didn't mean he would have blurted out direct and in a buttonholing, big-headed style the new, fascinating factor in his life. That would be crude, naive and naff. It could have undone the very effect Ralph wanted.

No, simply he would have let this information surface quite offhandedly in conversation, as though it were absolutely natural and didn't need to be flagged. It would have indicated a much changed social identity for both The Monty and Ralph himself. Yes, Harpur might have been surprised by such a development, but, if this kind of situation ever did come, the trick from Ralph's point of view was to behave as though the sterling, magnificent qualities now displayed had, in fact, always been present, but not easily detected because of competing influences, such as that oiled idiot popping .38 shots at the aerial William Blake.

Ralph found no seasonal incendiary items on his patrol and re-entered the club. He took off the winter gear and sat down at his accounting desk behind the bar. After that thought about the pitifully immature gunning of *The Marriage of Heaven and Hell* beard, he wanted publicly to reassert his belief in the steel sheet and its elite collage by placing himself at what some might judge an appallingly dangerous spot: hardly the behaviour of someone branded 'Panicking'. He believed it was Ralph W. Ember saying, 'Here I am in my customary, dedicated chair. Do your contemptible, malevolent worst. The captain's on the bridge.'

If Harpur had dropped in just now, Ralph would have acted just the same – taken up that position behind the bar, as a bold sign of his total faith in The Monty's and his own future. They would have talked in an entirely relaxed manner, Harpur with a glass of his usual disgusting, soak's tipple, gin and cider in a half-pint glass; Ralph opting as ever for Kressmann Armagnac, famed for that distinguished, understated black label, a connoisseur's choice, something a long way from Harpur's crude palate. Ralph let himself imagine their conversation, in the way he used to imagine conversations with Margaret when they were younger.

'Well, Ralph, the club is looking very fine, brass fittings agleam, panelling that tells as ever of a fine tradition and of enduring worth. This is a lovely refuge from the uncertainties, setbacks and stresses of life outside.'

'Thank you, Mr Harpur.'

'I think of it as a kind of brilliant and renowned communal hub. The Christmas tree modest in size yet indicating in its ungrandiose way a festival feeling shared with all your members and staff.'

'Thank you, Mr Harpur. It is my aim and indeed responsibility to make it so.'

'Although there are London clubs with, possibly, more famous names and of longer standing, such as The Athenaeum or The Garrick, in its own unpushy, welcoming, sincere fashion The Monty lies closer to its people's souls.'

'Thank you, Mr Harpur. One puts a great emphasis on sincerity. Without sincerity what have we? What we would have is mere show and duplicity. But I certainly would not claim this is all on account of one man, myself. We are a happy and fulfilled team, here. Everyone committed to the club and content to serve – lastingly content.'

'Perhaps at Christmas it really comes into its own, an essential, heart-warming centre.'

'Over the years we have built that kind of reputation. And, of course, *this* year it will be especially appreciated.'

Ralph thought that such a statement would be the muted, though intriguing, way to have tickled Harpur's curiosity. He'd be used to noting tiny, inadvertent hints given during interrogation. Well, this hint would not have been inadvertent but delicately schemed.

'In which respect, Ralph?' Harpur would probably say.

'The musical side.' (Keep it oblique, gradual, a sort of good humoured tease, a tantalizingly slow unfolding.)

'Musical in which respect, Ralph?'

'Classical.'

'I don't follow.'

'Orchestral.'

'To what effect?'

'Oh, yes, Mr Harpur, there's a notable musical function taking place in the city this year.' (Step by extremely unhurried step with these facts. Feed him bait. Lead him gently but steadily on.)

'In which respect, Ralph?'

'The Shire Counties Youth Orchestra.'

'Oh?'

'It's an honour for the city and, I'm happy to say, for The Monty also. Not *The National Youth Orchestra of Great Britain,* but still quality.'

'Yes?'

'A very worthwhile project, bringing out latent talent in the young, music being one of the arts where youthfulness is no bar to excellence. Think of Mozart and teenage genius.'

'Absolutely. But how does this affect you and The Monty, Ralph?' (No need to answer that at once. More evasive obliqueness required.)

'It meets in a selected city each year, has some lessons for the child instrument players who are housed in the youth hostel, and gives a concert at the end,' Ralph replied.

'Yes?'

'Certain facilities required.'

'Clearly.'

'A hall for their concluding performance.'

'Indeed.'

'Plus rooms for the coaching from known stars on various instruments, who are put up in local hotels – for instance, a trombone room, a flute room, a viola room.'

'Not easy to find such a building.'

'Fortunately these visits take place in the school holidays.'

'Ah.'

'Therefore, schools with their many classrooms and assembly hall, are empty, unused.'

'They take over a school, do they?'

'Corton House, which my daughters attend, will provide excellent facilities.'

'Great!'

'The children come from all over, not from Corton itself. The orchestra just needs the property. But Corton parents, as sort of third-party hosts, well-heeled mostly, or their kids wouldn't be at Corton – we, parents, have been asked by the head to help with the social side and, truth to tell, with a donation if they wish to aid with extras – soft drinks, snacks. Well, of course, one is ready to assist in both aspects.'

'So like you, Ralph.'

'This is elements of the community in constructive actions.'

'Grand!'

'And now – at last, you might say – we reach The Monty and its part in all this, a wonderful, significant part: post-concert, a little get-together here in the club, for the organizers and teachers only. Not the children, naturally.'

'Excellent, Ralph.'

'I feel it will give The Monty what one might term a new dimension, an artistic character, refinement.'

'How true – and well deserved, Ralph.'

'I want to develop The Monty, you know, Mr Harpur. You mentioned London clubs, such as The Athenaeum and The Garrick. And there are others – The Carlton, Boodle's. You very kindly said The Monty might have certain attributes these others lacked. Thank you. But they, in their turn, have attributes lacking to The Monty and this I would like to correct. I speak of cultural and social distinction recognized worldwide. In these aspects I feel The Monty may lag a little. To have these classical music stars as Monty guests – everything on the house, naturally – will be a significant step towards this change of profile for the club. It will give me a start. The usual membership will also be present on this occasion, naturally. It would be snobbish to ban regulars because of the special clients, and, obviously, I hate class distinction. There are, it must be admitted, some real rough-house oiks and slappers among the present membership. However, I believe in tolerance and sympathy, at least *pro tem*. But the highly-thought-of musicians will provide The Monty with a tone and grace it has not always enjoyed in the recent past.'

Ralph would have taken true pleasure in that type of intelligent conversation, and Harpur might have also; no need to speak of a possibly increased danger in the bar because of extra numbers; best keep the chat optimistic and happy. Harpur might have understood and supported Ralph's ambitions for The Monty and his clever, resourceful stratagem for getting it under way by entertaining the musicians. And, yes, maybe Harpur would relate the gist of the talk to Assistant Chief Constable Iles, relate it in such a form and with so much evident approval that even someone as thoroughly poisonous and gleefully harmful as Iles could see the merit in what Ralph hoped to achieve, indeed, *meant* to achieve. This projected attempt to transform The Monty was surely a supremely positive quest. All should be able to acknowledge that, Iles included.

Three women were fighting, silently, intently, on the floor over near a fruit machine, at least one of them wearing no knickers. Bad feeling

221

often followed a big jackpot triumph. Non-winners might claim they had been playing the machine for hours and losing, then somebody who's been watching comes along, craftily calculating that, after so much investment, a pay-off must be due. And those previous feeders of the slot feel cheated and enraged. The winner had obviously been loading the loot into her bag when the other two struck and one-pound coins were scattered across the bar floor now. She had a cut to her forehead. People stood around watching the scrap, shouting betting odds on the outcome, and encouragement to the contender or contenders they backed. Ralph left his seat and went and pulled the three apart and then on to their feet. 'Don't bleed on to a fucking pool table,' he remarked considerately. 'I had enough trouble with the Worcestershire sauce.'

# Twenty-Five

In the conservatory as the afternoon light began to weaken, Esther had a phone call on her mobile from Desmond Iles. It shook her a bit, pulled Esther out of her reminiscing and made things very present tense, very now and the dicey near future. In the past there'd been that Mondial-Trave situation needing careful, tactical management; and this call today from Des Iles would also require careful tactical management, though of a different kind. The relationship with him, if it could be called that, had always been difficult to define. But shouldn't she be accustomed to weird relationships, expert in them? Think of her and Gerald.

'Good to hear your voice again, Esther,' Iles said.

'Good to hear yours, too.' And it was at least half true. He could put on a mild, warm tone for her which she thought probably didn't match his more usual way with words.

'Can you talk?' Iles said.

'I'm home, alone. I was owed a couple of days off.'

'I've been going through a list of names,' he said.

'Oh, yes?'

'Something more or less routine, but then a surprise, even a shock.'

223

'Oh, yes?'

'I felt I needed to talk to you about it.'

'Am I concerned in it somehow?'

'Possibly. Obliquely. You'll be able tell me right away.'

'I'll try.' She'd been going through some names herself, most from way back – Mondial-Trave names. There was quite a crowd of them. The newspaper reports at the time had been fairly full and accurate but, of course, they'd depended on witnesses and on what the media were told by the official police spokeswoman. What the media were told by the official police spokeswoman, though, was what Esther had told the official police spokeswoman she could tell them. Neither the witnesses nor the media had seen things from the inside, as Esther had.

Standard procedure had required her to complete an A to Z account of the day's happenings and the run-up to them, giving all the names, including one of somebody missing. Naturally, she'd done a copy for herself and was reading it over when Iles called; her objective, as before, to see what she could learn from the report in case it might be useful now in her new and bigger responsibilities. Perhaps she'd need to set a trap again. The report could possibly give some tips on how to do it.

Her report had begun:

*The disorder in the Mondial Street-Trave Square area breaks into five principal stages. (Firms' names may be abbreviated: Pasque Uno to PU, Opal Render to OR.)*

*Stage One. Preliminary. Acting on informa-
tion received (from special source,
'Mandrake') and from concealed filming
(team commander Sergeant Fiona Hive-
Knight) two armed police units were established out of view at locations within easy
reach of the street complex named by
'Mandrake' as the probable ground for battle
between the Pasque Uno and Opal Render
firms. Observations recorded on film of
assumed familiarizing runs in a Vauxhall
(PU) and a Mazda (OR) by members of both
companies appeared to confirm the 'Mandrake'
information on the likely setting for the
conflict – Vauxhall: Dale Hoskins, head of
PU with three subordinates; Mazda: Piers
Elroy Stanton, head of OR plus an aide. Both
vehicles made there-and-back journeys along
Mondial Street, travelling slowly on what
appeared to be a thorough reconnaissance
exercise. All involved in these excursions
would know the area well already. But they
were looking at it now as a potential battlefield, not a trading locale. Different factors
became relevant.*

*Film also showed a possibly independent,
individual reconnaissance of the area by a
member of the Pasque Uno firm, identified as
Ralph Wyvern Ember (present earlier in
Vauxhall). He seemed to show a strongly
focused interest in the writer of this report
– self – who was also engaged on a personal
survey of the territory at the same time. It's
possible – probable – that I was recognized*

*and my purpose speculated upon; perhaps correctly speculated upon.*

*The police parties took up hidden positions in Dorothea Gardens and in a basement of the apartment block used for filming. Each unit comprised fifteen officers, seven handgun armed, one first-aid trained. The Dorothea party under command of Inspector Leighton Maliphant (armed), second in command, Sergeant Lisa Ohm-Reen (armed); basement party led by Inspector Jennifer Ash (armed), deputy, Sergeant Martin Wilcox (armed).*

*Stage Two. Both firms used stolen vans to bring their fighting groups to the confrontation site. The Pasque Uno team arrived at the southern end of Mondial Street, disembarked and moved on foot up Mondial towards the entrance to Trave Square. They were masked but those injured, killed or arrested subsequently were identified as Dale (Gladhand) Hoskins, leader (killed); Hector Lygo-Vass, driver (arrested); Gregory Francis Mace (killed)); Clive (Aftermath) Palgrave (killed); Quentin Stayley, second in command (arrested); Mimi Apertine, bodyguard (arrested).*

*All were handgun armed. Palgrave appeared to have some difficulty with his pistol and was delayed at the van. The rest of this party progressed along Mondial and turned into Trave Square, obviously searching for the Opal Render team. The Pasque Uno thinking seemed to be that if Opal Render were not evident in Mondial they must have chosen to make their arrival in the Square and come from there to confront PU in Mondial. This appeared to be an accurate estimate. The Pasque Uno countermove was to pre-empt any OR strike by advancing swiftly into Trave. The OR party comprised Piers Elroy Stanton, leader (killed); Luke Gaston Byfort, aide to Stanton (arrested); Corneille Jameson, driver (injured and hospitalized); Mary Zara Pill (killed); Jasper (Meticulous) Carp-Isis, body-guard (arrested); Leonard (Impish) Smythe (injured and hospitalized). All were masked and carried handguns.*

*Stage Three. Jameson, Byfort and Pill had left Trave and reached Mondial ahead of the rest of their group. They appeared to have come through from the back entrance of a shop in Trave Square whose frontage was in Mondial (Supervalue Grotto). They were still in the shop on their way into Mondial when the main PU platoon passed, making for Trave in their search. The OR trio remained unobserved in the shop. A Supervalue manager confirmed later that the three had moved through the premises and on to Mondial, threatening staff and ordering them not to interfere if they wanted to stay unhurt. When they emerged into Mondial they saw Palgrave running to catch up with his colleagues. He had become isolated and very exposed because of difficulties with his firearm. He must have seen the three OR personnel emerge from Supervalue Grotto and tried to take cover behind the pavement pillar box.*

Jameson, Byfort and Pill went into sniper-crouch positions and opened fire on Palgrave when he stepped partly out from the pillar-box cover. (Subsequent examination of Palgrave's handgun showed it had not been fired and was not functioning properly.) He was hit three times and fell dead there. Showing considerable courage two paramedics reached him only a few minutes after he was hit, but found him dead.

Stage Four. Both police groups were ordered to intervene from their cover in Dorothea Gardens and the apartment block basement. They called 'Armed Police' warnings twice before Sergeant Martin Wilcox and Sergeant Lisa Ohm-Reen opened fire on the three, killing Pill and injuring Byfort and Jameson (both hospitalized). The main Pasque Uno unit continued on Mondial and then into Trave Square. Several exchanges of fire occurred there. As a result, Piers Elroy Stanton, leader of OR was hit twice by nine mm bullets and died in the road near the 'Gleam and Smile' dental practice. Possibly suffering demoralization at the loss of their leader the remnants of the OR contingent – Carp-Isis and Smythe – were driven out of the Square and down towards the Red Letter public house. This appeared to have been a pre-schemed strategy by PU.

Stage Five. The Red Letter has a car park walled on three sides. It functioned on this occasion as a trap. The OR survivors who were forced into this enclosure were easily *picked off by PU weapons. Carp-Ises and Smythe suffered gunshot injuries, were hospitalized and subsequently arrested. Some desperate firing still came from the OR members, however, and it was during this final episode that Dale Hoskins was shot in the head. Landlord of the Red Letter, Clifford Grange, who had come out from the public house to investigate the disturbance in the car park, dragged Hoskins into the pub out of danger but he died on the floor of the snug.*

*All personnel as listed by 'Mandrake' were accounted for at the end of the action except for Ralph Wyvern Ember who, it is assumed, withdrew from the PU party, although originally due to take part, having been a Vauxhall passenger and conducting his own, unaccompanied assessment of the battle area.*

Esther was thinking about this missing name and the other names involved in the events of that day when Iles called wanting to talk about a quite different collection of names, or, specifically, one name: 'Gerald Orville Ludwig Davidson,' Iles said.

'What of him?'

'He's on a schedule I have here.'

'What schedule?'

'Is it *your* Gerald Orville Ludwig Davidson, Esther? Do I remember you referring several times to your husband as Gerald?'

'Would there be other Gerald Orville Ludwig Davidsons about?'

'Musician?'

229

'Destined to it by the christening. What schedule?' Esther replied. 'What's Gerald been up to, for heaven's sake?'

'Instrumentalists. We have a function on here – coaching of talented children.'

'Yes, I knew he was coming in to your domain.'

'Well, obviously we have to do paedo and other checks on the adults. There's bound to be a lot of fingering and close contact – helping girls get to grips with their violas properly: that kind of earnest, physical assistance and pressure, some of it quite possibly necessary and non-grope. But, just the same, we need to know who's likely to be doing one-to-ones with the kids. If music be the food of love how would you like a mouthful of this, my sweet little timpanist?'

'Gerald and I have our eccentricities, but he's not interested in underaged,' she said. 'He likes someone who can kick, claw and punch at least as hard as he does.'

'You.'

'Me. "Reciprocity" would be his middle name if he didn't already have others. And he's not a pink oboe man. Bassoon.'

'Fine. But I thought I'd ring to see if Gerald is Gerald. We did some routine inquiries. He composes as well as plays, I gather. And he's written something for their final concert. An all-rounder, indeed.'

'I'll have to sit through that.'

'Yes, well I wondered whether you'd be in the audience.'

'We stand by each other, you know.'

'Yes, of course' he said.

230

'It's not all mutual assault and battery.' She grew uncertain of the real, hidden theme of this conversation. Nothing much had happened between her and him when they last met. He'd unofficially helped her with what turned out to be a doomed and tragic undercover operation. Not anything more than a friendship? Professional collaboration?

'When I saw the name, I felt I ought to give a bit of advice, if you don't mind, Esther.'

'Shoot.'

'Our inquiries came up with the news that there'll be a post-concert party in one of the local clubs. It's called The Monty. All very hospitable and convivial, perhaps. But I get a feeling it's not an entirely safe place at Christmas. And I don't believe I'm the only one who suspects that.'

'Not safe why?'

'Sorry, I can't really say why. An intimation.'

'You suffer from those, do you?'

'These worries centre on the club. Ralph's a strange fellow.'

'Ralph?

'The owner. Ralph Ember. You'll probably meet him.'

'Ralph *Wyvern* Ember?' she said.

'You know him?'

'Not exactly.'

'I don't understand.'

'He missed an operation I ran in London. He should have been dead, or disabled or jailed. He'd disappeared, though.'

'I think I remember that interlude on TV News. Peckham? East Dulwich?'

'I was Gold.'

Iles went silent for a while. Then he said: 'His gang colleagues won't have liked getting ditched then. It upsets the agreed plans and causes a numbers problem – leaves a combat unit one short. Possibly, his absence indicates a rejection of those agreed plans – agreed by all the others – and he walks away. Not easily forgivable, Esther.'

'Betrayal?'

'Something like. He disappeared to here, maybe not immediately, but he's very much in place now,' Iles said. 'Yes, I've heard he had that London beginning, but nothing clear or proved. He's become a big trader – country house with paddocks, daughters in private school, Welsh cob ponies, fervent, very worthy letters to the Press on environmental matters, especially river pollution. All that might enrage survivors of the London battle. He vamoosed, abandoned them, and then somehow creates a fine, new life for himself. The club's a right dump but it turns a profit.'

'And dangerous, you say?'

'There've been incidents. Someone shot Blake there.'

'Blake?'

'William Blake. A decoration on the protective steel barrier he's installed at The Monty. A truly terrible beard injury. The mad blast-off was the kind of hilarious event that gets talked about, draws attention to Ralph. He believes, or pretends to believe, he can turn this den into somewhere as respectable and refined as the top London places. In a way, it's an admirable, wholesome ambition. I'm fond of Ralph. Daft determination. Ludicrous hope, but hope. He's in pursuit of a distant prize. In fact, it couldn't be more distant. Yet, he's not always daft. He possibly applied his brain to that proposed gun fight, decided it, not he, was crazy, and therefore doomed, and acted intelligently by opting out. That's how he'd see it, but not his chums of that era. I understand he longs to start The Monty's magical transformation by inviting all these heavyweight, distinguished musicians, festooned with respectability, achievement and artiness like Gerald to the *après-gig* rave.'

'Gerald would enjoy that. He adores kudos, as long as it's aimed at him. He doesn't get much of it these days. I provide some for him, naturally, but he doesn't really value that, regards it as only conjugal. He wants it from the world.'

'The point is, Esther, I can't really look in on The Monty do, to check things are going OK and peacefully, because it would unsettle, inhibit dear Ralph in front of his classy guests. I mustn't do that. He's liable to disabling panics. He might fail to make the most of this occasion. He thinks of me as a gross troublemaker, disrespectful, contemptuous – I don't know why. Just keep watchful. Tell Gerald to keep watchful. If you can, get into a part of the bar covered by William Blake. I understand the beard has been patched up admirably. Make good references about his literary taste and knowledge of the Romantics. The metal's thick enough to stop anything but a cruise missile.'

'Well, thanks, Desmond.'

'Old time's sake. And I must preserve Ralph. He's part of the atmos here.'

She found she was glad Iles wouldn't be at the party. If Gerald saw them talking together intimately in the club, with, obviously some shared past experience, he'd be almost sure to assume a major and secret link between them. Gerald was exceptionally good at suspicion. He could get very unpredictable, especially after some drinks following an exciting, adrenalined evening in the concert hall. It would be unhelpful if he fell into a rage fit and turned destructive, possibly trashing The Monty and causing injuries. At this time of the year, there might be a Christmas tree he'd adapt into a weapon. He could bring a true inventiveness to violence. She loved that in him, of course.

But Esther would almost certainly be trying for a chief constable post soon. It might not be a plus if interviewing panels heard she had a husband who went berserk in a notorious, underclass drinking joint. Some strands of liberalism were allowed in the police service these days, but not that many.

# Twenty-Six

As well as an entitlement to reserved seats at the youth orchestra's final concert, Ralph and Margaret Ember, and other parents who had made a donation to cover the cost of extras, were invited out to Corton school to see the tutors and young pupils actually teaching and learning all aspects of their instruments.

Ralph would admit he didn't know a terrific amount about classical music, but on the whole he was not anti. It could do no real harm. Radio Three was always there, but you could take it or leave it alone. A lot of the stuff had been around for centuries so there must be certain parts that were reasonably OK. He'd read somewhere that music by top people from the past was played in mental hospitals to help keep the patients more or less peaceable. This proved it had true useful-ness and was not just noise. And then, during the Second World War, a famous tune had notes at the beginning that imitated the Morse code, dot, dot, dot, dash, meaning V for victory. Britain broadcast it to Germany to scare Hitler. 'We're going to stuff you, Adolf.' Ralph had an idea this piece of music was actually written by a German. It must have been a real pisser for Hitler to have it turned against the Nazis.

Ralph had heard there was a lot of what was called 'in-house fucking' that took place in adult orchestras, such as, say, a harp player with a trombonist, two different sections of an orchestra, but, when it came to fucking, the instruments they played wouldn't be to the point. This sort of carry-on didn't seem to Ralph to matter, except it showed fine music even from centuries ago could get the people who made it very excited and eager now. Often the brass section of an orchestra had a French horn and this might be where the word 'horny' to signify dying for it came from. The French were famous for sex and intelligent music.

Ralph felt that to watch and listen to pupils and teachers actually working on orchestra skills was the kind of thing that could help him really well now with his plans for change at The Monty. It would show he knew about culture, and not just about culture as such but the way culture needed to be carefully prepared and created. It meant he'd have a practical grasp of culture, more than simply the airy-fairy word. At the club they occasionally had music, such as what were termed 'Golden Oldies', like 'Roll A Silver Dollar' and 'They Try To Tell Us We're Too Young', or numbers by Bowie and a girl from Iceland, though Ralph could be copped for performing rights and a payment for these. That kind of music was all right in its own category and a full bar chorusing 'They Try To Tell Us We're Too Young', regardless of age, could be quite impressive. He liked to imagine the Queen and Prince Philip having a little singalong together with this tune. But Ralph wanted to get himself, and therefore The Monty, associated with symphonies, rondos and intermezzos – that brand of much deeper thing.

He liked symphonies because they came in a collection of what were called 'movements', each movement commenting on the others and fitting in nicely with them. This suggested good order and control. Also, with concertos, the solo player would stick his or her bit in at just the right place when he or she got a wink from the conductor, and stopped at just the point where the orchestra would take over again. This meant the solo player couldn't hog the whole performance and behave like some superstar. Orchestras were a community.

So, Ralph decided they could accept the invitation and go to Corton to observe the courses under way. There had been a moment when he'd thought it might be best *not* to. The trouble was that Basil Gordon Loam, the dim prick who'd opened fire on William Blake, had three children at Corton and would most certainly have coughed a contribution, so would also get invited. And if he was invited he'd attend, no question. He loved to show he had funds. Well, putting three kids through Corton at £19,000 each a year, acted like a cash boast. This was a private school, yes, but not boarding, so 19K for just teaching, tuck shop and the sports field was pricey. The donation could be another bit of flashiness, because Loam would tell everyone he'd made it. 'One is only too glad to back worthwhile artistic effort.' Fuck off, you jerk.

Ralph didn't know where Loam's money came from, but that would be true of many members of The Monty. It did come, though. And seemed to keep coming. Probably quite a few Corton households had incomes it would be hard to explain. Not all of them did their share-out at the club after successful activity and selling to a middleman. Although for Ralph himself the fees were a flea bite and hardly noticed, he felt disappointed that, despite getting screwed in this way, the school did not teach the classical languages, such as Latin and Greek, but had stories to do with the one-eyed Cyclops and similar yarns, in English only. It was a mistake to put them into a lingo people understood. These tales were so stupid they ought to be told in words people had to struggle with and weren't quite sure about. The crappy quality of the tales wouldn't be so obvious then. There was another one about somebody pushing a bloody great rock up a hill but just when it got to the top it would roll back down again. Of course, no explanation came, in English, Latin or Greek, of why this chap had to push the rock up there. It was hard to visualize a shortage of rocks anywhere, unless the very big sort were needed to keep gypsies from setting up illegal camps.

What Ralph didn't want was this full-time nincompoop, Basil Gordon Loam, making more pleas at Corton for re-admittance to The Monty. It would be embarrassing if he started all that in front of unquestionably distinguished musicians. They'd be curious as to why he had been kicked out and might uncover the whole story of the shot beard and the inconvenient flying sauce. No doubt these celebrities would find the abominable

238

episode a big, unmusical laugh. It would be demeaning for the club and for Ralph, the very reason for seeking association with them torpedoed.

Or, of course, Loam might try an alternative and get all tough and angry, claiming he'd been victimized for what amounted to only a prank and arguing that nobody had been hurt by the pieces of hurtling glass, and stating he'd offered to pay for repairs. What Ralph had to remember was that Loam sometimes carried a weapon, and sometimes used it, as the beard damage proved. Suppose Loam, in a wrath-spasm because at Corton Ralph continued to refuse him restored membership, instead, gave him the big ignoral – and Ralph at Corton *would* refuse him restored membership and try to give him the big ignoral – suppose, then, Loam pulled out a pistol and in a paddy started targeting some of the orchestra's instruments. Admittedly he'd been drinking when he attacked The Monty's Blake. But that didn't mean he'd *always* have to be tipsy before opening fire. Anger and self-pity might be enough to take the place of alcohol. Ralph hated to think of one of the orchestra's drums ripped open by bullets; or a triangle hit by a .38 and giving out a lovely, melodious sound as a result, but from a disgraceful, extremely *un*lovely cause.

Culture had to be safeguarded. Ralph saw it as rather like care for the environment, which he was very strong on, such as river pollution. Basil Loam and his sodding firearm could be a pollutant. He and it should be shunted off to somewhere out of sight and kept there.

239

And, of course, Ralph had to consider that Loam might become even more vicious and malignant than that. What if in his fury he turned the Smith and Wesson on Ralph, and possibly Margaret? There would be a dark symbolism about this: the old style, violent Monty attacking the new, brilliant, emergent Monty – him, R.W. Ember, in a wonderfully aesthetic and educational setting. Ralph wondered whether he ought to take a shoulder-holstered automatic himself, entirely for defensive purposes. He had a duty to protect not just Margaret and himself but all the talented folk visiting, and their kit.

But Ralph greatly disliked the notion of going into a school carrying a firearm, just as he wouldn't be comfortable tooled up at home or in The Monty. This wasn't simply a school, but a school which, in term times, his daughters attended. There was something not acceptable about taking a pistol into the building. It would be to taint premises devoted to learning and, for now, music, with the unpleasant presence of an item designed to kill or disable, just as the unleashed Worcestershire sauce had tainted a pool table – and as that injured fruit machine woman might have, if she hadn't been warned by Ralph to keep her blood to herself.

True, Corton didn't do Latin or Greek, but it represented education all the same. One of his daughters had mentioned a civil war in British history with a rebel's head on a spike. Corton did all that type of thing. Ralph would not contaminate it by going there armed. After all, it wasn't totally certain Loam would be at Corton.

Even if he was – very likely – it didn't signify he would come armed himself, and, even if he did, he might not actually produce a gun and start shooting.

And he *was* present, as Ralph had guessed. He and Margaret had just come out from a classroom where they'd been watching and listening to a young lad being coached in bassoon playing by a musician who'd been announced by their guide for the evening as Mr Gerald Davidson. This had made Ralph get very alert and curious. The name, Davidson, was common enough, but it was bound to bring back memories of that woman superintendent in the days of the street battle in southeast London. This instructor, Davidson, wore a fairly foul red-dots-on-a-yellow-background bow-tie but, even in the limited time Ralph and Margaret Ember were present, had shown the learner how to get simultaneous passion, incisiveness and precision from what Margaret called his warm, lyrical, double-reed woodwind. Although Davidson's nose was not broken it had bruising of about two centimetres length, as if he might have been thumped by an elbow jab or a kick some while ago when he was down. He took no notice of Margaret and Ralph.

When they left the classroom and were about to be taken to the flute room by their guide for the visit, a young girl soon to go herself for saxophone coaching, Basil Loam seemed to be hanging about waiting for them in the corridor outside. He might have seen them enter. 'Why Mrs Ember, Ralph!' he cried joyously. 'Here's a pleasant surprise.'

241

'You're the mad, boozy fucker who shot *The Marriage of Heaven and Hell,* aren't you?' Margaret replied.

'What could be termed a *jeu d'esprit,* I think,' Loam said, chuckling in a dismissive sort of style.

Ralph thought Loam had just the kind of face you'd expect for someone who'd shoot upwards at totally harmless pictures; in fact, not simply harmless but significant, and part of a tableau much larger than a club in Shield Terrace. Of course, Ralph knew Loam *did* shoot upwards at totally harmless pictures, and to spot this tendency in his face now could be called a kind of cheating. Someone might ask why Ralph hadn't kept him out of the club if he'd been able to tell from his face pre-incident that he would pull out a gun and use it on the beard.

Ralph would accept this as a valid point. He decided that what he meant about Loam's face was that a disdain, even contempt, for ordinary, solid standards could be found in his face and this might at any time get transformed into an urge to damage a montage and cause ricochets. Snub, his features might reasonably be described as, his nose small and turned up at the end so you had the feeling you could look up his nostrils to the inside of his head and the notions he kept there. Ralph did not believe these would be civilized or even worthwhile notions

Loam's eyes were small. They had a glint that seemed to proclaim he was lively, mercurial, irrepressible. Ralph sensed that this glint wasn't spontaneous and natural, though, but had been worked on and contrived a bit at a time over the years. The eyes were blue-black and contained furtiveness. He was giving Margaret and Ralph some of that creepy gaze now. Ralph hated it when people put bits of French into what they were saying in English as Loam had done just now to Margaret as explanation for the Monty shooting. Ralph didn't understand what the phrase meant, but in his opinion if someone had to go into French to account for his actions it showed those actions lacked straightness. Although Ralph was in favour of classical languages being taught in schools, foreign words slipped into ordinary talk, possibly with an impudent chuckle, were sickening and signalled now not what the words were supposed to mean if they were spoken in, say, Paris but, in Britain, falsity and slipperiness.

'We have to get along to the flute,' Ralph told Loam.

'Yes,' their guide said.

'Ralph, I have to say I miss the club badly,' Loam replied

'You didn't miss the montage,' Margaret replied.

'I've found myself walking along Shield Terrace twice in recent evenings, just, as it were, to get a renewed glimpse of the building, an almost subconscious, compulsive, robot-like attraction to the spot.'

'Ralph won't mind you parading like that, as long as you don't try to get in,' Margaret said.

'I must be a sad, forlorn sight,' Loam said.

'I can bear it,' Margaret told him.

'A kind of yearning, a kind of haunting.'

'Tough,' Margaret said.

'Yet I'm not the only one who does it,' he replied.

'Does what?' Ralph said.

'Parades, as Mrs Ember calls it,' Loam said.

'Around the club?' Ralph said.

'Exactly,' Loam said.

'Who else?' Ralph said.

'Is it another what we might call banee?' Loam said.

'What banee?' Ralph replied.

'Twice I've noted him,' Loam said.

'Who?' Ralph said. He tried to keep his voice unflustered, steady.

'Ah,' Loam said.

'What?' Ralph replied.

'Are you saying, Ralph, it's *not* someone else you've banned?' Loam asked. He gave a short whistle. 'Why these secret visits, then? Someone casing the property?'

'Are you trying to scare us – scare Ralph?' Margaret said. 'This is some feeble attempt at retaliation, is it? Alarmist. You're the kind who would call Ralph "Panicking" behind his back. That's a rotten slander, not for one second justified.'

'Certainly not,' Loam said. 'As a matter of fact, I *had* wondered whether there might be a different reason for this person to patrol there – a more sinister reason. Well, look, Ralph, shall I accost him on your behalf next time and see what I can discover for you?'

'And you'd have to bring back a report, which would be your way to reinstatement at the club,' Margaret said. 'It's all tosh.' She turned to the

244

girl who was escorting them. 'Flutewards, dear,' she said.

They moved off with her. Ralph felt panicked. A sweat layer soaked his back and shoulders. There was a scar down one side of his face, long ago healed, but in his worst collapses of morale he had the impression that this ancient wound had opened up and was oozing something unspeakable on to his cheek and down on to his shirt. It wasn't, but he had that sensation now. He would have liked to ask Loam for more detail, might even have asked him to do what he suggested and question this unexplained figure. He could think of a string of possible names, above all Quentin Stayley's. Would he still have a ponytail?

The girl tapped the flute-room door and he and Margaret heard a fairly terrible, weak screaming sound coming from the instrument. 'We feel so privileged to be a part of all this, don't we, Ralph?' Margaret cried to the mentor and novice.

# Twenty-Seven

Harpur hadn't pushed Ralph entirely out of his mind, though, when he ditched his plan to talk caution and alertness to him and, with a sudden switch of direction, drove past The Monty car park. He did some inquiries and found that the club would host a celebration party for the youth orchestra instructors and other staff after the concluding concert performance. A day before this event he went up to Iles's suite at headquarters. 'There's a bit of a do for the musical lot at The Monty tomorrow night, sir,' he said.

'Yes, I know.'

'Oh?'

'I felt sure you'd catch up on things eventually, Col. Plod and more plod gets you there ultimately.'

'Thank you, sir.'

'It's mentioned in your CV documents: "An ultimately person. Never overhasty. In fact, slow."'

'Right.'

'But what's it to you, Harpur?'

'I thought I'd do some mingling with the festive crowd at the club.'

'Why, Col? You hope there'll be spare pussy around in a liquored-up, music-juiced, exuberant, gasping-for-it state?'

246

'I'll go armed. There might be something,' Harpur replied.

'What makes you say so?'

'Well, as starters, your intimations, sir. These are famous for their accuracy.'

'True. And?'

'Sir?'

'What else?

'Not sure.'

'Your brilliant private source let you down on vital details, did he? So sorry, Col.'

'It's just to show my face.'

'Well, yes, it's the kind to scare most people shitless.'

'Thank you, sir. I'll be recognized by most of them. They'll see we're watchful, holiday season or not. A deterrent.'

'If you meet a woman called Davidson give her my regards, will you? She might have bruises and/or scars visible, so she'll be easy to identify.'

'Your regards?'

'Yes, I think "regards" is at about the right level of familiarity.'

'Oh, I'm sorry about that, sir.'

# Twenty-Eight

One of the most useful things about Esther as a wife of a professional musician was she didn't detest *all* classical stuff, at least not to throw-up level. For instance she would sit through this youth orchestra concert tonight and keep a look of real interest and even appreciation on her face more or less the whole time and especially, of course, for Gerald's item. There would be no bored-as-buggery shifting about on her chair, no get-lost-for-God's-sake splutter-coughs. And, in any case, Mahler: she could spot something quite close to being a tune in a piece of his they did. She thought it might be that theme from the *Death In Venice* film, where Dirk Bogarde lusts so feverishly after the blonde boy that his mascara melts, dowsing his face, and puts the kibosh on his chances. She'd bet Mahler never thought his symphony would be just right for runny cosmetics.

Then the Elgar: taking into account what composers could be like, the bombastic prats, she thought he had things reasonably tidy and genial. He didn't go blasting off with brass and timpani, or not in this extract, anyway. Gerald's own composition seemed OK and got good applause. He'd told her his was a gavottish fantasia after Poulenc – 'quite a way after,' he'd said. The orchestra was children only, except for the conductor, so Gerald didn't get to play any of his opus himself, but he'd written a very nice three- or four-minute solo chunk for the youngster bassoonist.

Esther felt pleased Gerald's work earned a decent reception. He hadn't been all that keen to take the youth orchestra offer. 'Hackery,' he'd told Esther. 'Poor for my reputation. I'm on a Haydn to nothing.' His reputation was at its best a year or two or five ago, so he was very sensitive to any signs of a further shrinkage. He'd discovered, though, that all the other tutors brought in for the youth orchestra session were unquestionably top bananas, and top bananas today, not the day before the day before yesterday. This allowed him to respond to the youth orchestra's call and agree the fee.

Yes, he could grow touchy about reputation and honour. He still steadfastly believed he had some of both in the music game. She thought this admirable and quaint. It would probably save him from complete break-up. 'Don't part with your illusions because if you do you will exist but cease to live.' Where did that quotation come from – the economist, Keynes? Twain? Gerald had a good, nicely shaped, middling honest face which seemed to her the right sort for someone who wrote gavottish fantasias, but also had charming reserves of very realistic violence.

She'd arrived a couple of hours before the concert, in time to have tea with Gerald at his hotel, The Mandrake. That name reminded her, naturally, of the source who'd fed her the first tips about the then-approaching clash between Pasque Uno and Opal Render at

Mondial-Trave. Not long after that conflict he'd been hit by a stolen car and killed while out walking his Rottweiler. It might have been an accident. The driver was never found. Legend said the mandrake plant shrieked if pulled from the ground. Esther had felt like shrieking on his behalf when she heard of his removal. She didn't go to the funeral.

In the hotel lounge, Gerald said: 'I've felt like a fucking animal at the zoo. People come in and stare at me when I'm doing my teaching.'

'Did you have that bow-tie on?' Esther replied.

'Woman boasting that she knew the bassoon was a double reed. He, I could tell, very aware of my nose damage – staring, wondering.'

'I'm sorry. I always try to avoid thumping your lips so the nose is rather liable to get it.'

'I gave them the freeze. Maybe it was wise not to protest. I found out afterwards that this particular couple had chipped in big towards orchestra costs and would be giving us farewell hospitality at a club they own. It'll be a fleapit probably, but I suppose they mean well.'

'Name Ember?' she said.

'Ember, yes. Their guide introduced them.'

'Ralph and wife.'

'You know them? How the hell?'

'He was a mini-crook in London and now is a maxi-crook here.'

Gerald grew agitated and pink verging to red, almost matching the dots on his tie. 'Who told you this?' he said.

'I knew the first bit from when I worked there. As to the second, there's nothing provable, I imagine, or he wouldn't be acting the generous host now.'

'And am I, Gerald Davidson, supposed to accept hospitality from such a one?' he said.

'Well, yes. But think of yourself as an artiste, a touch of the Bohemian in your character, an *essential* touch of the Bohemian in your character. You're not one to kowtow to the tedious dictates of the law and conventions.'

'True.'

'Nobody who cared what other people thought about him would wear a tie like that.'

During the concert, she saw Ralph W. Ember, last in her view via security film. He still looked remarkably like the young Charlton Heston, but had picked up a long facial scar from somewhere. She had an idea he saw her, too, but made no sign. He and what Esther took to be his wife – small, pixie-like, blonde – had front seats, obviously reserved for those who'd coughed aid, sort of patrons of the arts.

# Twenty-Nine

Harpur went late in the evening to The Monty. He had a Glock nine mm pistol buttoned down in a shoulder holster. He went direct from headquarters. If he'd worn the armament at home Jill might have spotted the bulge under his jacket. Not might: would have. There'd have been questions.

Of course, the club was full. What sounded to Harpur like trad jazz boomed from the audio system. On these special occasions Harpur knew that the usual checking of membership at the door became pointless because so many regulars brought friends and relatives with them. And so, the risks. Ralph would know this, too. He busied himself behind the bar, helping out. Harpur thought he looked genial and relaxed. But Ralph was a trouper, could put on an act. He'd had plenty of practice. Harpur felt sure Ralph regarded most Monty members as rubbish. A club host had to do the hospitable role, though, and Ralph did it perfectly. He was in shirtsleeves so might not be carrying anything. That seemed to Harpur optimistic and casual. But there were little self-protection pistols around, small enough for a woman's handbag. Possibly Ralph had one of these in his sock or trousers pocket.

He smiled what could be mistaken for a genuine welcome and seemed about to put Harpur's regular gin-and-cider tipple on the bar. Harpur stopped him. 'Not now, Ralph,' he said. It was a way of telling him, without actually mentioning the danger, that Harpur wanted to keep his mind clear and reactions sharp. Bluntness might have shattered Ralph's cheery pose. It would have been callous.

Harpur's eyes inventoried the crowd. He saw some faces he knew, and many he didn't. Among those he did know were a few he and his department had sent to jail, and would probably send to jail again. And he also saw Mansel Shale, square-built, ferrety-eyed, with a clump of dark hair and wearing one of those old style, thick, woollen suits he fancied, perhaps hoping to be mistaken for a member of the squirearchy. He was standing not far off and by himself at present. Shale ran the other principal recreational substances firm in the city. Ralph and he had somehow worked out a successful coexistence agreement, so Iles let them function. 'Manse!' Harpur said. 'Merry Christmas.'

Shale nodded towards the holster hillock. 'Expecting trouble, Mr Harpur?'

'Ralph certainly knows how to put on a party,' Harpur replied.

'Are there people gunning for him?' Despite the voices-din and music-din, Harpur picked up a sadness bordering on despair in Shale's words. There was a sad story centring on Manse. Not long ago, his wife and young son had been shot dead by mistake in Manse's Jaguar.[3] The real target had been Manse, and the executioner had

[3]  See *I Am Gold*

expected him to be driving, not his wife. In his grief, Shale had withdrawn from the trade for a while and turned religious. But he'd recovered from this lapse and was back in business now, though for ever mentally scarred. 'Who?' Manse asked.

'Who what?' Harpur said.

'Who wants Ralph dead?' Shale went silent for ten seconds and then supplied his own answer: 'Well, I suppose plenty want him dead. You're here to save him? That's princely of you, really princely.' He paused again and lowered his head. It was as though he would like to ask why nobody princely had been there to save his wife and child.

Abruptly, Shale jerked his head up. 'Christ, is this it?' he said. He was staring across the bar to the club's main entrance. A man wearing a scarf to hide his lower face and carrying stiff-armed ahead of him what looked to Harpur like a Browning automatic pistol had entered the club and scuttled to his left obviously seeking a line of fire that would skirt the *The Marriage of Heaven and Hell* obstruction and give a gorgeous, clear volley-route to Ember. The man yelled, 'A traitor to glorious Gladhand and to me! Panicking Ralphy, it's time for you to panic again.'

At once, Harpur went for the Glock but knew he was taking too bloody long to get the gun from its nest, sober or not. He glanced towards Ralph and howled 'Get down!' But Ralph stood there full on to the intruder, scarlet-shirted chest wide open for whatever was coming, as if he thought he deserved it. Harpur had the pistol half out and was turned towards the gunman now.

The jazz still rolled on, but the crowd had gone totally silent. Harpur heard a shout above the music. It seemed to come from behind the man about to aim around the Blake at Ralph.

Iles, in a tremendous, grey, three-piece suit and striped tie, loped in from the club entrance. He bellowed again, 'Unarmed police! Drop it! Ralph is precious to us!' and the man glanced back, was put off his purpose for a moment. A moment would do. Iles hit him an immaculate, full-power, right-hand karate-chop to the neck and then, as he tottered and collapsed, gave him a kick in the face on the way down, deftly placed to smash at least his jaw and possibly a cheek bone. His automatic fell from his grip and Iles kicked that, too. It slid out of reach on the bar floor. The gunman lay at least unconscious, possibly broken-necked. Iles kicked him thoughtfully twice more in the head, seeming to aim especially at the man's ponytail. For a couple of seconds things seemed to Harpur very unChristmasy.

The music had reached the end of the tape. The crowd stayed quiet. Iles said: 'A bit damn slow unbuttoning, weren't you, Col? I bet you were quicker getting my wife stripped in some damn grubby rooming house or lay-by or abandoned property.' Spit-froth, always at the ready, fell from the Assistant Chief's mouth on to his magnificent Charles Laity, kick-prone, black, lace-up shoes.

'We weren't expecting you, sir,' Harpur replied.

'I had an idea you might fuck up, Col. Decided I'd better show.'

'You got here an exactly the right moment, Mr Iles,' Shale said.

'It's a habit of mine, Manse,' Iles said. His tie had gone a bit skew-whiff during that necessary encounter and the Assistant Chief straightened it now. Most likely those stripes signified some eternally non-Monty type, exclusive London club, or a fine rugby union side. He bent and, removing the scarf, had a close look at the man's disfigured face. Cuckold-rage saliva fell on him, too. 'Don't recognize. Someone from your adventurous past, Ralph? Or perhaps a relative of someone from your adventurous past.'

'Possibly,' Ralph said.

'I believe you almost sympathized with him. You let down pals back then, did you? But we have to take care of you, Ralph: a titan of the local scene,' Iles said. He went and recovered the Browning and without much originality at all fired a shot up at the Blake. Everybody knew something similar happened before. The ricochet knocked a bauble from The Monty's stunted-looking Christmas tree near the door. Iles said: 'I can tell you from experience, Ralph, they don't have fun like this at those select London clubs such as the Athenaeum, not even at Yuletide.'

Harpur, gazing at the ruined bauble on the floor, thought it said something about the fragility of peace on earth and of human merrymaking. Iles often sniggered at him for turning philosophical. Harpur reholstered his pistol and went to pick up the bauble. The bullet had knocked it shapeless, and unfit to go back on the tree. Harpur put the wreckage on the bar near where Ralph was sitting at his desk. 'Do you know our friend?' Harpur asked, nodding towards the flattened visitor.

256

'He was the one who started all the damned obnoxiousness, Mr Harpur. He's probably not long out of jail.'

'Which particular obnoxiousness?'

'The names.'

'Which?'

'You're very kind, Mr Harpur.'

'Am I? In which way?'

'To pretend you don't know.'

'Don't know what, Ralph, or which?'

'Names,' Ralph said.

'Names?'

'Spoken behind my back.'

'Ralph Wyvern, do you mean?' Harpur replied. 'Surely they're used openly.'

'You're very kind, Mr Harpur.'

'Again? In which respect?'

'"Panicking Ralph." Or even more disgusting, "Panicking Ralphy".' His voice gave that 'y' on the end a kind of whiplash frightfulness.

'You mean people refer to you as "Panicking Ralph" or "Ralphy"?'

'You're very kind, Mr Harpur.'

'In which respect, Ralph?'

'Pretending you didn't know.'

Iles joined them. 'Congratulations on a magnificent, auspicious session, Ralph,' he said.

'Which?' Ember replied.

'Tonight. The musicians and so on,' Iles said. 'A truly refined atmosphere, not always easy to achieve, but a skill that seems to come naturally to you, Ralph.'

'He recognizes the previously troublesome guest,' Harpur said.

'Really?' Iles replied.

'Apparently he devised some monstrous nicknames for Ralph,' Harpur said.

'Really?' Iles replied.

'You're very kind, Mr Iles,' Ember said. Harpur thought this didn't sound as if Ralph actually believed it, or came anywhere near believing it.

'In which respect, Ralph?' Iles said.

'Pretending,' Ralph said.

'He remarked the same to me,' Harpur said.

Iles looked outraged by this. He would detest anything that made him and Harpur sound equal or even similar whether during a game-playing conversation like this or in more serious conditions.

'Pretending what, Ralph?' the ACC said.

'That you're ignorant of these nicknames,' Ralph said.

'Which?' Iles said, with a very puzzled yet considerate smile.

'"Panicking"?' Ralph said.

'"Panicking"?' Iles replied. 'Who's panicking?'

Harpur said: 'He believes people call him "Panicking Ralph" or even "Panicking Ralphy", behind his back.'

Iles put extensive puzzlement onto his face now. 'Why would anyone do that? Should I have kicked the bastard some more? If Harpur didn't have such palsied hands we might not have needed to neutralize that sod by unarmed combat because he'd have had a couple of rounds in him and been dead.' Iles began to slaver. 'Mind you, Ralph, I'm quite sure Harpur's hands would find their appalling, efficient way around my wife's

258

body in one of their degrading shag crannies. Oh, yes, his fingers—'

'I took what I considered to be a totally rational, indeed, inevitable, decision during a certain period in my life, and recommended others should do the same – to avoid disaster,' Ralph replied. 'And it was this entirely justified opinion of a situation that caused this man, Stayley, to misrepresent my revised thinking, in view of fundamentally altered facts, as cowardice, as panic.'

'Ludicrous,' Iles said. 'Neither he nor anyone else will call you "Panicking" henceforward.'

'As a matter of fact, the person responsible for my amended estimate of risk is here tonight with her hubbie – one of the gifted musicians,' Ralph said.

'Yes?' Iles replied. 'Well, I think we've shown the backbiter – Stayley, you say? – I think we've shown Mr Stayley that it's extremely unwise to go about trying to shovel contumely on to you, Ralph. I'm sure Harpur would agree if he knew the meaning of "contumely" – insolence, Col.' As far as Harpur could make out, the pony-tailed Stayley lay totally still where he had fallen and might be dead. 'When you speak of the person responsible for your rethink, Ralph, whom do you mean?' Iles said.

'Davidson.'

'Oh, Esther,' Iles said.

'You know her, sir?' Harpur said.

'Must go and have a word. She'll be surprised to see me, I expect.'

Iles left them and Harpur watched him push

259

through the crowd towards a slightly long-faced, tall, strong-jawed woman and a man in an exceptionally offensive bow-tie. The woman smiled at Iles as he approached. She didn't appear to introduce him to her 'hubbie', if that's who he was. She and Iles talked vigorously together. The 'hubbie' looked on, and looked on looking furious.

# Thirty

In the morning at The Mandrake Esther went downstairs first, leaving Gerald patching himself up, while she looked for the manager to apologize and settle the account. The hotel's name continued to bring back memories for her. She thought it a deep irony that one of the deaths at Mondial-Trave had been caused by Sergeant Martin Wilcox, who'd objected so vehemently to her ambush plan. Circumstances took away choices, didn't they? He'd been ordered to use his appropriate skill – gunnery – and he'd used it.

Likewise, the media had sounded off for a while about police warring tactics, but had gradually come to accept that if people wanted peaceful streets they'd better realize that peace didn't come by wishing. It might have to be fought for and won. The educated niggles in the leader columns had faded away nicely.

The Mandrake manager was about five foot six, bouncy, cheerful, his white shirt brilliantly laundered. He had a greying moustache that had width and vibrancy; his teeth not too good, but treatable, probably. 'There are some breakages in our room, three-twelve,' she said. 'Obviously inadvertent, but I hope you can give me a quick estimate of the cost and I'll do a cheque to cover our stay and the accidents with the curtains, the basin in the *en suite,* and the TV set. I think the sheets will wash out fine if you put them through twice, and the mattress is absolutely OK.'

'Well now, as a matter of fact, Mrs Davidson, Assistant Chief Constable Iles is well known and much esteemed here.'

'Yes, I'm sure.'

'And perhaps I'm at fault in calling you Mrs while giving Mr Iles his full title. You, I understand, are at an identical rank: Assistant Chief Constable Davidson.'

'Mrs will do. My husband remained very excited after the lovely time with the orchestra last evening, and hence the hand basin broken away from the wall. The basin itself is wholly unsplintered I think. It's just the fixing to the wall that's fractured.'

'Assistant Chief Constable Iles rang, you see,' the manager replied. They talked standing in the lounge. Other guests were seated nearby, reading newspapers or chatting. The manager lowered his voice. 'Yes, rang particularly. Very early.'

'Particularly what?'

'Concerning possible damage.'

'How do you mean?' She spoke at normal level, didn't see why not.

'He said there might be some.'

She quietened. 'He told you in advance we'd trash the room?'

'A possibility. Only that. He has intimations, I think, and he was with the two of you last evening, I believe. He seemed to have noticed some indications.'

'What indications, for God's sake?'

'He thought possibly some resentment.'

262

'What resentment? Who did the resenting?'

'I think Assistant Chief Constable Iles would answer, "Your husband". He insists that all this be dealt with very privately and I think I sense that you would like that, too. He says you might be thinking of promotion and unfavourable matter should be avoided. He doesn't want you incommoded in any way and certainly not bothered with the cost. I'm to bill him personally when the work has been done, the envelope marked "Strictly Confidential and Private" and sent to police headquarters, not his home. And I think we'll forget about the accommodation charge, if you don't mind. It is a privilege to have any friend of Assistant Chief Constable Iles staying at The Mandrake.'

'I knew someone called Mandrake. He's dead though.'

'It's not a common surname. Assistant Chief Constable Iles said not to trouble your husband with any of this.' The manager's voice had dropped even further. 'Your husband is a virtuoso, I understand, and shouldn't be exposed to banal, dismally workaday pressures. We have to cherish our stars, don't we, Assistant Chief Constable Davidson?'

'Well, yes.'